# Brothers

# and other stories

# by
# Tom Hernandez

COVER BY RYAN BOYCE
AUTHOR PHOTO BY MEGAN JOHNSTON

ISBN-13: 978-1-7331766-2-0

# BROTHERS

*To Tim and Paul Hernandez*

*and Chuck Pelkie, Paul Spencer,
Jeff Palmer, and Jay Baaske*

*Brothers, all*

# ACKNOWLEDGEMENTS

As always, many have gently guided (and sometimes aggressively pushed) me along my writing path. Thanks to one and all:

- My wife Kellie, my most trusted reader and critic.
- My daughters Emma Williams and Olivia Hernandez, my greatest inspirations.
- WriteOn Joliet - a more talented, supportive, good-humored, and encouraging group does not exist.
- My friend and mentor Denise Baran-Unland whose boundless patience and talent are fuel for my fire.
- And Riley Jean Williams, my light, my love, my heart.

TOM HERNANDEZ

# ALSO BY TOM HERNANDEZ

*Chocolate Cows and Purple Cheese, and other tales from the homefront (essays)*

*Abundance - a collection (poetry)*

*The Edge of Middle - thoughts from the top of the hill (essays, poetry and short fiction)*

*The Acorn Wars – (novel)*

*The Weekly Fruit and Vegetable Report – (essays, poetry and short fiction)*

# INCLUDING TOM HERNANDEZ

*Write Where We Are – WriteOn Joliet Inaugural Anthologies (2017-2021)*

*Cheetah Stories: a collection of short stories, poems and essays based on one silly prompt – a WriteOn Joliet anthology (2019)*

*Let there be no strife, I pray thee, between me and thee…for we be brethren*

*~Genesis 13:8*

# BROTHERS

# CONTENTS

Author's Note                                                      12

## FICTION

Brothers

- Mickey Blake                                              17
- Rebecca Blake                                             22
- Dalvin Grayson                                            25
- Peter Blake                                               32
- Janeen (Blake) Roberts                                    36
- David (Rosie) DeLaRosa                                    42
- Madame Marguerite Thornberg-Tonelli                       47
- Aisha Shah                                                51
- Richard (Rickey) Blake *(read by Aisha Shah)*             55
- The Hon. Robert Roy                                       59
- Mickey Blake (continued...)                               62

Bad Medicine                                                       77
New York Style, With Strawberries on Top                           81
The Editor                                                         86

## ESSAYS

The Love of We                                                     91
Musical Therapy                                                    98
Finding Joy                                                       104
Overcoming                                                       109
Baby, I'm a Star!                                                113
Sod in the Front, Seed in the Back                               118
Let It Go!                                                       122
The Balcony                                                      126

# BROTHERS

# AUTHOR'S NOTE

Inspiration, like fire, can be both wonderful and dangerous.

For example, the title novella was inspired by Edgar Lee Masters' classic "Spoon River Anthology."

"Spoon River" paints, one piece at a time, a picture of the life of a small town through first-person monologues and short, free-verse poetry. Each entry sings the town's bright joys and whispers its gossipy secrets.

I first read this book and performed several of its roles in a theatrical production in high school and have been fascinated by it since.

Fast forward. I wanted to write a story about two brothers whose already-complicated relationship becomes even more challenging when one creates a terrible moral dilemma for the other.

Not a bad idea, but there was nothing especially original about the concept.

Then, Inspiration came along.

I got the idea to tell the brothers' story entirely through first-person monologues by people in their lives, ala "Spoon River."

And here we are.

"Brothers" has no direct exposition. Rather, each character shares details, memories, and secrets that, together, tell the tale.

"Brothers" therefore, is as much a writing experiment as it is a story.

The reader will decide if it is successful.

TOM HERNANDEZ

# BROTHERS

TOM HERNANDEZ

# Mickey Blake

The first time I killed my brother, I was about 12 years old.

He'd just thrown a baseball at me as hard as he could. We had been playing long toss after a game of rundown with a neighbor had broken up.

The rules of the game called for us to take another step toward each other with each toss. Boys being boys - and we were definitely "Old School" boys - the rules meant everything. As we kept closing the gap between us, one step at a time, he kept whipping the ball a bit faster.

I was a small kid, but I loved outdoor activities and could hold my own playing most sports, especially baseball. I was never going to win a Gold Glove, but I was decent enough to play some Little League outfield, even some infield in a pinch, although it was much easier to catch high flies than hard grounders skimming across the grass, especially since they'd sometimes catch the lip of the infield turf or skid across the dirt and skip over my glove into my arm, chest, even my face. My hand-eye coordination hasn't always been great, which is maybe why I never played seriously past Little League.

I yelled at him to slow it down and stop throwing so hard.

He yelled back at me. Suddenly he was all angry, teasing me, condescending. He said, "What's wrong, you pussy? Are you scared of a little old ball?"

The next part, I'll never forget. I was thoroughly confused and simply asked him what'd happened? He answered me like I had asked the stupidest question in the history of stupid questions. Without any emotion at all, like some a machine or something, he said, "Nothing at all." Then he whipped the baseball again, only about fifteen feet away now. I barely got my glove up in time to keep the ball from sailing over my right shoulder into the alley separating our house from the neighbors' back yard.

Thinking back now, I don't know why I didn't just hold the ball, turn around and go home. Instead, I threw it back. A little harder, but still not much more than a fast toss. The ball arced gracefully into his glove below his waist. He continued mocking me.

He said, "Oh, big man! Look at that Major League curveball!"

We moved another few feet closer. Another hard throw came at me so fast you could hear it sizzle. My glove snapped shut on its own from the speed of the throw.

I told him to slow it down. I tossed it back. Took another step. We stood about 10 feet apart.

He screamed at me. I'm not kidding. He yelled at the top of his lungs, "Fuck you, you big baby!"

I didn't know what in the world was happening. I asked what the hell I did and swore right back at him, matching him F-bomb for F-bomb. Like all kids, we loved to swear. Especially the "F" word. That was the big one. The worst one. The best one.

But he said that nothing was going on. Nothing was any different that would have caused him to hurl a rock-hard baseball at my head for no good reason in the middle of an innocent game we played all the time

Now I was really confused. He threw the ball back again as hard as if he was perched in center field trying to throw out a runner at home.

Except that the ball didn't have the hundred feet or so between center field and home plate to slow down.

And I didn't have five or six seconds to figure out where it was coming from or headed, adjust my catching hand, position myself to catch it, and pretend to swipe smoothly down across the runner's leading arm just before his stretched-out hand touched the dirt-covered front of home plate, prevent the winning run from scoring and save the mythical game while the crowd erupted in delirious cheers for their Diamond Hero.

Despite other issues, Rickey and I liked playing together. We talked a lot, dreaming of seeing ourselves in the Big Game, pulling off miraculous plays just like that.

Kids just being kids, playing around, having fun. But he wasn't playing around, and I wasn't having fun.

Standing less than ten feet away, the ball caught me flush on my right cheek as my head instinctively, defensively swiveled away from the throw. My glove rose a millisecond too late. All I could do was cover my fractured cheekbone. I crumpled to the ground and started sobbing. I heard something that sounded like a wounded animal, screaming in pain.

*"You fuckingfatassholesonofabitchmotherfucker!"*

At least, those are the words I meant to say. The words I heard myself saying in my head. What actually came out of my mouth, through grass and dirt, as my face swelled into a Macy's Day Parade balloon version of my 12-year-old self, was so slurred no one could have understood a word.

But anyone - anyone with a heart, that is - would have at least tried to understand what I was saying.

They would have dropped their glove, run over, kneeled down, put their hand on my back, tried to help me sit up, hold my arm as we walked back home, gingerly so as to not jostle my head and face any more than normal walking was already doing. And maybe, just maybe, apologized for an accident. An errant throw in a game between brothers that got a little out of hand, for whatever reason. Begged my forgiveness. Even cried with me and pleaded to coordinate our stories so he wouldn't get in trouble with our parents.

But not my brother. Not Rickey.

Lying there, from under my gloved hand, I saw his shoes approach, then stop an inch from my face.

He asked me, if I was OK.

I tried to say, "No, you moronic jackass! Clearly, I am not OK." But an anvil of pain was sitting on my cheek, pinning my head to the ground. The words were trapped inside my swollen, shattered mouth. I was crying so hard. My face was burning with fury and confusion and fear. It wouldn't have mattered anyway. His shoes waited about two seconds before leaving.

Oh, I've killed my brother many times. Or, at least thought about it…how I would do it, how it would feel to not have to worry where he is or how he's getting by…

Which, I guess, is why I am here today Your Honor…

# Rebecca Blake

Well of course they hated each other!

At least, growing up they did. Who really knows why? I kind of blame their parents. I mean, who names their kids Michael and Richard - Mickey and Rickey - dresses them like twins even though Mickey was a couple years older, forces them to do all the same activities in school, and doesn't think about or realize that other kids are going to tease them? How hard their lives are going to be, always competing with each other for everything?

But it was more than just that, obviously. From the first time I met them, they were constantly at each other's throats. Calling each other names. Hitting on each other's girlfriends (yes, me too - but I told Mickey about it and played it off as innocent flirting. I didn't want to hurt his feelings any more than Rickey was already trying to do.) Stealing each other's money and records and even clothes. Actually, that was kind of funny, since Rickey was a good six inches taller and fifty pounds heavier. He couldn't have worn Mickey's clothes if his life depended on it. He just liked doing stuff to get under his brother's skin.

Mostly, it didn't amount to much. But sometimes, a comment would cross the line, or one or the other would push too hard with a joke, and they'd fight. Oh boy, would they fight. I personally witnessed several knock-down drag-outs that ended with them both covered in blood. In fact, Rickey knocked one of Mickey's teeth out one time. Not one that anyone could see, but still and all... To this day Mickey never got it fixed. Every now and again he complains about it hurting. I tell him to go see a dentist, but he doesn't listen. I mean, who am I? Just his wife, the mother of his children. What do I know, right?

Honestly, I think he kind of considers it some weird badge of honor - proof that he took Rickey's best shot and survived. Plus, now that they're adults and mostly get along, it makes for a heck of a story around the dinner table. The kids all love hearing about how Uncle Rickey knocked their dad loopy but couldn't make him fall.

That's the kind of stupid brother stuff that I don't understand and never have understood. How can boys fight like the world is ending, bruise and break each other's faces and bones and teeth and whatever else, and then just walk away and laugh about it? Seriously! We grew up across the street from the Blakes. I literally saw them beat each other to a pulp in the street because one of them had thrown the Frisbee too far, and then get back up and keep on playing like nothing happened.

So why are we here today? It's hard to say. Obviously, Mickey is my world. The man of my dreams, the father of my children, all that stuff. It's sappy, but it's true. I've been head-over-heels, mad-crazy-deeply in love with him since my dad took us on our first date when were fifteen.

And despite everything he's done over the years, I love my brother-in-law. He would move a mountain for me and our kids. He adores his niece and nephews, and they love him, too.

They both have a dark side that sometimes takes over every part of them, like a demon in one of those horror movies. Especially when it comes to being honest about themselves. I mean, *God forbid* either one *admit* that maybe, just maybe, they were both wrong in some argument, or that they have both made mistakes in life.

On the other hand, no matter how bad it gets, even when it seems like they could kill each other, if anyone else says anything bad about one of them, the other will be the first one to defend him.

Listen, I am not saying girls are perfect. *Far* from it! Maybe it's because I'm a girl. Or maybe because I don't have any brothers, I don't know…All I can say is, boys are just, well, *strange*.

# Dalvin Grayson

Man, to this *day* I still don't know what happened when "Johnny Football" came back and found his windshield in a million pieces all over his car.

All I know is, I picked up Mickey the next morning, we pulled into our usual spot in the school parking lot, a few spaces from where "Johnny's" car was parked the day before. All the broken glass was gone. We heard through the grapevine that "Johnny" filed an insurance report and got it fixed. Nothing else came of it. Except that I learned two hard life lessons the hard way that day. One is, people are who they are. Nothin's gonna change that. And two, if your back is up against the wall, everyone, even your best friends - even your brothers - will cut you quick as they can pull the knife.

Listen man, I know what it's like to have brothers. I got one of each, older and younger. I mean, I love both of my brothers, but I can tell you for certain, it ain't always easy.

I was closer to Mickey, but I hung with him and Rickey both, for a while. Mickey and me was in the same grade in high school. Rickey was a year behind. But they did everything together - at least 'till they got to school. Once they came through those doors, Rickey did his own thing. I don't know sometimes how he survived, pulling all the crap he did. He just lucky his dad never found out. 'cause if he did, Rickey probably wouldn't have made it past freshman year. But you know, none of us never said nothing. We was too afraid. At least Mickey and me was. I hung around a lot for a few years. Their mom and dad started calling me their "dark-skinned son," the "cousin from out of town," stuff like that. I never really liked it, but, you know, what could I say? It was a different time, man. Anyway, the point is, I saw a lot.

One thing I knew, Mr. Blake had a temper. He was old school. Career Marine. Worked at the train yards for a few years after he retired from the Corps. All about respect and discipline. Didn't no one want to cross him. One time he caught Rickey in outright, bald-faced lie. Listen man, Rickey was lying big time, sure as he was standing there, right to his daddy's face. He knew it. We knew it. And his dad knew it.

He listened for about a minute. Then, faster than I ever saw anyone move, before anyone could say or do anything, Mr. Blake smacked Rickey. Hard. Grabbed him by the hair, telling him, "Don't ever lie to me again." Sounded like some kinda wild animal growlin' or somethin'. Like Mickey and me wasn't even there.

We disappeared for a while. Came back later, we all had dinner just like normal. Mrs. Blake was always inviting me to stay for dinner. You would'na known nothin' had happened except for the big ol' lump on Rickey's cheek. Listen man, we all had our own things that if our parents found out, we all coulda been dead, no question. You know, stuff with girls, bein' places we shoulda never been at, drinkin', smokin', maybe a little more for a few people. Dumb kid stuff. You know how it is. We were young and full of ourselves. Didn't never think nothin' coulda happened to us. But to this day I ain't never seen nothin' like that. And I don't think that was the first or last time, either. I'm no expert, but I think that stuff affected Rickey, you know, in his head. Maybe it was why he could be so mean sometimes…but that's another story, I guess.

Anyway, the three of us did a lot of stuff together, at least for the first couple years. We was all in the high school band. Rickey was cool, but he was never as heavy into music as Mickey and me. In fact, that's really how we got tight. Didn't take long for us to realize we both liked jazz and blues.

He told me about Big Band cats he liked. Benny Goodman, Tommy Dorsey, Glenn Miller, Sinatra, dudes like that. I mean, they were OK and all, but everything changed when I introduced him to all these Black musicians he never heard of before. Pretty soon, it was like him and me were like "brothers from another mother." I never in my life saw a white cat try so hard to be Black! At least, in terms of music. If we hadn't been so tight, I woulda laughed at him. But, you know, I was kinda proud I'd opened up his mind to the Truth: Black people invented every kind a' cool sound there is, starting with jazz. That's ours man. We let white people in the door, let 'em come along for the ride, but it's always been ours.

He loved every bit of it. I mean, he was *passionate* about anything having to do with African American culture. I loved him for it. I did! He went way deep, started wearing Dashiki shirts to band practice and stuff. Mickey was a *sight!* In some ways, Mickey was more a brother to me than either of my own blood brothers. I can't even count all the hours we spent talking about music, listening to records, analyzing and dissecting every note and lyric. We thought we was the shit! Oops, sorry Your Honor. What I meant to say was, we thought we knew everything there was to know about everyone who ever blew a horn or played a guitar or sang a note: Miles, Dizzy, 'Trane, B.B. King, Duke, Basie, Ella, Billie, and R&B like Brother Ray, James Brown, Aretha, Stevie. Oh man, then I really blew his mind when I turned him on to Prince. Makes me laugh even now, just thinking about it.

Mr. Blake used to drive us all to school before we could drive ourselves. We hated that bus, and he didn't seem to mind. School was on the way to his work. We used to drive Mr. Blake nuts with our music talk. But once I got a car of my own, I drove us everywhere. We even triple dated a few times. Now *that* was a trip! Mickey and Rickey would always fight about who got the back seat. Of course, it was my car, so I was stuck driving, like some sad chauffer or something.

It was about that time when Rickey kinda started goin' his own way, but Mickey and me stayed real close for a long time. Until near the end of our senior year.

I'll never forget it. We had just gotten done with school. Mickey's girlfriend had broken up with him and he was just not in a good place. I think they had finally gone all the way, then she dumped him for a jock. That hurts a hundred different ways when you're kind of a small guy and a band geek, too. Don't get me wrong. Mickey was cool. A real "big fish" in our "small pond," you know what I'm sayin'? But, when it come down to him and the star quarterback? Well, you know how that story goes, every single time.

Anyway, we come out of school, and "Johnny's" car is still there in the parking lot. We'd been at band practice, so it was late. No other cars around. Just mine and "Johnny's." Mickey saw that car and before I knew what was happening, he started running to the parking lot, crying, screaming, "MF-er this, MF-er that."

Now, you know, we was teenagers. Young men. Cool cats. Musicians. So, we always acted a little crazy anyway, you dig? But not like this. He charged at that car like it was going to start itself up and drive away. He was kicking at the tires and fenders, talking about, "You stole the one thing I love!" and crazy stuff like that. That car ain't done nothin' but turn over that morning and sit there all day. Then, out of nowhere, Mickey picked something up. A brick or big rock or chunk of asphalt or concrete, I'm not sure, but he yelled at the top of his lungs, "I'll kill you before I let you have her you F-ing jock a-hole!" The next thing I knew, the windshield exploded into a million pieces all over the front of that car.

We both just froze. I think we were in shock. I didn't know what to do. Call the police? Get a teacher? Book out of there as fast as we could? The school had security cameras, but we always heard those things hardly never worked. So, chances were, they didn't see anything. Or, maybe they did. How could we know?

Mickey turned to me. He's fairly pale, even for a white dude, but he was whiter than I'd ever seen him. To my dying day, I'll never forget what he said. "Dalvin, you're my best friend. I love you like my own brother. Hell, truth be told, I love you more than my own brother." That didn't surprise me. He'd said that kind a stuff before, especially after fighting with Rickey, which they did a lot.

But I never in a million years expected what he said next. "If anyone asks, I need you to say you did this."

I thought, "What kinda crazy cracker shit is this?" I think he saw the confusion on my face because he started talking real even, real smooth. Like nothing was happening and we was about to start discussing the latest George Clinton record or something. He said, "If anyone finds out I did this, I could get expelled. I could lose my scholarships. I could go to *jail*. I'm going to be the first person from my family to go to college. And I don't want to even think about what my dad will do."

Man, I'm not gonna lie. I must a stood there for a full minute before I realized my mouth had been hangin' open. Finally, some words came outta my mouth. "Yea man, but all that shit could happen to me, too," I said. I mean, I was the first one from my family to be goin' to college too. Maybe not the big shot college Mickey went to, but still.

He just looked at me like we were on different planets or somethin'. "Well, I mean, it wouldn't affect you as much as it would me, because...well, it's not that people would *expect* you to do something like this, but it wouldn't surprise them as much if *you* did something like

30

this, because, you know…"

He didn't say it. He didn't have to. I was as Black as he was white. I knew exactly what he meant.

I told him not to worry about it. Said I got his back, all like that.

We walked back to my car and got in. He took a deep breath and thanked me. "I love you man. You know that." I looked past him back at "Johnny Football's" car. The parking lot lights had just come on. Everywhere you looked, little bits of glass shined like diamonds. On the hood, in the front seat, on the parking lot circling the front end of the car. Like our guilt was twinkling under those lights. I started the car and pulled away, slowly, not wanting to attract attention.

I told him, "I know man. I love you too." But I didn't look at him. I didn't want him to see the tears in my eyes. I just said what I'd said a million times before. "We're brothers."

# Peter Blake

Yeah, they're my brothers, but you gotta understand, we're not exactly close.

Fact is, I haven't talked to either of them for months. Don't plan to, either. I don't know what's going on here. Don't care, really. They didn't give a crap about me when we were kids. Why should I care about them now?

It's not like we spent a lot of time together growing up. I mean, Rickey and Mickey were always together. Inseparable. If someone didn't know better, they'd swear the two of them were twins. But I came seven years after Rickey. Then our sister, Janeen, then Dylan, the baby. I was the "Elder of the Others." That's what we used to call ourselves. The three who probably were mistakes. At least, I probably was. But then after our parents had me, I guess maybe they figured it was OK to keep going. Janeen was born sixteen months after me, and like clockwork, Dylan barely a year later.

We all lived together, of course, at least until Mickey moved out when he was about nineteen. But you'd never have known it. M and R – that's what I called them - never paid any attention to me and Jan and Bob (that was my nickname for Dylan.) They were like two strangers living under our roof, eating our food, watching our TV to the three Others. Adults we didn't know. Seriously, I can probably count on less than one hand how many times they even talked to us, much less played or did anything with us. That includes holidays.

None of us knew M and R very well then, and I still don't. Jan's always been, I guess "closer" is the right word, but she always kinda took care of all us boys and our dad, especially later after Mom got sick. Still does, God love her. But Bob and me, we still kinda keep to ourselves when it comes to them. A lot of water under the bridge. Maybe too much.

I guess I understand, to a degree. They were so much older. What were they going to do? Take us with them on their dates? Especially Bob. He was so cute as a kid, with that curly blond hair and big, brown, puppy-dog eyes, he probably would've climbed on top of one of their girlfriends and had his way before they even knew what was going on! Ha! Now *there's* a thought.

We never really wanted anything more than what little brothers usually want from their big brothers. I admit, we weren't always angels either. We caused some trouble for them, too, a couple times. But still, they didn't have to be so mean about it. And I don't just mean Rickey.

Rickey was no sweetheart, but I'll say this for him: he

always got a bad rap for having a temper, but Mickey was worse, if you ask me. Rickey came after me, too. Plenty. But he was flashy and loud. He'd scream and punch and kick and break things. Sometimes even Dad couldn't get control of him. When Rickey was mad at you, you knew it, and you got out of the way as fast as you could if you knew what was good for you. He'd fight with anyone. One time he even got into it with Jan, until she scratched his face and kicked him in the nuts. I mean, well, you know, down there. He didn't mess with her much, after that.

But Mickey was quiet and cruel.

He would wait until no one was around or paying attention. Then he'd sneak up on you and twist the skin on the back of your arm, or pull a handful of hair, or bend your fingers back. Just mean, pointless stuff like that.

I'm not playing the victim here, but I'll tell you something. For some reason, he seemed to have it out for me more than the others. He'd come up behind me and whisper something to hurt me like, "You're the perfect argument for birth control," or "Dad should have pulled out one minute sooner."

One time - totally serious - he actually said to me, his own brother, "Why don't you kill yourself, so someone doesn't have to spend a buck for a bullet."

Come on! Who says stuff like that? Who does stuff like that? I never did a goddamn thing to either one of them. How could I? I was seven, eight years younger. I was smaller. I kept my distance. We almost never crossed paths except for dinner.

But the worst part was, then he'd laugh. He'd always laugh. Like other people's pain - *my* pain - was funny. One time I cried and told my parents. My dad beat the holy hell out of Mickey. Left welts on his back from his belt. You know what Mickey did? He came into Bob's and my room that night and put a pillow over my face and just kept saying, "Talk again, you bastard, talk again."

When he finally pulled the pillow away, I could see his eyes were shining in the dark and they looked wet and swollen. Like maybe he'd been crying.

Frankly sir, they can both rot. As far as I am concerned, I've got a little sister and a little brother. Anything else is just bad genes and paperwork.

# Janeen (Blake) Roberts

Just for the record, I want to say, it's important to remember that no one is as good as they think, or as bad as someone else thinks.

Much as I love my brother Peter, I will also tell you he's always been a bit of a whiner when it came to our big brothers. I'm not saying he's lying, but, well, let's just say he sometimes exaggerates when it comes to Mickey and Rickey.

I love my brothers. All four of them.

In their own way, each one is very special to me. Maybe that's to be expected, me being the only girl and all. I was their sounding board when it came to girlfriends. Not so much with Mickey and Rickey. By the time I was a teenager they were already pretty far along in terms of their social lives. With them, I was more just the "bratty kid sister." Believe me, I played that part to the hilt! I used to love to interrupt them when they were down in the basement with their dates, or just hang around, talking to the girls, hogging all their time, until they would scream at me to go away! I knew what they were up to, but I wasn't going to just let them have their way. What fun would that be?

But I was the "designated interpreter" for Peter and Dylan. I'd tell them what their girlfriends were thinking, what they meant when they said or did certain things, or more to the point, what they *didn't* mean. I mean, who knows the deeper meaning behind a hair flip or if they really thought you were funny when they laughed at your stupid joke than another girl? And trust me, there were a lot of stupid jokes. I've been surrounded by boys my whole life: my brothers, our dad, my husband and our four sons. But sometimes I just don't understand how the male species can be so incredibly blind, dense, and stupid and still manage to survive.

Well sir around this time, when I was 13, our mom started getting sick. Her legs and hips always hurt. Or she'd say that her skin felt like it was tingling or burning, or her joints were always sore and tender. Which all made it hard for her to stand or move around. Eventually we found out she had bone cancer.

Mom being Mom, never wanting to admit she was in pain or had any problems, she waited a long time before she would see a doctor and the cancer spread very fast. By the time they knew what was going on, there wasn't much to do. Mom got chemo for a couple months, but that just made her worse. She died about seven months after she was diagnosed.

Her death nearly killed Dad. He didn't know what to

do with himself. Or, with us, to be honest. What I mean is, Mom and Dad were what you'd call "old school." Mom ran the house and the family. Dad's parenting pretty much consisted of him working and putting a roof over our heads. When Mom died, a lot of her responsibilities just sort of naturally fell to me as the only girl in the house.

Listen, I know how that sounds in today's world, but back then, it made perfect sense, and I never really minded. Dad made sure I still had time for school and a social life, and my brothers all made sure the boys didn't get too friendly! They really took care of me, and I did my best to take care of them. Even today. Mickey, Peter and Dylan are all married, so they don't need me so much now, but I still do what I can for Rickey, even though he has a girlfriend.

My husband, Eddie, he's got the kindest heart. He understands me trying to help Rickey here and there, as long as he doesn't bother us too much. Eddie's friendly enough with Rickey, but they don't exactly see eye to eye on a lot. And, honestly, Rickey does kind of ask for a lot. Sometimes it's just a few dollars, sometimes a place to crash.

One time, he wanted me to cook and freeze him a month of meals. I didn't see the harm. It seemed like a small thing to me, but Eddie said absolutely not. We actually fought about it. Eddie said, "We work hard to make money to buy that food for *our* family!" Maybe it was just the proverbial straw, you know? He wasn't totally wrong. Rickey will never get rich, bouncing around from job to job like he does, but he shouldn't count on me for everything, either.

What I want to say, umm, the whole reason I am up here, is just to, I don't know, not *defend* Rickey. Not at all. He's made some bad choices. No one can deny that. We all do. That's just life. We make our bed and then we sleep in it. Mom used to say that Rickey's bed was always a little messier than anyone else's.

But I think it's also important to understand that underneath everything - the womanizing, the violence, the lying and cheating - Rickey is a good *person*. Not always right or law abiding, or ethical or even moral, but, you know, *good*. Good soul, good intentions. It's just that his follow through isn't very good.

He'd hate me saying this and deny it 'till the day he dies, but the fact is, I think he's always been a little bit lonely. In the couple years he still lived at home after Mom died, we talked a lot. Sometimes about everything, sometimes about a lot of nothing. You know how it is between siblings. But every once in a while, he'd tell me stories about how he never quite felt connected to anyone. Not even Mickey, and they shared a bedroom their entire childhood.

He told me how they'd lay awake, Mickey bragging about this girl or that friend, this idea or dream or thing he wanted to do, this good grade he got in school, things like that, on and on, whispering across the room about one big deal thing after another.

I guess you could say Rickey held his own in the dating department. He had a lot of girlfriends, if you want to call them that. There's another word for a lot of the women he saw, even back then, that maybe we don't say while the kids are here. Just suffice to say, they weren't the kind you got close to.

But Rickey said he never really felt like he had anything to say because he didn't have any real friends or dreams or goals. All he wanted to do is get to the next day, find some way to survive, and do it all over again.

Wait, that's not entirely true, now that I think about it,. I remember one time, he told me he really wanted to go to aviation school and become a pilot, maybe buy his own plane and start one of those "puddle jumper" services. He took a few flying lessons, but nothing ever came of it. Typical Rickey. To this day, I don't know what happened. Although I do have my ideas. He let slip once that he'd been dating the daughter of his flight instructor. They broke up and then he stopped taking lessons, or maybe it was the other way around. Either way, he never flew again, far as I know.

But like I said, he wasn't a *bad* guy by any stretch. He was always trying to do the right thing. Here's a good example. A couple years ago, Rickey actually took me to dinner. He even *paid*. I literally could not believe it! 'Course, it wasn't anything fancy, just burgers and beers, but the gesture was sweet.

After a while, he said something I'll never forget because it just kind of came out of nowhere: he said, "I love all our family, but you're the only one I ever really respected and admired. Because you don't judge me. I look in your eyes and I see Mom looking back, loving me for who I am. If Jesus was a girl, He'd be you."

Let me tell you, I nearly fell on the floor, and it wasn't because of the watered-down booze, either! Rickey never opened up to me like that. Not before, not since. It still makes me cry a little, just saying it out loud. I used to think it was so out of character for him, but maybe that's the point. Maybe it wasn't out of character at all.

# David (Rosie) DeLaRosa

Dude, what's *happening* here? Really, I mean it. I don't understand. I know some big decisions have to be made, but I've been sitting here for hours, listening to you people bash Rickey and Mickey, decide who was the good brother or bad brother, slicin' up their relationship and personalities like some kind of meat or somethin'.

All I got to say is, who cares? No, I'm serious. We're amigos, man. Buds. *Familia.* None of that matters. At least it shouldn't. Not at a time like this. Who really cares how they felt about each other as kids and who was mean, and who was nice, and who stole the other one's girlfriend or…whatever! Jesus!

You know what I remember when I think about Mickey and Rickey growing up? Being together! All the cousins at their house, playing in their yard, every day in the summer, seemed like. Officially, there's nine of us. But dude, whoever could make it out that day plus all our friends from the block, everyone counted, everyone family, Didn't matter who your momma and daddy was.

Man, that was a great time to be alive. We'd all kind of just come together first thing in the morning, soon as we could get out of the house after breakfast. Didn't really matter who it was, we'd all be running around, screaming, playing tag or hide-and-seek. Even the girls when they were *brave* enough to mix it up with us boys!

Sometimes there'd be enough of us to play two whole teams in baseball. Their yard backed up to an open field. Lots of room, dude, and we needed it, too! Sometimes there was fifteen, twenty kids. Little guys, six, seven years old, and us older kids. Even the teenagers. They mostly left us alone, but when they could be bothered, they hung around, too. Mickey, Rickey and me, we was about ten or so. Still riding bikes, no cars yet. Girls too, I mean, our girl cousins and their friends.

You know what? There were no fights, no hard feelings, no name calling...well, that's not exactly true. Sometimes they'd tease *me* because my last name means "Of the rose," or "From the Rose." Some of my cousins called me "Rosie" instead of my given name. Some still do. Really though, dude, I never cared. They could joke all they wanted. Later, my girlfriends, they liked it a lot. Sounded exotic. And "exotic" meant action! Dude, I think I got the last laugh on *that* one! Anyways, my point is just nobody got *seriously* hurt, you know what I mean?

We got some bumps and bruises. How could you not with a yard full of kids? Once, when we was playing hide and seek, our cousin Frannie ran into the steel laundry pole trying to get back to Home Base. Broke her arm and everything, dude. Man, that was funny. Not at that exact moment, but, you know, later. She went down so fast, BOOM! Like a bomb had hit and sucked all the air away and took all the sound with it. Then a few seconds later, she started crying.

Frannie was cute and all, and she grew up nice! But back then, she had this squeaky voice that just got squeakier the louder she got. Dude, seriously, it was like nails going through your brain! She screamed until they got her in her dad's car. She was *still* screaming when they turned the corner down the block. I bet she screamed all the way to the hospital. I gotta give it up to her, though, Frannie was tough. She came back the next day. Everybody signed her pink cast. She couldn't really run around with us, so we didn't hear from her much again until the cast came off a few weeks later. So, I guess, we all won! Just kidding, Frannie, you know I love ya!

Anyway, my point is just that whatever hard feelings there were between any of us, didn't go beyond the normal stuff that all kids got, especially boys. At least, boys who grew up back then before everything got so goddamn touchy-feely. Oops, sorry for my language sir, but you know what I mean. Now, you can't say *anything* without steppin' on somebody's toes and getting sued.

Just so's I'm clear, I spent more days and nights than I can even count with Mickey and Rickey over the years. Through junior high and high school. Especially in high school once Mickey got a car, and later, when we was in our early twenties. When Mickey went away to college for a couple years, it was more just Rickey and me, but the three of us always got together when Mickey came home. We were inseparable. Three crazy vatos on the town! The "Three Amigos," my dad would call us. Like that dumb movie. Except we were a lot funnier than those guys.

Dude, we did a lot of stuff…Maybe I shouldn't talk about this with a judge in the room, huh? Just teasing, your Honor. We never did nothing terrible, just trying to impress girls and each other. We might have crossed a few lines here and there, but some people might say some of those lines were too tight, you know what I mean?

Mainly, we talked. A lot. You have no idea how long a night can be until you're busy trying to fill it. I loved my uncle Joe, but all that stuff everyone has said today about him was true. He could be really tough on *everybody*. Man, he was even hard on my mom - his own sister - because she married a Spanish guy. Like, not even a Mexican or Puerto Rican. Literally, a guy from Spain. No offense to my Mexican and Puerto Rican hermanos y hermanas, of course!

Lots of times, Mickey or Rickey left that house to get out of Uncle Joe's way or didn't go straight home after work or a class or a date. They'd call me, and the three of us would meet up at a park or a bar, or see a movie, or just hang out in Mickey's car if we couldn't do nothing else. Sometimes it was just one of them and me. But usually, it was the three of us. They were always together if they could help it.

I know you've heard a lot of stuff about how they maybe sometimes didn't get along or fought or whatever. Listen, I ain't saying either of them was perfect. But no one is talking about how they supported each other through everything, dude. *Everything*. Beatings, fights, bad relationships. It's true, what Rebecca said. They could cut each other down to bloody stumps. But if you tried to get between them, boy, you better hope God is awake and still likes you. Kinda scary even for me, and I'm related

Case in point: a couple months ago, Mickey had some money problems. A few gambling debts that got a little out of control. I know this probably sounds weird since Mickey was the "successful" one in everyone's eyes, and Rickey had a hard time just keeping a job. That's all true.

But it's also true that Rickey had no problem lending whatever money he had to whoever needed it. That's right, including Mickey. How much don't matter. It probably wasn't a lot for you or me, but it was for Rickey. He didn't care. He wanted to help his brother, no matter what. It's true that Rickey technically owed Mickey and was kinda-sorta paying him back for bailing him out that time he got arrested, but still. And no one ever knew. Except me.

Can I say one more thing before I give up the floor, judge?

Peter? Dude, I am sorry for you and Dylan. I love you. You know I do. You were a sweet kid and you're a decent young man. You're like my own *hermanos*, but get over yourself! What are you now? Like, thirty? Thirty-two? It's time to grow up. Sometimes life doesn't break the way you want. It's nobody's fault that your mom and dad decided to have kids so much later in life.

So, stop blaming them like they did something wrong to you. Not when Rickey's laying in a hospital bed and can't speak for himself.

# Madame Marguerite
## Thornberg-Tonelli

My name is Marguerite Thornberg-Tonelli. You may address me as *Madame* Thornberg-Tonelli.

You have asked me here today to speak about the Blake brothers. I do not recall very much about them as young men individually. However, I do remember them as students in my music classes. Over my forty years as an award-winning music educator, I am proud to say I instilled the love of music and passion for the performing arts in thousands of fine, upstanding young men and young women.

Please do not be mistaken, I did not misspeak. I *rarely* do. All my pupils were indubitably all fine young men and young women. But of course! I insisted on it! Anyone who wanted to study with me had to rise to my high standards. I made a point to identify and treat and respect them as the talented creatures they, and I, believed them to be. In return, I insisted that they behave accordingly and earn the high stature I afforded them. Any students who did not comport themselves appropriately soon found themselves relegated to study hall, or worse, physical education.

Both Michael and Richard - I do not use nicknames, I find them exceedingly *vulgar* - were decent, hard-working students, as I recall. Richard, particularly, evokes fond memories. He had the voice of an angel. I can admit it now without shame or concern, being many years beyond any connection with him: I had something of a "musical crush" on him. Nothing *inappropriate*, mind you, but my heart simply turned to jelly when he sang.

Each word, every syllable danced off his tongue, out of his mouth, and through the air, and landed gently on my anxious ears. Such beauty! Such grace! Such skill! Richard exhibited an exceptionally rare vocal command and subtlety for even the most talented professional such as myself, much less an adolescent in training.

My heart floods with pride even now, though I truly had little to do with Richard's inherent talent. I am not what one might call a "person of faith," but I think it is appropriate to say his was a gift from God. And I shared and enjoyed and even envied that gift for the two glorious years Richard sat in my class.

Michael, bless his soul, tried very, very hard to contribute. Indeed, sometimes *too* hard. Sadly, he just could not sing. Even if his life depended on it. At one point in his sophomore year, it became sadly, undeniably clear that, Michael simply and utterly lacked the gift of voice. This, despite my best efforts in the classroom, countless hours of personal lessons and years of skill and expertise, mind you. Yet, he was a wonderfully talented musician, so I encouraged him to join the band that accompanied our swing choir. That was, I thought, a clever, respectful way to honor and support Michael's love for music without doing irreparable harm to our program.

However, the same could not be said for Richard. For some reason I could never quite grasp, Richard never wanted to join any of our external performing groups. Of course, he was a wondrous presence in the classroom, but he disappeared the minute the bell rang. That was all the stranger, considering that Michael was - how shall I say this? – omnipresent. It was almost as if they were each other's polar opposite.

As absent and mysterious and intractable as Richard was, Michael was available, energetic, and willing to do anything to garner my attention and, dare I say, affection and approval. I know this may sound somewhat gauche coming from an accomplished and dedicated educator, but his attempts to ingratiate himself were sometimes irksome. Yes, that is *definitely* the word for it. Michael's musical enthusiasm knew no bounds. Normally, one would praise a student for such dedication, such spirit. Even encourage it. However, one does not have to be a *beloved and eminently skilled* teacher such as I, to know that sometimes too much of a good thing is, truly, too much.

He commanded everyone's attention incessantly. I am sorry sir? Did I misspeak? No, as I said before, I do not misspeak. I choose my words deliberately and purposefully. and I said precisely what I meant. He *commanded* attention - both drawing and organizing it around himself until it could be unbearable. As a very small example, once, although we had, I thought, safely tucked Michael away in the band, he continued singing. Badly. And loudly. So loudly that I raised my own voice which I never did, to protect my delicate vocal cords.

*"Please stop singing, Michael."* I directed, as firmly and clearly as possible. "You are *overwhelming* the rest of the group."

He merely scoffed - yes, literally scoffed. Then he said, both haughtily and condescendingly, "I suppose you'd prefer my idiot brother to sing a few love songs, wouldn't you?"

Naturally, being adolescents, the class laughed hysterically, much to my displeasure and chagrin. I am embarrassed to this day that I did not immediately chastise and correct their bad behavior! Attacking such a gentle soul! I held my tongue, struggling to maintain my professional decorum, only to watch poor Richard melt into his chair. Soon after, as I recall, Richard dropped choir altogether.

Nothing I did would entice Richard to add his majestic voice to the choir. Such a *shame*. Such a *loss*. For our music program, certainly, and our school, but also for himself. I always sensed a void in Richard that I truly believe music could have filled.

I understand that you asked me today to assess Michael's character, and whether he is the best person to care for Richard now. Although I make every reasonable and appropriate effort to maintain contact with all my students, I honestly cannot say.

What I can say with *absolute* certainty, is that the world missed out on something very special in Richard Blake.

# Aisha Shah

Most of you don't know me, and that is understandable, and acceptable. I am not interested in anything you have to say. I'm only here to give this letter Rickey wrote after the first time he tried to…well, you know.

Oh, a thousand pardons. I see by the looks on some of your faces, perhaps some of you *don't* know this isn't the first time Rickey grew so tired of everything and everyone, especially his so-called family, that he tried to end it all.

That first time, he did the stupidest thing ever, sitting in his car in the garage with the motor running. As if no one would hear the noise or smell the fumes in the house. Luckily, I did. I pulled him from that car with nobody's help, and you know that he is not a small man. Just me, pushing and dragging him into the kitchen, his clothes stinking of gas. Calling 911 with one hand. Slapping and shaking his head with the other. Trying to not wake my son.

And do you know what the first words out of his mouth where when he woke up? Not "Thank You, Aisha," or "I am sorry, Aisha." No. I'll never forget it. The first thing he said was, "Don't tell my family." You did so much damage to that good man, you hurt him so badly, he didn't want to tell you anything. Not even how depressed and confused he was. Please do not misunderstand me. He was not embarrassed about his depression at all. We talked about it quite often. But because he didn't want you to use it against him. He was so tired of you making him feel like he couldn't do anything right, and Mickey couldn't do anything wrong.

That is how I got to "know" many of you before I ever met anyone. Him telling me how ashamed he was of many of you. But he should not have worried about me telling you. I would have never talked to any of you about anything before, and I certainly won't after I leave here today.

Of course, I might feel differently if any one of you ever made me feel welcome the few times Rickey tried to include me in your family. The first time he brought me to his parent's home, I brought Hussein, my beautiful little boy. I was reluctant but Rickey insisted. Unfortunately, the look in his father's eyes told me immediately that I was right to be concerned. His father barely spoke to me at all except to pester and tease me about my name. I explained that "Shah" is a very old, very traditional, honorable name given to Muslim royalty and rulers. It meant nothing to him.

I will have you know that I am also a successful, accomplished, intelligent woman, but I am sure Rickey's father wouldn't have cared about that either. It did not matter that my husband was an American citizen who proudly served this country's military before dying of cancer five years ago. No, all his father saw was another brown-skinned, foreign, single mother.

Your Honor, it is very important for you to know the Rickey that I have come to love. I met Rickey three years after my dear husband died, and since that beautiful day, he has brought light into my lonely life. But more important than me, he loved Hussein as if he were his own son.. I am not sure if I will ever marry again, but if I ever consider it, I pray he would be a man like Rickey. A good, decent, caring, and kind human being to stand with me as a husband and father for my children, inshallah.

How do you explain to a child about things that even grown-ups do not understand? What does an eight-year-old know of racism, or religion, or politics? All he knew was that this wonderful, sweet man with the quiet spirit loved him and treated him like his very own son. A boy needs a father. Especially a boy who feels out of place in his world and in his skin. Rickey became that man for my son. He gave the love that only a father can give a son. Rickey made him feel special. Strong. Smart. Valued.

Then, the first time he was in your family home, Hussein may as well have been invisible. You treated the dog better. Hussein was so confused and heartbroken. He thought he had done something wrong. You don't treat anyone like you treated me, but especially an innocent child.

Did any of you ever wonder why I never brought Hussein for another visit? Probably not. You never wanted us there in the first place. But if you did, well, now you know. Praise Allah for Rickey. When we got home, Hussein cried for an hour before he fell asleep in Rickey's arms.

In time, some of you at least tried to pretend to accept Hussein and me, for Rickey's sake. I appreciated the effort, but I knew the truth. Once I saw that look in his father's eyes, I understood the racism and all the other nonsense Rickey had been raised with. He was shamed and pained by it, but I have been living with it my whole life.

Still, I am an adult. When you treated my little boy like he was a filthy street beggar, well, let me just say, you were lucky Rickey was there, because if he had not been, I might have done something to justify his father's fears.

Forgive me, Your Honor, I did not intend to speak like this. It is not my place, or my way, usually. My emotions have gotten the best of me as, I am sure, is the case with most mothers.

As I said, I am here only because Rickey asked me to give this letter directly to Mickey if anything bad ever happened to him.

I never intended or expected to cross paths with any of you again. In my heart, I would not cross the street to spit on any of you if you were on fire. But he made me promise on the soul of my son. Our love for him compels me to honor his request. May Allah forgive your sins

# Richard (Rickey) Blake
## *(as read by Aisha Shah)*

*Mickey,*

*I was gonna start this letter with "Dear Michael James Blake," just to drive you nuts, like when Mom would do when we were in trouble. But I don't want to piss you off any more then usual since I need to ask you a favor. Lord knows I don't want to get the "Great Michael Blake" mad! Just teesing, brother! I am sure your face is turning eight shades of red right now! Well, at least I don't have to listen to you bitch about my gramer and spelling since this is probably the last thing I will ever right. (Ha ha, I know its "write." Just wanted to make sure your paying attention.)*

*Anyway, no jokes I hope your doing alright. If your reading this letter, that means I am probably not doing so hot. I made Aisha promise to give this to you if something bad ever happened to me, or if I ever did something bad again. If that has happened, then I need your help.*

*Please don't go getting all crazy like you usaly do. Its not like I never asked for your help before, or that I haven't helped you too. Its just that this time might be the last time. And I really can't go to anyone else.*

*I guess I will start by saying I hated you when we were kids. A lot. You probley know that now, if you didnt know it then. Not that you were perfect. I always hated the way you talked like some kind of college profeser, or worse then that, talking down to me like I was to dumb to understand your big fancy words. But you didn't do to much wrong to me. Mostly it was everybody else who did shit, wich I then took out on you. Always comparing me to you, pushing me to be more like you. Act like you. Do better in school like you. I gotta say that shit got old real fast. And it never ended. Not even when you went away to college. Really, it was worse because I didn't go away. Especialy with mom and dad, and dad worse of all. I could never do anything right as far as he could see. But YOU could never do nothing wrong. So, yes, I couldnt stand you a lot of times growing up because whenever I saw you, I saw the person everyone wanted me to be, and I couldnt ever figure out why I wasn't good enough just being who I was. Inside, I new it wasn't right or fair to blame you, but what else was I gonna do? Hit dad? Scream at the teachers? So, I just kept it inside or took it out on you. I am very sorry, from the bottom of my heart. I mean it. I now its to little to late, but this is the best I can do.*

*The truth is, deep down I love and respect you. Always have. I hate to say it because I don't want to enflate your ego which is already fuckin' huge, but your kind of my role model. The way you always came across to people as confident, strong, smart. You could talk to anybody about anything especialy music. Even if I was better then you, at least when it came to singing. Still I could never do that. I always admired that, but I was jelous at the same time. I never been able to be so open like that about my feelings. I guess I was always scared someone would push back and Id look like the ignorant fool people always said I was. But you? Mickey, you just have a amazing way of shining. And not just that, but you honestly care about people, even people you dont like or dont deserve it. (Hint, hint, like me.) You are the only one who stood up for me, no matter what, even when I was nocking you down. You never really gave me a hard time about, well, lots of things I did. Hell, you even helped with a few.*

*Remember that time we drove through that bad neighborhood at night? I told you to pull over by the street sign and I got on top of the car and broke the sign off. Richards Avenue! Come on, man, I know it was stupid but I had to have it! I couldn't really see anything because the I was kinda looking up into the street light, but when I looked down, I saw those two giant guys siting on their porch. That old guy starting yelling and the other one ran toward us. I dived through the window into the back seat like Starsky and Hutch and screamed at you: "Drive! Drive!" You peeled out of there so fast it smelled like a tire factory had berned down! Oh my god! I never been so scared in my life! Then when dad found the sign in the garage where I hid it, you told him you were holding it for that black kid you used to hang around with in school. You saved us a hard core ass whipping that day for sure.*

*Then there was that time I got that girl pregnint. The pilot's daughter? Remember I used to tell you she loved to test out my joystick? I kinda wasn't kidding. We did a lot more stuff in that plane when it was on the ground then when it was in the air, and you now what happened. You took us to the doctor, you paid for the entire thing, and you never said another word about it. I now I paid you back, but I can never really repay you, because I now what you did goes against what you believe and your church stuff.*

*You did so many other things for me. Sometimes I wondera why. Did you feel guilty? Or that you owed me something? Who knows? All I'm trying to say is I never thanked you, but I never forgot, either. So, I guess, now is as good a time as any. Thank you. Mostly for understanding when I left the car running in the closed garage, and forgot to get out first. I now how angry you were. I don't blame you, but you never really hassled me about it. Lucky for me I guess, Aisha was there.*

*That's kinda why I am writing this letter.*

*Some days, I feel like I am sitting on a cloud. Things are actually kinda good for me lately, with Aisha and Hussein. He is such a sweet, sweet kid. I never saw myself as a dad. Never really wanted to be one, considering our dad. I don't pretend to be his father. His dad was a good man from what Aisha says and I don't want to disrespect his memory. But there's just something about the way he looks at me that makes me feel halfway human.*

*But other days, I just want to dig a hole climb in and never come out. I can't really explain it. Accept to say I just get tired of everything. Living is hard work. I am so tired, so worn out. I don't want to fight no more. I just give up in my head and my heart. I just want to sleep. I want to die. There. I said it. Not pulling any punches. I don't blame you, or mom and dad, or anybody really. I don't understand it myself, Mickey, so dont get mad at me.*

*I aint saying I am going to do anything, but if anything bad happens to me, whatever it is, I want you to make sure that I can die in peace. You step in. that's the favor. That's what I am asking. I except the idea of my own death, so just let me go. I now it will be hard but that is my wish. I want you to make any dicisions. I don't want to burden Aisha with this. She's already lost one husband. I don't want to break her heart twice.*

*I love you. I trust you. I now you'll do the right thing.*

*Sorry to put this on you, and sorry it took our entire life for me to write this letter! Your a pain in the ass, but your alright, for an older brother! Thanks for everything.*

*Your brother, Rickey, or as mom would say, "Richard Adam Blake"*

# The Hon. Robert Roy

I must reiterate that this is not a court proceeding. I cannot make, or compel anyone else to make, this decision for Michael or the Blake family.

Rather, I am here today merely to offer whatever advice and guidance I may as a family friend.

First, we must establish the facts, which are these: Richard is on life support, having apparently tried again to take his life. Second, according to medical information provided by the family, he is essentially "brain dead" at this time and is not expected to recover. And, most critically, third, he did not leave a "Do Not Resuscitate" order or a living will, does not have a spouse, and his parents are also both deceased. The only direction we have as for how to proceed, in as much as it can be considered such, is the letter that Ms. Shah so kindly and bravely read for us.

Assuming Richard did in fact write the letter - and we have no reason to think otherwise - and that it does in fact reflect his clear-minded and sincere interests at the time of its writing, then it is Richard's stated wish that his eldest brother, Michael, make any and all critical decisions about Richard's health and medical issues and ongoing care.

I have listened very keenly to all the statements about Michael's and Richard's relationship in the context of establishing whether Michael has the mental and emotional wherewithal to decide whether to continue life support for Richard, or to disconnect those systems and let his brother pass.

Some of you are opposed to any such action and would rather leave such weighty decisions to the medical professionals. I understand and respect your position.

I also understand and respect that some of you wish to respect Richard's last wishes, to the extent we have them, and at very least support the idea of Michael making this extraordinarily difficult choice on his brother's behalf.

Your memories and perspectives about their relationship speak to the unique bond between them that would inspire one to make such a request of another. However special their own relationship was or is, the request itself is not uncommon. Indeed, in many ways we often put our lives in the hands of those to whom we feel closest, often just emotionally or symbolically, but sometimes literally and legally.

Although I am not a member of the Blake family, I have seen up close in my courtroom more times than I care to remember the devastating pain that extended illness or imminent death can bring to a family. I have also seen how these exact challenges as we face today can, and sadly often do, divide and even sometimes destroy families. As a human being, I sympathize and empathize with everyone involved with this agonizing dilemma.

To whatever extent my words and experience may give you clarity and strength, please do not let one tragedy cause another. So often - too often - we are the victims of nothing more or less dangerous than ourselves.

That said, I have reached a conclusion in my unofficial capacity as arbiter and advisor.

Based on my thirty-seven years of service as both legal counsel and judge, it is my considered opinion that Michael is more than capable to decide whether to continue life support services for Richard.

Michael, please know that whichever path you choose, my heart goes with you.

# Mickey Blake (continued...)

...I don't deny it, I absolutely I have wished my brother dead many times in our lives. But to ask me to really end his life? This is just beyond the pale.

Of course, this doesn't surprise me a bit. And it shouldn't surprise anyone else, either. This is classic Rickey. He does something dumb or harmful, then asks someone to get him out of the mess he created. I know that sounds terrible, but it's true. Whenever he got into a jam - in school, with girlfriends, at home with our dad, on the job (whenever he worked, which wasn't all that much), he'd inevitably screw something up and come running for someone to rescue him. Usually, me. And of course, I would answer.

I know he had a hard life. But I never intentionally did anything to hurt Rickey or make anything worse for him. I always did my best to be the Big Brother. To show him the right path and teach him the right things to do. Just go to class. Or show up on time to work. Or save a little money here and there. Or something as simple and obvious as don't sleep with the boss's daughter.

Hey, I understand he believed I caused some of his problems and the pressures he felt being my little brother. I admit, I cast a big shadow sometimes. And our mom, God bless her soul, just made it worse, always comparing him to me. All those teachers criticizing him when he wasn't me, never appreciating him for what he was, or could do. I get it. I always wanted to scream at them, "Stop it! Let Rickey be Rickey!"

But is it my fault that I was actually successful in life? Jesus Christ, just follow the rules a little bit and things tend to turn out ok more than not. Really, is that so hard? And even if it is, why should I have to feel guilty for being a good person and working hard and making a little something of myself? I'm not responsible for all his failures and screw ups! It's just not fair.

Sure, he could be kind and caring and thoughtful, just as Janeen and Aisha said. He was a great uncle and brother-in-law (when he wasn't flirting with my wife.) He was a terrific father figure to Hussein. Truth be told, when we weren't fighting, I loved him more than just about anyone else. We understood each other in ways that, I don't know, went beyond words. Often, we could just look at each other and know what the other one was thinking. So, before you all think, "Oh, what a jerk you are, Mickey," know this: I loved - sorry, *love* - my brother very much.

But this? You're asking me to do something that's just…I know this will sound harsh, but I think suicide is the coward's way out. It's selfish. Rickey knew that. He knew, or knows, how I feel on the matter. We talked about it after the first time he tried to take his life. Boy, I must have really hit a nerve with that one. I never saw him so mad at me. He kept screaming, "You don't know how I feel!" Whatever! I was furious, too. I told him, "I may not be inside your soul, Rickey, but I know what I know. And I know that God - whatever you call it, whatever you believe - didn't give us Life so we could just throw it away when things get hard." *Life is hard.* That's the point. What comes *after* life is easy. But life itself? We must muscle through. Surviving is the first step to succeeding. If I had a dollar for every time I have said that, I could have retired early.

You know what he said to me? "Surviving for what? Succeeding for what?" Maybe for the first time ever, I didn't know how to respond. It was like the words were trapped in my mouth. The only thing I could think of, was to tell him that he was a good person, to remind him about Aisha and Hussein, and to insist that *I* loved him if *no one else* did...I did my best, but really, words are too small to fill a hole that deep.

So here we are. Rickey asking me to get him off the hook again. Thank you, Aisha, for being so brave and thoughtful as to share his letter. I know it wasn't easy for you to be here. I hope you know, no matter what else has happened or will happen, you are always welcome in *my* family.

Please, all of you! Stop looking at me like I have some big magic solution. I don't know what to do any more than you! How can *anyone* ask *anyone* to intentionally end someone's life? Especially my own brother? I mean, what gives him the right?

Rickey and I have a love-hate relationship, that's for sure.

And yes, I have been mad enough to want to kill him myself. Choke the living crap out of him. Or bash his head in with a baseball bat. Or shoot him, or stab him. It didn't really matter as long as he died. All the times he stole my girlfriends, always telling me when he'd slept with them. Or embarrassed me in front of my friends saying something disgusting or acting like a jerk. Or stealing money from me. Or worse, if you can believe it.

But that was all kid stuff. It certainly doesn't mean I actually want to see Rickey die, much less cause it myself! Or any of my brothers or sisters. Not even you, Peter.

I know what Rickey said in that letter. But who knows what he really meant? He wrote that at another very bad time, so maybe it's not one hundred percent totally accurate. And if it is, it breaks my heart to think that my brother hurts that badly.

I truly, honestly want to give him some relief. Some kind of peace. Even if he never knows I did it. I want so bad to fix everything wrong in Rickey's life. But I just can't...I can't...do this.

Good God in heaven, forgive me! I just want one more chance to talk to him again, to tell him that he is wrong! That life is worth living. That people *do* love and respect and admire him for who he is. Does that make me the selfish one? Am I a coward now, too?

I know he will be angry with me. Probably won't ever talk to me, if he talks to anybody again. But he said he trusted me to do the right thing, right? That's what he said in his letter? "Do the right thing?"

Hopefully, one day, I'll be able to explain to him why this *is* the right thing. Not just for now, but for always. Maybe he'll understand. Probably, he'll just blame me for whatever else goes wrong...

But I cannot think that far ahead. I cannot think about anything beyond this moment, this act. No matter what else happens, it is my job to protect Rickey whenever I can, even if that means protecting him from himself.

That's what brothers are supposed to do, right?

I mean, isn't it?

# BROTHERS

# TOM HERNANDEZ

# <u>STORIES</u>

TOM HERNANDEZ

# <u>Bad Medicine</u>

*"Happy birthday, dear Dad/Grandpa/Uncle Joe, happy birthday, to youuuuuuu!"*

The group of well-wishers hung on to the last word for what seemed like eons in Joe's ears. The notes mixed with the antiseptic smell in the air that crept into his room at the assisted living facility where his family had parked him ten years ago. They'd expected him to die much sooner. And why wouldn't they? After all he was 107 when they brought him here. Any reasonable person with any kind of respect for normal life would have died by now. Given up his spot in the daily bread line. Turned over his table in the Restaurant of Life.

But not Joe.

Here he sat. Still able to walk the halls. He didn't even need the hand under the elbow that most of the residents, all much younger than him, needed if they could walk at all. Not that he saw much of his family. Except for "official" visits like today or a holiday when relatives were invited to have lunch with their resident (on his tab, mind you) he rarely saw, much less walked around the halls with many of them.

Still able (and very happy) to chat up and wink at the women, young and old, although he'd never done anything beyond flirting the few times when circumstances had led in that direction. Not for lack of ability or interest. Joe still had both. He might have been a little slower on the draw, but he was certain the old "love gun," as that silly band KISS had sung a million years ago, could still fire a round or two. Rather, no woman, no matter her age, even looked at him, much less saw him as an interesting, capable, viable partner of any kind, much less physical.

And still sharp as a new tack fresh out of the box. That expansive family? He still called every one of his seventy-two kids, grandkids and great grandkids by their proper name, no hesitation at all. And don't get Joe started on current affairs or politics or sports or culture or – most especially – music and movies. He could back just about anyone into an inescapable conversational corner, tongue-tied and feet tangled in their knotted, and often only half-tied rhetorical rope. Nothing worse than an ill-prepared or lazy adversary, Joe often chastised after winning another argument.

Still, most days, Joe Barker was not happy. Especially on his birthday.

"Hey there, Dad," his son, Matty, said. "How are you feeling today? Doctor says you are doing great, for a man your age. Heck, you're doing great for a man of *any* age!" Matty dropped the zinger loud enough for the room of relatives to hear. As planned, it drew the fawning, cooing, polite but insincere laughter he intended. It almost seemed like he was waiting for a drummer to add a rim shot. *Ba-doom-doom. Csssss!* Matty was the youngest of the four kids he had with his wife, Claire. He was far too old to still be called by the diminutive nickname, but it stuck, glued to him by eighty years of life. It was both ironic and sad, Joe thought, since the older kids – Joseph Junior, Monica, and Jean – had all died long ago. Matty, the "baby," was now the adult. Had been for many years. Except when visiting Joe, Matty was usually the oldest person in the room. Heck, Joe's youngest great grandchild was twenty-nine, and carped incessantly about turning thirty, like that was something worth complaining about. Joe appreciated Matty's high spirit and good nature. He loved his son's sincere, well-intentioned effort to inject some levity to counterbalance the wailing sobs from the old woman across the hall that hung in the air like smog. But Joe couldn't look past the very old elephant in the room.

"Matty, you know how I am. I am here. I am awake. I am healthy. I am breathing. I am hearing, talking, eating, reading, listening to the radio when I can get Alexa to answer me, watching television when I can find something that interests me. But I don't want to be."

"Dad come on now," Matty interjected. What was coming was inappropriate for the day and the room of guests who'd gathered, no matter how many times they'd all heard it before. "We have talked about this."

"Yes, son, we have. So, you should know by now how I feel," Joe said. Eyes turned toward his rising voice, still as clarion and crisp as that of a man half his son's age.

"I want to be dead. Like everyone else of my generation. I should be in the ground or in an urn on top of your fireplace. Instead, I am here."

"But Uncle Joe, we all love you," said one of his nieces, Catherine. "We don't want to lose you any time soon."

"Catherine, sweetheart, I appreciate the sentiment. I really do. And I love you for saying it," Joe said, smiling at the beautiful middle-age woman. "I know you all mean well for me. But I want to be dead. I'm not sad, or depressed, or suicidal, I promise. It's just the natural order of things. A man my age should be dead. And I would have been if not for that stupid COVID-19 vaccine."

Few in the room had lived through that god-awful pandemic. Fifty years ago, an unknown virus gobbled up and shat out most of the world's human and financial resources for nearly three years. They had not lived through the plague, yet not knowing its reality didn't make its truth any less real.

"I did what I - what we were all - supposed to do," Joe said, with the practiced flatness of tone of someone who'd told the story many times.

"I wore my mask, I social-distanced, I stayed away from everyone I loved for months at a time. And then, the first vaccine came out, a month before election day that first year, just like you-know-who said."

A glancing smile broke quickly across Matty's face. To this day, his dad refused to speak the former president's name as if in ongoing protest.

Joe looked around the room, filled with everyone with even a scintilla of concern or affection for him.

"To this day, I don't know what was worse – him winning re-election, or the millions of people who died after taking that first vaccine. And not just died. But died horrible, painful, terrible deaths because they had been willing to believe anything anyone said, just to get it over with faster. So they could stop wearing masks and go out to dinner."

Joe's bony, knobby index fingers waved in front of his face, making air quotes. "I cannot even begin to put into words how angry and betrayed and guilty I felt, because I'd been 'smart enough' to not take that first vaccine. I knew it wasn't safe. How could it possibly be? They rushed it into production as soon as soon the government waved all the safety regulations. Any fool would have known it wasn't safe." Joe took a deep breath. "Except those that didn't. Including your mother. She believed everything that man said. Boy, we fought so much that first term…" Joe's voice trailed off, drowned under a wash of memories. "Look what her faith got her."

A tear crept into the corner of Joe's 117-year-old eye. He quickly turned in his chair toward the wall and wiped it away.

"Dad, I think it's time for us to go," Matty said softly. He and his father had had this conversation so many times over the last half-decade that it'd taken on a life of its own, breathing its own sorrow into the air around Joe. The loss of his mother was the real source of his dad's bitterness, at least as much as the politics of a plague that killed many millions of people, including two younger cousins, Matty knew. "You need your rest."

Joe's head swiveled back like he'd been slapped. "Rest? Rest? *Rest for what?* To play another round of Old People Who Should Be Dead Bingo?" he yelled. "Matty, you cannot possibly understand what it means to be so old that the oldest people around me are considered youngsters by comparison, and yet I can't die! I have absolutely nothing in common with anyone. I am utterly and literally alone on an island. It's not that I have lost touch with the world, Matty. The world has lost touch with me"

"But Dad, you could have taken your chances with the next four vaccines. You chose not to," Matty said smoothly, trying to calm his father.

"And it's a good thing, too, seeing as how they all failed. It's like the virus kept getting smarter every time and laughed at us with each new vaccine. Ah, but then they came out with a sixth one. And every scientist and doctor worth their lab coats said this was the one. *This one* would cure COVID forever -- and not just the current strains. It would even prevent new strains that hadn't even formed yet. Well sir, that sounded too good to be true, but I figured, what is there to lose? The sixth time must be the charm, right?"

Matty dropped his head. He'd heard the inevitable answer to this rhetorical question a thousand times before.

"It worked, all right," Joe said. "Only too well! Now I am trapped by my own bad luck and some sick, twisted cosmic irony! Here I am, a living, breathing testament to the power of modern medicine!" Joe shouted. His vitriolic cynicism was as clear as the spittle now on his lips. His anger drew surprised glances from a few people floating around the edges of his room.

"Dad come on. You know there's nothing to that. There is no proof that the vaccine caused you to live longer, or stop your natural aging, or whatever it is you think happened. It could have been a fluke. It could be that you've got incredibly good genes. Maybe God has a reason for keeping you alive so long. Who knows? Yes, there were problems with the first six vaccines, but the next one worked the way it was supposed to. Maybe not for everyone, but at least for a few people. The others who lived all had happy lives and eventually died just like we're all going to do" Matty said. "Including you." His voice carried just the faintest wisp of exhausted exasperation.

Joe shifted in chair. Several relatives had quietly slipped out of the room, lingering now outside the open door or down the hall near the dining room. Those remaining watched the ballgame on the television. "Bears are losing again," Joe noted to no one in particular. "Some things never change."

Matty lifted and gently held his father's right hand. He spoke respectfully, but firmly, as if reprimanding a child whose countless good deeds far outweighed this one bad one. "Dad, all we know, all any of us care about – " Matty waved his right hand over his shoulder toward the thinning herd as it now issued a collective groan at yet another Bears fumble – "is that you are still with us. For whatever reason. It doesn't matter. Your life is a blessing.

And we cherish it."

Joe quieted for a few seconds, reflecting on the journey he'd taken, but would have never wished on anyone. A wistful chuckle escaped through a melancholic smile. "A blessing? Hmmm…fifty years of memories that no one else understands, of a colossal human disaster that we brought on ourselves." He stared at his and his son's hands, intertwined. "Somehow, this blessing feels more like a curse." He raised his eyes to his Matty's face. "Son, you are a caring and conscientious man. I have always been most proud of your heart. So, I know you understand when I say this: I love you, but I don't want to see you ever again."

A loud cheer erupted behind them – thankfully, loud enough to hide Matty's gasp. The Bears had scored a rare touchdown.

"Now Matty, I don't mean to hurt your feelings. I just want to be left alone until I die. Lord knows when that will ever be, or how it will happen. I don't want to bother you with all that." Joe smiled and winked at his son. "Plus, at your age, you shouldn't be driving anymore." The attempted joke fell flat. Matty stared at his father, unsmiling.

"Matty, all I do anymore is sit around here and review my life. My freakishly long life. You know I'm not particularly religious. Never have put much stock in all that 'Invisible Man' stuff, but sometimes I think that if there is a God, He was using that virus to teach us a lesson in humility. You know, they called it a 'novel' virus because it was new. But really, there was nothing new about the situation. As usual, we humans saw something small and thought we could just crush it under our giant feet." Joe said.

"Six times, we rushed. Sacrificing safety for speed and profit," Joe said. "Six times, our arrogance told us our size and strength would win out. That our superior firepower would win the war because it always had  But none of that mattered to the virus."

Matty had long been in awe of his father's wit and intellect. But he was astounded by the words Joe now spoke.

"Dad," he nearly whispered, "to be fair, the scientists and doctors finally got it right with the seventh vaccine."

"Great!" Joe said, looking away. "Lucky Number Seven, I guess."

Joe took a deep breath. For the first time in many years, he called his son by his adult name. Decades of kind, mature patience with his father had earned him this small token of his father's respect.

"Matthew, here is what I have learned these last fifty years when I should have been dead and spending eternity with your mother," Joe said, wryly.

"*I* won, I suppose, but *we* failed," he said.

"Our leaders failed us, our doctors and scientists failed us, the media failed us. Heck, even that God of yours failed us. But mostly, we failed each other. As individuals, as a community, as a species. And why? Because doing the right thing took too long and was inconvenient."

Now Joe stood, walked to the door, and stared down the hall. A man who looked older than Joe toddled down the corridor, clinging shakily to a sparkling, aluminum walker. He turned and reached back to his son, hugging him with all his might.

"I don't believe in much these days, Matthew, but I have come to believe that God of yours gave us that virus to remind us that we're supposed to find our strength by working together," Joe said.

"But we didn't. We never do. Instead, we died from something too big to kill. Our hubris and greed." Joe exhaled deeply. He slumped into his chair like a deflated balloon.

A groan rose from the remaining visitors. The Bears had lost again.

"I guess God just gave us a taste of our own medicine."

# New York Style, With Strawberries

He quivered with the last, convulsive, knee-weakening explosions of their lovemaking.

His fingers released their grip from her shoulders and slowly slid up the back of her taught neck, offered a quick scalp massage, then reversed course, heading firmly down his wife's beautiful back.

His manicured nails gently scratched as they descended below her shoulder blades, through the deep middle regions and settled in the small, just above the top of her round, slightly flushed backside.

He continued this sensual denouement for several minutes as his own love exhausted itself inside hers. Then, he positioned his hands just beneath the wings of her shoulders, fingers splayed, and pressed firmly until they popped, loudly, decisively.

Her head sagged with laughter at the familiar announcement of the end of their coupling. "Oh my god," she said, giggling. "I can't believe you still do that after all these years."

"It's all the built-up tension." He backed away and rolled back into his place in bed, the blanket and sheets off, waiting for the sweat on his glistening skin to dry, lying next to the only woman who'd ever made him feel so full, so crazy, with love.

He always craved her heat. Was always trying to hold her tighter. But sometimes, like now, it seemed they were so close that only their souls separated them. She was not the only lover he'd ever had. Just the best. The one that he'd bet his life on, knowing he'd never want to cash in these chips.

She could hear his smile as much as see it in the darkness. Funny that a gesture so out of context would continue to amuse and bind them. "You drive me so wild, I get so crazy, all that energy's got to release from someplace."

"Yea, well, I'd think it'd maybe release from someplace else." She swatted at his bare thigh. "And cover your nakedness up there, or at least dry it off. I don't want to roll over into a wet spot!"

Now it was her turn to tease a bit, both producing and eliciting love-filled laughter. She turned toward him and ran her fingers first around, then up from his navel. Her sharp nails cut a path through his thick and slightly graying chest hair, then playfully pinched his right nipple.

"Ouch! Stop that! You know I bruise easy," he whined. "Plus, I am done. The tank is empty. Nada. That's it."

"Of course!" she said, now nibbling his ear. "That's what you men always do. Tarzan swings off to another branch and leaves poor Jane hanging."

His brow furrowed in confusion. "Wow! That's quite the image! But I'm not sure it's completely accurate. Last time I looked, Jane was swinging pretty good on that vine. In fact, I think she got to the top of the tree at least twice!"

"Well, you never did that, you know, thing you did tonight before. That was amazing!" She lay her head on his chest and breathed deeply.

"Likewise. What you did had me shaking in my boots - or would have if I'd been wearing any!" He gently stroked her hair as her head rose and fell with his words. "You know what I was thinking about, you know, *during?*"

"No, I couldn't even imagine," she teased. "What were you thinking about, you know, *during?*"

"I was thinking that was the best..."

"I know! Me too! The best se..."

"...cheesecake I've ever had."

Her words crashed into the back of her teeth, causing a massive pileup in her mouth. She finally extricated her tongue from the wreckage, raised her beautiful nude form onto her elbow so that she stared directly into his deep, brown eyes.

*"Excuse me?!* The best *cheesecake?!* Is that some kind of weird, twisted, macho male code for that little trick you did?"

He stared back at her, his face blank as a new brick wall.

"Code? No. I mean it. The cheesecake I had for dessert today after lunch. It was fantastic. The best I ever had. Firm, sweet but not too sweet, giant, ripe, strawberries on top, the juice dripping down."

"I don't mean to ask a silly question," she said, hoping her calm tone would keep check on the firing pistons in her brain, "but what in the hell brought that to mind?"

"Well, us. You. Me. Our lovemaking. Trust me, this is really a compliment for you."

Confusion pulled her eyelids taught. "Uh-huh. I can't wait to hear this one..."

"See, I always have to think of something else to distract myself so that I, you know, don't finish too soon. I want to make sure you get your fair share of pleasure, too."

"Well thank you for that, I guess..."

"Tonight was so good – you were so beautiful and we were on fire! I try to find something commensurate to the task at hand. Usually it's baseball, or some movie, or work. But tonight was really, really, *really* good. I had to dig deep."

"And tonight, it was cheesecake?"

"Uh-huh."

"Is that why I heard you making 'yummy' sounds just before…"

"Um, maybe?"

She locked eyes again with him to make sure, if only in her mind, that he wasn't crazy as an outhouse rat. Uncertain, she rolled out of bed. Beads of perspiration still glowed on her breasts in the moonlight from their interlude.

"Where are you going?"

"Well," she said over her shoulder, "all this talk about food – and our workout -- has made me hungry."

"Hey! If you're going to the kitchen, would you bring me a slice of that cheesecake? I brought some home. It's in a leftover box the fridge." He smiled his sexiest, most alluring smile.

She guffawed. "Are you serious?"

Without warning, he quickly lunged across the bed and smacked her bare behind and smiled again.

"I told you. The best, ever!"

# The Editor

*My writers group challenged itself to write the best complete story possible — beginning, middle, and end — in 200 words or less. This is mine.*

"Trust me," the Editor said, "It's better."

The Writer couldn't believe his ears. "You clearly do not understand the art and majesty of what I have written," the Writer said. "The subtle simplicity. The layers of complexity. The poetry is nearly perfect. The metaphor is virtually mystical. Hinting at a higher Truth but leaving it to the Reader to discover and accept. Correct my spelling if you must, but don't change my words."

The Editor resisted the urge to shake the Writer until the rocks which had so obviously clogged his brain rattled to the floor. Instead, the Editor smiled. Inhaled, then exhaled. Lavender suddenly perfumed the air. The Writer seemed to calm.

"I share your concern for your story," the Editor

said. "It is important. Which is why you must let me make a couple minor changes. Cut a few words, trim a sentence or two. I know poetry and metaphor because *I am* poetry and metaphor."

The Writer relented. "Fine. But I get final approval. And credit."

"Of course. As usual." The Editor blinked. Words danced and shuffled.

*"In the beginning, when God created the heavens and earth…"*

"Hmmm…" The Writer nodded. "You're right. It *is* better!"

TOM HERNANDEZ

# ESSAYS

# TOM HERNANDEZ

# The Love of We

I have not written a single non-work-related word for nearly two months.

Not for lack of interest or inspiration, mind you.

In fact, I have fought the urge to write a poem that has been swimming lazy laps around my brain for a couple of weeks. It is highly critical of God and the current Oval Office Occupant, and I didn't want to offend those friends who believe in either or both, all whom I otherwise admire and respect.

I have struggled to stay above the strife (or at least not add to it) as the entire world deals with the fallout – physical, emotional, spiritual, financial – of the worldwide COVID-19 pandemic.

Still, it's been a difficult time, concrete-hard, for me as for many.

I felt like the undersized, but quick-cutting football team running back who has finally broken through the line, zigging this way, zagging that way, hips twisting, knees high, legs pumping, evading linebackers twice my size.

The goal line was in sight. The winning touchdown and all the attendant glory only yards away, nothing ahead of me but screaming fans.

Then, wham!

I was blindsided and tackled by an unseen cornerback. No touchdown. No winning score. No glory. Only pain, turf and stars.

As I lay on the ground, the officials kept their yellow flags in their pockets as every defensive player on the field and, it seemed, a few from the sidelines piled on.

I struggled with sleep-stealing financial concerns for my two daughters and their families; not seeing our granddaughter for more than six weeks; my own blues from lack of socialization with friends and family; the murky, bottomless depths of uncertainty about and concern for the future.

Then it got worse.

Every jaw-droppingly stupid utterance from Donald Trump, a man with a narcissistic need to be in the spotlight. Blammo!

Every one of his gob-smacking, forehead-slapping denials of a comment despite video proof of their utterance. Pow!

Every ridiculous bit of his "cheerleading" to try to ignore and deflect and minimize the seriousness of the situation. Smash to the kisser!

Every childish fight picked with other leaders who dare to cross his constantly shifting, arbitrary political line in the sand. Gut punch!

Every attempt to blame everyone else, anyone else, for seventy days of misdirection, lies, obfuscation and political gamesmanship, while thousands died from a mystery virus. Another shot to the ribs.

(By the way, how many shades of cynical or paranoid does one have to be to suggest, much less think, that this pandemic is a political scheme or hoax?)

And worst of all, his calls to "Liberate" states, prompting people to take part in armed protests of *his own administration's* health directives intended to keep people from dying. Proving yet again that he was most concerned with how he looked to his rabid cult -- and even then, only when the stock market started to tumble. Because those are his only real priorities: money, and image. Especially *his* money, and *his* image.

Each one felt like another cleated foot on my throat. Another body jumping on my back, pinning me to the ground.

I was so anxious, so overwhelmed, so conflicted, that I literally could not catch my breath under the crushing weight of fear, confusion, frustration, anger and lack of human decency.

Then, I read a recent issue of Time magazine.

The special subject, "Finding Hope," featured article after story after essay from writers, doctors, elected officials, religious leaders and social and cultural icons, each promoting a simple, essential premise:

We cannot recover from this pandemic alone.

We must work together as individuals, families, communities, professions, governments, faith systems, public and private sectors.

We must believe that we will return to "normal" – whatever that will look like – only when we share responsibility for each other, rather than thinking only about our singular interest.

Yes, it will be hard.

Yes, it will be painful

Yes, many will suffer financially, emotionally, psychically, spiritually.

And yes, many will die. Maybe, with any luck, not as many as various models and experts have predicted. But more than any rational person would dare call acceptable if any one of the suffering or dead belonged to them.

Interestingly, not one writer took or demanded credit for any idea, development, or policy (much less petulantly whined about not getting enough praise.) Not. One.

For the record, I do not hold Trump responsible for the pandemic. That's silly. However, I do hold him responsible for his own actions, the same as I'd do with any adult or child.

His self-centered, "I! I! I! Me! Me! Me!" behavior is stultifying. It is such a shallow, pathetic, transparent cry for legitimacy in a world in which even he knows he doesn't belong, that one might pity him under normal circumstances.

But nothing is normal these days, and his behavior affects the rest of us.

Trump's callous, callow, even cruel example followed only too gladly by his minions has made a tremendously difficult situation exponentially worse.

Simply put, Trump has pitted the One against the Many.

Listen, I don't pretend to be above self-interest. I want what's best for me and mine the same as anyone else.

But the Time magazine issue reminded me there's more than just "Me" to consider.

If "I" is my only focus, my only concern, my only priority, then others suffer.

"I" fuels fear. Anger. Greed. Hatred.

The power of "I" is its ability to divide. And in the darkness of that division to build walls between "Me" and "Them," defined in any way that helps me keep whatever I think is mine. Race, religion, gender, wealth. Even health.

"We," on the other hand, calls us to give. Love. Sacrifice. Even suffer.

The power of "We" is the life-sustaining energy that comes from combining whatever little bit I have with someone else's, so that what we create together is not only more, but also better and stronger.

"We" in its purest essence cares most about Unity. "We" knows that Unity can be hard, but that hardness smooths the rough edges of division. That hardness is often its own best reward.

Of course, it goes without saying that everyone can follow who they want to follow and believe what they want to believe. As Americans that is our right – even if we are wrong.

What does need to be said though, is that we as humans must be about more than our rights. We must be about our responsibilities, too. Rights are individualistic. Responsibilities are communal.

I am as scared, angry, frustrated, nervous, confused and concerned as anyone else with a functioning head and heart.

Still, right now, in the face of a once-in-a-lifetime worldwide crisis, I choose to believe in "We." I must. It is the only way I will see clearer, sleep better, breathe easier.

The strength of "We."

The dream of "We."

The love of "We."

Hmm…I guess I didn't need to write that poem after all.

# BROTHERS

# Musical Therapy

Truth be told, I've been a wreck for months.

My anxiety is sky-high, my creativity ocean-floor low.
All thanks to an invisible virus and the all-too-visible
havoc it has wreaked on our world, our country, our state,
our community, our families, our spirits.

This damn virus has killed more than 283,000
Americans, *and counting*, crippled the economy and created
a world of confusion, politically charged misinformation,
and paranoia. (Hey, what do you know? It's not fake, not
a hoax, and didn't disappear on November 4th ...)

Many days, like many people feeling the same way,
the stress caused by this emotional/spiritual dragnet has
also pulled me down physically. I sleep. Eat right.
Exercise when I can. Yet I often go through the day
feeling like I've been through three rounds with Mike
Tyson in his prime.

But I am never completely down. Because when all

else fails, I always have my secret weapon: music.

Reading is relaxing. Writing is rewarding. But music is magical.

It soothes me, sapping away the angst, or filling my mental tank. Speaking to the crisis du jour or the eternal human condition (both usually having something to do with love and relationships of one kind or another) I listen to a wide and eclectic range of music.

My collection numbers in the tens of thousands. Songs spanning everything from jazz to country to folk to rock to blues to R&B, soul, funk, classical, marching band, opera  You name it, I've probably got it somewhere, or had it at one time or another.

I am, literally, that guy who had hundreds of LP records (including some 78s from my grandmother) and 45 singles, replaced them all with cassettes, replaced those with CDs, only to replace them with thousands of digital songs on my iPod and now my phone.

(A few years ago, as CDs replaced vinyl, I carted hundreds of albums to one of those shops that buys used records and sold them for a couple hundred bucks. Now, vinyl is considered "vintage" and I no longer have a record player. Just my luck…)

So, with 2020 nearing its very welcome demise, Thanksgiving just behind us Christmas just down the road, this is a good time to thank some of those who gave me my love of music.

Starting with my mother, who introduced me to jazz-influenced crooners like Frank Sinatra, Ella Fitzgerald and Tony Bennett, romantic singers like Tom Jones and Engelbert Humperdinck, and of course, Elvis. For her, nothing and no one surpassed Elvis. The day he died, it was like the earth had stopped turning.

Then there's my junior high band director John Knudson, for the gift of Big Band jazz (Benny Goodman, Woody Herman, Glenn Miller); and my two high school band directors Mike Fiske (funkier, more mature jazz like Spyro Gyra and Maynard Ferguson); and the iconic Ted Lega, who turned me on to classical music ("Carmina Burana") and taught his students life-long life lessons about perseverance in the face of difficulty.

My high school buddy Anthony "Gook" Gray turned my whole life around when he lent me his cassette tape of this skinny African American musician who dressed weird and sang dirty lyrics. His name was Prince, and the album was "Controversy."

Prince took (and continues to take) me in every possible direction down every musical street there is including funk (James Brown) and soul (Ray Charles and Aretha Franklin) and rock (Jimi Hendrix.)

Another high school buddy, John Quirk and I explored every piece of jazz and blues we could lay our hands on, especially when we worked together at Musicland in the Jefferson Square Mall, neither of which exist now.

John Coltrane, Miles Davis (who singlehandedly changed popular music three distinct times), Dizzy

Gillespie, Charlie Parker. Howlin' Wolf, Muddy Waters, B.B. King, Buddy Guy, and the late, great, Walkin', Talkin' Stevie Ray Vaughn (and Prince too. John was as big a fan as me.) Our "erudite" conversations filled countless high school, college and post-college days and nights.

Early in our marriage, my wife, Kellie started listening to "modern country" – Shania Twain, Sarah Evans, and especially Kenny Chesney. I liked some of it, and soon gravitated more toward the more "traditional" sounding country artists like Alan Jackson, the Dixie Chicks, George Straight and Reba McEntire – you know, anything with a twang.

But of course, if you're going to listen to country music, you need to listen to COUNTRY music: – Merle, Willie, Kris, Loretta, Dolly, Hank (Senior and Junior), Waylon, and the biggest big dog of them all, the Man in Black, Johnny Cash.

My best college buddy, Chuck Pelkie, opened the universe to me when he introduced me to Dylan and Springsteen. I will always remember the first time I heard "The River" by Bruce. I sobbed – I am not kidding, tears ran down my face -- at the story of a young man who got his girlfriend pregnant, was forced into a life-sucking job, "and man that was all she wrote."

And Dylan? Well, there aren't words to describe Dylan. He is as significant as the Beatles in terms of his impact on popular music. A case can easily be made that he's even more significant than the Beatles since they were trying to emulate him when they wrote "Sgt.

Peppers."

Chuck has kind of soured on both Bruce and Bob in recent years, and not without some justification. However, he's continued to expand my musical horizons, introducing me to John Prine, Jason Isbell, The Avett Brothers.

I could go on and on – John Lennon's solo work, the Rolling Stones, Led Zeppelin. Each made a huge impact on me, opening my mind to new thoughts. New ideas. Experiences unique to one person or group, and experiences shared by all people and groups. What separates and unites us.

I turn 55 in January.

Still, whenever I stumble across a new artist – the Mavericks, Lukas Nelson and the Promise of Real, Lake Street Dive – I feel like a kid again. I want to share that joy and energy that comes only with discovery even as I revel in it.

I have shared my musical passions with both my daughters over the years. We may not always like the same things (Exhibit A, Your Honor: Jesse McCartney and The Backstreet Boys) but I am proud to say our girls have very well-rounded musical tastes.

These days, you'll find me explaining the unique Lennon/McCartney dynamic or dissecting the differences and similarities between the Stones and Beatles or singing an Aretha song or dancing to "September" by Earth, Wind and Fire with my granddaughter.

You may think that's a lot to lay on a two-year-old. You may be right; I may be crazy (Billy Joel.)

But in a world of talent-less garbage and profit-driven mimicry, I want her to understand the good stuff and where it comes from.

I want her to know the magic of music, and to feel and trust in and rely on its essential life-altering, life-giving power, especially in dark times.

Just as I have. Just as I do, even now.

# <u>Finding Joy</u>

What brought you joy today?

A new friend regularly posts this question/challenge on her Facebook page. Already something of a community activist and good-hearted person, she'd been doing it for a while when, in July, she had to have emergency brain surgery.

As you'd expect, she was temporarily down but not for long. A few weeks later, she resumed her near-daily inquiry as she started her journey toward recovery.

What brought you joy today?

Amazing, if you ask me, that she continued asking, picking up the pieces of her life after such an ordeal.

That she even asks it at all is even more inspiring considering the nightmare that 2020, and, frankly, the last four years, has been for many.

Truthfully, the first couple of paragraphs of this blog sat on my computer desktop for several weeks.

I couldn't bring myself to talk about "joy" as Donald Trump worked overtime in plain view to dismantle and destroy our entire American democratic system, while millions of fellow citizens encouraged his lunatic ravings.

I couldn't see "joy" beyond the hundreds of thousands of deaths tied to a worldwide pandemic -- not to mention the ancillary crush of collapsing economic, social, and governmental systems.

I couldn't hear "joy" over the clanging of cynical, politically motivated indifference, and deliberate attempts to mislead, misinform, and ignore.

What brought you joy today?

A deceptively small and simple question with big and complex answers. Perhaps too big, I thought, as I kept trying without success to get past the start of this essay.

Then, this week, as I started to take a much-needed break, it dawned on me. Joy flickers softly at first, then soon burns so brightly that you cannot see past it. Still, like most important things, one must be open to it. Must want to see it. And in so wanting, must almost will it to life.

What better time then, to talk about joy, than Christmas week when a baby turned out to be the light of the world?

So, on Christmas Eve-Eve-Eve, here are some of the many small (yet big) things that bring me joy:

- The shining eyes, silly laughs, and unfiltered love of a child – not that one, but our two-year-old granddaughter. Her natural exuberance and adventuresome spirit are a magical tonic to my tired heart.
- The raft of memories of my dad, who passed away in January 1997 at the sad, young age of 51. They seem to pop up these days when I least expect -- or perhaps, when I most need them – bringing a smile, a quiet laugh, or even a tear. He wasn't a perfect human, but he was a great father. I miss him.
- The courage of those fighting this pandemic. Yes, of course, I refer to all the essential medical workers, police, fire, etc. But I am thinking specifically of the four nurses in my family. They probably had some idea that something like this could happen. They likely had some training. But reality always overpowers anticipation and speculation.
- The commitment of the teachers working through remote learning. In my other life, I have heard, seen, and shared dozens of stories of teachers leaving their contractually limited duties in the dirt and finding ways to connect with children who desperately need it, at a time of extreme disconnection.
- Not to mention the thousands of families and students who likewise have made tremendous

sacrifices to fit the very square peg of daily schooling into the very round hole of "regular" life in 2020.

- The friends, spouses, significant others, etc. who stand by, ready to bolster our spirit, boost our energy, and sometimes even give us a much-needed kick in our spiritual backsides. "Support" and "encouragement" come in many shapes and sizes.
- Adult children whose every success proves the value of love, discipline, respect, and faith, and erases my many parental failings.
- The easy serenity, awareness, and acceptance that comes with long-term relationships.
- The coworkers big-hearted enough to tolerate the occasional (but always unintended) outburst, as layers upon layers of calcified frazzlement explode.
- The 81 million people who said, clearly, firmly, and beyond question, enough is enough.
- Those willing to tolerate and forgive our external nonsense because they know our internal truth.
- The peace brought by a quiet evening (or afternoon, or morning) spent reading.
- The awe and humility that comes with admiring someone else's talent and artistry.
- The grace of holding another hand, hearing another voice, healing another heart.

And most especially, those who seek and find and celebrate joy itself, wherever, whenever, however they can.

They shine a light on, and into a world too easily and

too often consumed by darkness. They remind me every day of my opportunity and obligation to do the same.

So, what brought you joy today?

# <u>Overcoming</u>

Truth is, I was scared.

Not of anything external.

But rather, of myself.

Or, at least, my likely response to something external -- that being the whole wide world around me, and the continuing political and social lunacy incited and inflamed by He Who Shall Not Be Named.

No need to rehash the last four months, much less the last four years. He will do that himself, either in person, online, or from prison, repeating the same Lie ad nauseum, until it no longer fattens his wallet.

The point is, like a rotting, stinking, zombie, every time we reasonably think that thing is dead, it pops back up.

Here we are, more than four months after one of the most divisive national elections ever, followed by weeks of discord, 60-plus failed court cases, and finally a terrifying, treasonous attack on the Capitol by insurrectionist trolls, and it still won't die.

Each passing day of non-passage brought more worms of frustration and fear and concern for the lasting evil this one man wrought.

They burrowed so deep into my tired writer's brain that I haven't been able to write much of anything. Every attempt, no matter how innocent or unrelated the topic, veered off onto some trash-covered back road of angry abstraction.

So, rather than expose the dark spots on my soul, I just stopped writing.

And for that, I say, shame on me.

Now I don't want to suggest I came to this point of self-correction purely due to my own intellect or intuition. Far from it.

This time, as with so many others, I saw the truth only through a friend's eyes.

Just recently, I was kvetching to a dear and respected friend and fellow writer about my self-imposed writer's block (I won't name him here, to protect the innocent.) Turns out, he'd been suffering the same blockage.

Interestingly, we share many connections, but our politics differ. Yet, he too hasn't been able to sort or sift, much less dispose of, his own anxiety over the impact of the recent presidential election.

He admitted he too, had "opted out" of the writing game rather than lose the intended message or open himself to potentially cruel criticism.

I've said it a million times if I've said it once: there is more that binds us than divides us.

This revelation – that it wasn't just me – was just what I needed to clear my mental clog.

Knowing that someone else shares your struggle is often ennobling and emboldening. It brings strength like braiding cords into a rope. It brings courage like linking arms against an opponent.

Yet, knowing someone agrees with you isn't enough.

One must also choose to act – and more importantly, accept responsibility for choosing.

I believe to the core of my burdened bones in the grace of giving. "Charity" is a soul function that both defines and measures our humanity.

But Giving and Getting are equal parts of the equation. Frankly, too many people ignore the "getting" part because they fear, or are too lazy to deal with, the responsibility that comes with accepting someone else's reflection, nudging, guidance, or even criticism.

And for that I say, shame on them.

Look, it's simple: if a gift horse appears and nips you on the nose while you dither around checking its teeth, don't blame the horse.

So, with gratitude for my friend's camaraderie, I

hereby reclaim my God-given voice and promise to use it to say whatever I feel like saying, however I want to say it.

If you agree with me, fine. If not, fine. But you-know-who created problems that, we now know, won't go away anytime soon – maybe by accident, maybe on purpose.

Either way, there's so much to do to fix what is so clearly and awfully wrong right now, and the first step is to speak the words.

About the state of the world, or the state of my spirit.

About things that lift up or things that pull down.

About the flowers of spring or the flowers of death.

About everything terribly important and nothing terribly consequential.

Whatever the subject, I have a voice and I will use it.

I must overcome any obstacles.

Even those self-imposed.

And I will.

Because I am a part of We.

And We must overcome.

And We will

# <u>Baby I'm A Star!</u>

I have always wanted to be a rock star. (Indeed, I have been for a long time, if only on my ego's giant stage.)

Finally, I really am – and believe it or not, no thanks to my good friend, KISS lead singer Paul Stanley. (We met a few years ago at a book signing - his, not mine.)

Rather, my stardom came because of "Doc" McStuffins.

"Doc" is a seven-year-old African American girl who likes to fix toys, dolls, and stuffed animals. (Doc's real name is Maisha, like that of Dr. Myiesha Taylor, an emergency medicine physician in Sunnyvale, Texas.)

Doc is the latest of the long line of Disney Junior's megastars.

But much more important, she is our 3-year-old

granddaughter Riley's current favorite television character and role model.

For those unaware, Doc's toys come to life through her imagination (and a "magic" stethoscope) and present all manner of toy traumas needing her medical expertise. Doc and her assistants – a hippo, dinosaur, stuffed lamb, and a paranoid snowman, among others – then treat them, dutifully recording their diagnoses in Doc's "Big Book of Boo-Boos."

Recently a coworker mentioned her 10-year-old daughter had outgrown her Doc McStuffins diagnosis table and cabinet and offered it to me.

As a proud, card-carrying Papa, I had only one choice.

I graciously accepted the gift and set it up in our family room. Kellie, my wife (and the best Nana, ever) and I couldn't wait to see the look on Riley's face on her next weekend visit when she walked into that room.

Needless to say, 3-year-old smiles don't come much bigger or brighter.

What I didn't know – and Riley soon discovered – is that the cabinet was filled with toy medical implements: a stethoscope, giant syringe, a blood pressure cuff with a needle that spins wildly every you pump the air pressure. Every kind of tool that a "doctor" would need.

Riley spent the rest of the day – and hours on subsequent visits - poking and prodding us. Pounding our knees and elbows. Peering into our eyes and ears. Listening to our hearts. Monitoring our blood pressure and pulse. I can't swear, but I am almost sure that she checked my blood pressure more that first day than has been done in my entire 55 years on earth.

Heck, if my real doctors paid this much attention, I wouldn't mind paying the deductible nearly as much.

After dropping Riley off that Saturday evening, Kellie and I were both elated and amazed at the incredible joy this used toy brought our sweet girl, from whom joy already overflows.

Then, Kellie said something that hit me like electroshock therapy (which Doc does not perform, thank goodness.)

"You were the rock star today."

Her simple, easy smile bespoke her sincerity. Knowing the strength of her own special and strong bond with our granddaughter, I knew she wasn't being in any way sarcastic or envious. There's no competition between us (only one of my wife's countless qualities.) Just stating the fact: on that day Papa had brought the roof down.

Like many things in my advancing middle age, those words meant more to me than maybe were intended or understood.

To paraphrase a cliché, if I'd have known that being a grandpa was so awesome, I might have tried it before being a dad.

Don't get me wrong: I was a decent dad. Not perfect. Who is? Parenting – like most "adulting" – can be very hard work. Mentally, physically, spiritually, and financially draining. But even decent dads do some "undecent" deeds, now and again.

I had (have) a short, impatient fuse and a long, flaring temper. I am reluctant (trust me, that's the fairest, most accurate word I can use) about change. I do not tolerate fools or foolishness, and I am the sole judge of both in my world.

I am eternally embarrassed to admit our kids saw all of that, and more than once.

(For the record: I think I've improved a smidge since our girls reached young adulthood. On a scale of 1 to 10, I'd say I'm now a solid 7. I love this stage of our relationship, being able to talk about everything with two intelligent, thoughtful, caring young people. It expands and energizes my mind and soul.)

Yet, as a grandparent, I can be a better Me.

Absent the parental pressures of providing housing, financial support, clothing, etc. the focus shifts completely to the purest interests of the heart: blowing bubbles, swimming, exploring the garden, taking long walks down a new path, visiting museums and parks, napping, tickling, snuggling, singing songs we've sung a million times at the tops of our voices.

And of course, sharing a bowl of ice cream on a warm Saturday afternoon.

My good friend Paul Stanley may pack in 25,000 screaming KISS fans, their faces made up in white and black and red Kabuki makeup to look like his or the other band members.

He may have sold 100 million records and helped pioneer arena rock.

He may be a talented songwriter, singer, and performer worth hundreds of millions of dollars.

He can keep it all.

Because, in the eyes of my favorite 3-year-old, baby I'm a star!

# Sod in the Front, Seed in the Back

Four whitewashed walls. Attached garage. A modest 1,375 square feet of living space. Roof thrown in for free!

No basement, no attic, no central air. No fence. No lawn, only sod in the front, seed in the back.

It wasn't much to look at. But for us - a pair of new parents, two small kids, and a 10-pound Shi Tzu - it was perfect.

It was our first house. We planned to move in three to five years when the kids got bigger. After all, 1,375 square feet doesn't leave much room to grow, and 3-year-old and 1-year-old daughters are all about growth.

Twenty-six years later, we are more salt than pepper. More aches than energy. Lasting memories outweigh likely adventures. The babies are now thriving young adults with families of their own.

We have survived a recession, a pandemic, several job changes, major health issues, bereavements, estrangements, separations, and innumerable life upheavals. And worked our figurative fannies off to beautify, improve, maintain, protect and extend our little corner of the world. Tens of thousands of dollars and countless hours spent picking and pulling and painting and pounding vegetables and weeds and walls and nails.

We never did move. And now, our first house is our forever home.

Thoughts of "home" – literal and metaphoric – come to mind as we watch our youngest daughter and future son-in-law take on the many challenges of home ownership.

They bought their first little house about two years ago. Showing us pictures the first time, almost glowing with pride and excitement, they said it needed a bit of work. The previous owner had quickly fixed up and flipped the property.

I am now sure someone coined the term "fixer-upper" specifically for this house.

And that the previous owner was a liar, cheat, and thief. If there is any real justice in this greed-infested world, he'll get his share someday in a moldy, leaky, dank corner of hell reserved specially for people who look to make a quick buck selling moldy, leaky, dank houses to young, eager, unaware couples.

Still, they persevered.

Using the unwelcome extra time (and some of the welcome extra money) the pandemic produced, they fixed what they could. Friends, family, and very kind contractors not hell bent on turning every dime into a dollar helped finish what they couldn't do alone.

Now, as they plan their wedding in October 2022, their first house is also their first home. Not because of what they got when they signed on the bottom line, but because of what they have created together, since.

Then, there was the dead tree.

Two of our very closest friends who have become family, planted an autumn blaze maple sapling at their then-first home, also about 26 years ago.

The tree bloomed and grew. Its branches literally and symbolically intertwining with every aspect of their young marriage and family. They welcomed and provided perches for myriad birds and innumerable squirrels – including the several that their dog successfully chased down and sent on to whatever follows tree life for squirrels.

It offered shade and shelter, beauty and inspiration, its thickening trunk a tangible anchor for the spirits that drifted under and around and into its arms.

Then, a vicious storm broke off a limb. Time and Mother Nature said the tree was damaged beyond saving, forcing our friends to cut it down recently. The loss was palpable and heartbreaking, as much for the giant presence lost as for all that it represented. (Full disclosure: one of our friends wrote a candid, sad, and beautiful blog about this experience.)

Like those who've never owned pets and are confused by the love humans have for their animals, some will be surprised to know how very seriously our friends took this loss. Until you understand that the tree was not just a tree, but a living, breathing element of their life – their home.

In the same way, those who have never lifted a hammer or slung a paint brush or dirtied their knees, hoping against hope that the picture balances the room, or the color matches the vision in one's mind or the flowers/grass/veggies eventually sprout and survive the ever-hungry critters in service to a mortgage payment, may have a hard time understanding the idea of a home as anything other than a dwelling.

The difference is as simple as the deceptively profound lesson learned as a very young journalist about word choice: a house is a collection of wood and glass and metal  A home is what you make of it. A building, versus what is built.

A house is filled with things. Transient. Impermanent. Replaceable. A home is filled with the stuff of Life seen by the soul. Joy and sorrow. Gain and loss. Laughs and tears. Most importantly, the love that exists between those who share its space for a purpose greater than themselves.

The saying "Home is where the heart is," is a cliché for a good reason: because it is true.

# **<u>Let it Go!</u>**

You know the old saying:

"Don't let the _____ get you down!" (insert your euphemism of choice based on your level of vexation.)

Whatever you call them, I've been surrounded lately by (euphemism of your choice.) And I've been letting them get me down.

I'd love to say you can't really blame me. After all, either by nature or nurture, design or default, these (euphemisms of your choice) say and do things purposely and strategically designed to flatten my psyche, injure my ego, and sap my spirit.

Some are misguided, some are confused. Many have been snowed under by an avalanche of anger triggered by a fat, orange Sasquatch. Still, whatever their motivation, they chew on my confidence like a rodent gnawing on a power line.

Yet, honestly, it's not their fault.

How can that be, you ask with an abundance of (much appreciated) concern for my well-being (or well-earned uncertainty about the point of this entry into Tom's Journal of Middle-Age Miasma.)

Well, upon some serious therapeutic self-examination, I realize that, as is usually the case, I am to blame.

The key word in the saying, "Don't let the ____ get you down," is, "Let."

Are the (euphemisms of my choice) really doing all those things that lead to me feeling badly about myself? Absolutely! Although I am in my middle 50s, my approaching and imminent dementia isn't so bad that I am imagining things yet – voices in my head be damned!

However, "letting" something happen is often our own choice.

I have long been a strong and vocal proponent of "personal accountability."

For example, as a thinking – and, hopefully, thoughtful – human being, I am well aware of the evils we have, and continue to, commit against each other.

I am ashamed of and regret the resulting waves of repression, oppression, poverty, resentment, division, and societal decay that have rolled onto our historical beach. I try to understand and, whenever possible, speak out against the many things wrong with our world and help fix them in my own miniscule ways.

(Without getting too much into the weeds, these tiny actions of candor and conviction on my part are exactly what some of those (euphemisms of my choice) have criticized me for.)

Yet I also stand firmly on the conviction that, all things being equal, one must also be brave enough to take responsibility for the things one can control. Blaming others for problems of your own making only exacerbates the problem.

I cannot single-handedly control or change the world (although I will keep trying.)

But I can most certainly can control and change my world – which is to say, Me.

This nugget of wisdom came back to me recently from my two of my most trusted resources: my wife, and a children's cartoon.

Sure, this behavior from others is often hurtful, and my frustration is real and significant. Yet, ironically, I give it weight, I assign its value, I make it real by how I respond.

Fight against it? Sure.

But let it darken my mental and emotional doorstep?

No more.

Instead, I will re-commit myself (because I am often a slow learner with a spotty memory) to do what my wife and Elsa, from the Disney movie "Frozen," recently reminded.

I will just "Let it go."

Easier said than done? Yep.

Worth the effort? Most truly good things are.

All those (euphemisms of my choice) can keep right on stirring pots overflowing with a bitter soup of their own recipe. That is their right. But don't expect me to taste it.

Not even a sip.

# The Balcony

Michael Myers, the Living Dead, Evil Incarnate, the soulless, faceless one (unless you knew that he was actually wearing a modified William Shatner mask), pawed at the slatted closet door.

Inside, his terrified, traumatized older sister Laurie (Jamie Lee Curtis) did her desperate best to disappear into the corner, having tied the sliding doors shut with a flimsy scarf or belt (yet Michael couldn't just yank that door open...hmmm...maybe Evil Incarnate isn't as smart or strong as we think.)

Finally, Michael gives up trying to open the door, smashes through the slats, turns on the lightbulb, reaches for Laurie. She somehow turns the light off while fashioning a poker out of a wire clothes hanger.

She stabs Michael in the eye. He drops his 12-inch butcher knife, in pain, maybe confused that someone, anyone, much less his sister, had somehow disabled him, even if for only a second. She picks it up and stabs Michael again in the chest or throat.

He backs away from the door.

Not hearing anything, Laurie exits the closet, sees her brother lying on the floor, and thinks he is dead. (Silly girl, have you never seen a horror movie?)

She turns away, the bedroom still dark. Michael stands. Laurie doesn't hear him and starts to leave the bedroom, only for Michael to grab her from behind!

Suddenly, from the bottom of the stairs, Dr. Loomis (Donald Pleasance) shoots Michael.

(Side Note: Dr. Loomis is perhaps the unluckiest psychiatrist ever, inheriting Michael as a patient just after the pre-teen had gone on a Satanic killing spree dressed as a clown on *Halloween*. Side-Side Note: really, have none of these people ever watched a flipping movie?!)

The undying hulk releases Laurie and stumbles back into the bedroom. Loomis chases Michael back into the room, firing five more shots into his one-time patient.

The doctor's gun finally empty, Michael falls through a door onto the balcony, and tumbles over the balcony railing. He crashes to the ground, lying there in a twisted, lifeless, unmoving heap.

He is dead. He must be, right? I mean, how could anyone survive a stabbing, six gunshots, and a two-story fall to the hard ground below? Not to mention a nasty poke in the eyeball.

"Was it the Boogieman?" Laurie asks the doctor.

"As a matter of fact, it was," he says, in a pathetic attempt to assure her that the living evil that was once her little brother, is now dead and cannot hurt her anymore (and a great bit of ironic foreshadowing of what would become a cinema franchise with a dozen entries as I write this.)

Then, he looks over the balcony railing at the ground below and sees...

Nothing.

Michael is gone.

I do not remember now, 43 years later, if my brother and/or I actually screamed, but it seems that we may have. And if we didn't, it wasn't for lack of cause.

We had just watched what would become one of the classic cornerstones of horror cinema, the original "Halloween." I was 12, my brother 11.

Our dad had brought us with him to his part-time job as a projectionist at what was then the Mode Theater, hidden in the shadows of a dark, dilapidated corner of downtown Joliet. The downtown was a ghost town in the late 1970s, close to death itself thanks to the life-sucking draw of the vampiric new malls on the other side of town.

The theater had reached the point in its dwindling existence at which it usually showed R-rated, soft-core sex-type stuff. Stuff our mother wouldn't let us see, like "Saturday Night Fever." She was a bit of a prude. Ironically, now she just loves, loves, loves, John Travolta, for his dancing.

The Mode was dank, moldy, dirty, sticky, and empty most of the time. We could eat all the popcorn and soda we wanted, and we had free run of the theater so long as there weren't too many people around.

Our dad wasn't much of a movie buff. He liked Westerns – especially John Wayne to the point of adulation – and war movies. Loved silly comedies with the likes of Abbott and Costello and the Bowery Boys. And revered all the various James Bonds, especially Sean Connery.

But he really loved horror films of every kind.

We spent many a Saturday night curled up next to him in our parents' bed watching the old "Creature Features" program.

In the dark, often peeking out from the sheets or hiding behind his arm, we learned to love all the Universal monsters. Vincent Price. The "modernized" Hammer Films versions of classics like Dracula. Even the weird, nuclear-era stuff from the 1950s and 1960s about giant lizards and killer bugs.

So, when this new movie called "Halloween" came out on Halloween weekend, there was no question, much less paternal debate, about him taking us to see it.

And see it, we did.

We sat in the balcony – the kind found in old movie houses and theaters like the Mode. It connected to the projection room where Dad waited for the fuzzy little dots to appear in the corner of the movie screen telling the projectionist when to manually change out the reels.

We watched this cheaply made film featuring unknown or barely known actors. that would redefine and reinvigorate the horror genre.

It set a new cinematic standard by combining innovative, gory shock with the most essential, basic, time-worn element of all: suspense.

As with Hitchcock's classics and modern masterpieces like "Jaws" and "Alien," etc., "Halloween" reminded us that the scariest scares always come from the unknown. The biggest screams came not when Michael Myers killed someone in yet-another weird way. Frankly, that gets tiresome after the shock value wears off.

Rather, they came when the audience didn't know where he was. Did someone just duck behind that hedge at the end of the sidewalk? Who is that stranger standing right behind Laurie?

So, we sat, cinematically stuck to our seats (and probably literally, too, considering all the pop and gum and candy and who knows what else had been spilled there.) Entranced. Enthralled. Too scared to look, too amazed to look away.

Then, Loomis emptied his pistol into Michael.

And we breathed again for the first time in what seemed a horror-filled eternity.

Then Loomis looked over the balcony railing, only to see Michael gone from the spot where he'd lain only minutes before.

We turned to each other. Eyes wide. Mouths gasping with the terror-infused, joyous squealing that surviving such an experience yields. In my blurred memory, one or both of us said, "Holy shit!" (whispering, of course, so Dad wouldn't hear.)

Then, we inched up to the front of the theater balcony.

We carefully, cautiously peeked over the railing at the chairs and floor below, and saw…

Nothing.

The credits rolled.

The "Halloween" theme tinkle-tinkle-tinkled through the empty theater.

We waved to Dad in the booth, and smiled.

TOM HERNANDEZ

## ABOUT THE AUTHOR

Tom Hernandez is a writer, public speaker, performer, and communications professional. His writing explores the many complicated facets of life: marriage, family, relationships, identity, aging, parenting, faith, social justice, and politics. He and his wife, Kellie have two adult daughters and a granddaughter. They live in Plainfield, Illinois with their dog, Daize.

www.tomhernandezbooks.com

# Deadlines:
## Murder and Mayhem on the California Coast

## Volume #1

Central Coast Mystery Writers

Edited by: Susan Tuttle,
Barbara M. Hodges, Marie Marcy

ISBN: 1-941465-16-1
ISBN-13: 978-1-941465-16-5
A WriterWithin Publication

# Deadlines:
## Murder and Mayhem on the California Coast

### Volume #1

# DEDICATION

This volume is dedicated to the Sisters who began it all:
Sarah Paretsky, Nancy Pickard, Charlotte MacLeod,
Kate Mattes, Betty Francis,
Dorothy Salisbury Davis, and Susan Dunlap

Thanks for making it easier for all women who love to write
and read the mysterious and the arcane.

# CONTENTS

A Blast from the Past by Diane Broyles    Pg.  1

A SLO Death by Candace Sargent    Pg. 10

Figment by Susan Tuttle    Pg. 32

Mistaken Identity by Paul Alan Fahey    Pg. 35

Little White Pills by Judythe Guarnera    Pg. 48

Metaphor for Murder by Sue McGinty    Pg. 53

A Murder Most Fowl by Ruth Cowne    Pg. 71

Murder Under the Oaks by Susan Tuttle    Pg. 74

Pushed Down and Tucked Away by
Cora Ramos    Pg. 104

The Canine Caper by Sue McGinty and
Victoria Heckman    Pg. 110

Jack's House by Paul Alan Fahey    Pg. 132

Rockin' the Casbah by K.M. Kavanaugh    Pg. 142

The Writer by Susan Tuttle    Pg. 173

Twenty-one Days and Counting by
Barbara M. Hodges    Pg. 176

Authors Showcase    Pg. 183

# FOREWORD

Just a few thoughts you might find interesting before you begin reading.

All the writers contained herein are members of the Central Coast Chapter of Sisters in Crime (SinC), a national organization that promotes mystery writers. We run the gamut of sub-genres: cozy, hard-boiled, detective, police procedural, Private Investigator, even paranormal and satire. If we can put a mystery in it to solve, we can write it.

We chose the title of this anthology, "Deadlines", for three reasons. As writers, we are always under one deadline or another in either finishing a story or editing it for print. It's also the name of our Chapter Newsletter. And it's a fun play on words, since we specialize in making all sorts of things dead—on paper, that is.

Putting together an anthology like this is a labor of love; love on the part of those who write stories for it, and love on the part of those who do the work of collecting and editing the stories and formatting the volume that you hold in your hands. It's a lot of work for everyone involved. Luckily, it's work we all love to do.

This particular labor of love was made both easier and harder because of the amazing group of mystery writers who submitted stories. Easy, because there was so little for the three editors to do: a little tweaking here, a suggestion or two there. But also hard because all the stories were phenomenal. It was impossible to turn any of them down.

What is it about the California Coast that inspires mystery? Believe me, when it comes to murder and mayhem, the California Coast is the perfect place to commit both! As you can see in these stories, there's no shortage of inspiration: the ocean, dunes, and hills; the history; the people, birds, and animals; the weather, the traffic, even the shopping.

We've mixed the stories up for you, some nice and long, some short flash fiction and some in-between, just for variety and the fun of reading. That's the best thing about an anthology; if you've a little time, you can read an entire story in five or ten minutes and get full satisfaction. When more leisure rolls around, you can immerse yourself in the longer pieces, wallow in their atmosphere for a more extended period, and still have the satisfaction of finishing the story before daily life once again intrudes on this fictional world.

Best of all, at the end we've listed ways to get in touch with these authors, so you can let them know you enjoyed their stories, follow their blogs and/or, sign up for notices of future releases, find their current books, post reviews, and more.

Now you've reached another Deadline: it's time to sit back, turn the page, and enjoy a little Murder and Mayhem on the California Coast!

Your Editors,
Susan Tuttle
Barbara M. Hodges
Marie Marcy

# DIANE BROYLES

Diane Broyles worked for ten years as a writing consultant in the field of marketing communications and several years as an editor. She has written journal and newsletter articles that have been translated and published in French and German. For nine years, she chaired a critique group of fiction writers and is currently active in a small line-editing group for mystery writers.

The idea for "A Blast from the Past" came to Diane Broyles after learning that Stephen King's inspiration often comes when he asks, "What if?" TV documentaries about the many children who report having imaginary friends gave Diane cause to wonder, What if these friends are actually real and from another planet?

# A BLAST FROM THE PAST

by
Diane Broyles

Kaley emerged from her new condo with the last empty packing box and a shopping list in hand. She locked the door behind her and breathed a sigh of relief. A condo of her own, an assistant manager's job at San Luis Obispo's

Marriot Hotel and no more school. She had finally become one of the Big People, her mother's name for adulthood. She dropped the packing box at the curb for pickup and checked her shopping list: first, a new necklace, the treat she'd promised herself once all unpacked. Then a new pair of sandals, a much-needed TV and a birthday cake for her mom.

She started her errands at Unique Selections, her favorite shop for beads and stones. An unusual pendant was what she was after. She walked the aisles of crystals hanging from chains. Jade and amber stones enticed her from display cases. On top of a counter, the glimmer of a hanging pendant of translucent blue and brown stone laced with gold caught her eye. She reached for it and bumped hands with a woman who was after the same pendant.

"You look at it first," the woman said, handing it to Kaley.

Intrigued by the woman's unusual eyes, Kaley accepted the necklace and held it to the light.

"It's beautiful. Isn't it?" the woman said.

Something about her seemed familiar. Surely Kaley would have remembered someone with such interesting eyes. And she was so tiny—hardly five feet tall.

"Very pretty," Kaley said, handing it back.

The woman fingered it, placed it on the counter and surveyed the area around her. "This is my first visit to this store. They carry such a wide array of gems."

"Yes," Kaley said. "And Frank, the manager, is a very knowledgeable gemologist."

A short, lean man approached them from behind the counter. "Hello, Kaley. May I help you ladies?" He adjusted his small, wire-rimmed glasses. His vest covered a pin-striped shirt with sleeves rolled up to his elbows.

"I was just talking about you, Frank, and how well educated you are in your field."

Frank ignored the compliment. He seemed more intrigued by the ring worn by the woman beside Kaley. "I've never seen a stone like the one you're wearing," he told her.

*This is a first*, Kaley thought. *Frank can name every gem there is.*

"May I see it up close?" he asked.

"Of course," the woman said, removing her ring and giving it to him.

He studied it. "If you don't mind, I'd like to inspect this in my workroom."

A nod from the woman and Frank hurried off. The woman picked up the pendant she and Kaley had both admired and handed it to her. "You buy it," she said. "I'm just looking."

Pleased by her kind gesture, Kaley introduced herself with the intent of starting a conversation.

"My name is Silica," was the response.

*An unusual name*, Kaley thought, *for a woman with unusual eyes.* "Are you new in town?"

Silica looked surprised at the question. "Yes," she said. "Just visiting California. San Luis is a delightful place."

"Would you like some suggestions of some sights to see?"

Silica's smile was warm. "What I'd really like, Kaley, is a pair of new walking shoes. Where can I find a good shoe store?"

Kaley glanced at Silica's feet. Her dark gray shapeless shoes lacked style and looked as if they were made of tire rubber. "As a matter of fact, I'm on my way to Takken's shoe store. I can take you there if you don't mind a short walk. Where are you from?"

"I'm from—" Just then Frank returned with Silica's ring. He was shaking his head. "This one has me stumped. I can't find it online and it's not in any of my books. Can you tell me what it's made of?"

Silica hesitated. "I'm sorry. I don't know. It . . . it was a gift." She took the ring from him and put it back on. Turning to Kaley, she said, "How about buying that pendant? And then let's go find that shoe store."

Kaley paid for the necklace, put it on and left the store with Silica.

Once at Takken's, Kaley purchased a pair of sandals as Silica tried on walking shoes. Kaley still felt a kind of familiarity with Silica. Maybe because she'd been easy to talk to on their walk.

Silica pulled a pair of Nike's from among the boxes the shoe salesman had set before her.

"Those look comfy," Kaley said. "Try them on."

Silica slipped off her strange rubber-like shoes, revealing opaque black stockings peeking from beneath her long dark skirt. Her feet appeared quite flat and her middle toe looked the largest. Kaley could have sworn she had three large toes instead of five. Of course, with the dark stockings, she couldn't really tell.

Kaley checked her cell for the time. She was running late. She'd need to put off buying a TV and instead go straight to the bakery to pick up her mom's birthday cake. "I'm sorry I have to run," she said, standing up. "I'm so glad to have met you."

"Yes, it's good to see you again," Silica said.

"Again?" Kaley turned. "Have we met before?"

Silica grinned. "I don't think you'd remember. We were very young. Your mother would know."

"I'm sorry I don't recall," Kaley said, "but I'll be sure to ask my mom. I'd like to stay and talk, but I'm late. Enjoy your vacation." She picked up her new sandals and set off for the bakery.

\* \* \*

Kaley didn't bother to ring the bell at her parents' home. Birthday cake in hand, she walked in and shouted, "Happy birthday, Mom!"

Her mother appeared from the kitchen. "What a nice surprise!" She took the cake box and put it on the counter before smothering Kaley in an embrace. A familiar hint of lavender reached Kaley's nose.

"You look pretty as ever," Kaley's dad said, coming from the living room. He gave her a bear hug.

Over milk and cake, Kaley updated her parents about her unpacking progress.

"Excuse me, dear, but isn't that a new necklace you have on?" her mom asked.

"Yes. Isn't it pretty? I just bought it at Unique Selections, where I met the most intriguing woman."

Her mother raised a brow. "What do you mean?"

"She was so tiny and had the strangest brown eyes flecked with green. She seemed familiar—like I knew her from somewhere I couldn't place. And she had on a ring with a stone that was so unique that Frank couldn't identify it."

"That *is* unusual," her mom said.

"The woman told me she knew me from my childhood."

"What was her name?"

"She called herself Silica."

"Strange name. Was she about your age?"

Before Kaley could answer, her dad interrupted. "I remember someone you called Silica."

"I did? I don't remember her."

"You're right, Bob," her mom said. "She wasn't a *real* friend. She was imaginary." She turned to Kaley. "You used to come in from your tea parties in the backyard and tell us all about what Silica did at the party. You couldn't have been more than four."

"Sometimes we'd look out the window," her dad said. "You'd be talking a mile a minute, serving make-believe tea to someone who wasn't there."

Kaley moved her chair closer to the table. "I'm at a loss. What did I tell you about her?"

"You said she lived in Arcadium," her dad said. "Remember that, Jane?"

Her mom nodded. "We never heard of Arcadium. It was a weird name for a four-year-old to make up. We checked at the library and could find nothing."

"Did I describe her?"

"Only that she was your best friend," her mom said. "Oh, and you said she looked different from you. We laughed when you told us she took off her socks in the sandbox and she only had three toes on each foot."

Kaley sat up. "Three toes? Are you sure?"

Her dad chuckled. "We got a kick out of that one. You used to play with frogs. We thought your friend might be a frog. That made more sense."

Kaley wished she could remember. "Whatever happened to Silica?"

Her mom looked to the ceiling as she seemed to recall. "One day you came in from the yard with a sad face. You said Silica had gone home and wouldn't be back for a long time. When we tried to console you, you said you knew Silica wouldn't forget you because she said she'd be back when the Big People found out where she lived."

"The Big People? So that's where that term came from."

"You gave us some concern," her dad said. "We thought maybe Silica was real and she'd been abducted. Maybe she'd been warned not to talk to any adults or, in her mind, Big People."

"Yes," her mom said. "We thought she might have been abused and waiting for the Big People to rescue her. We didn't know what to do, so we threw a neighborhood block party and asked questions. No one had any children you recognized as Silica. And none knew of a child called Silica or a place called Arcadium."

"Did you call the police?"

Her dad shook his head. "Your mother wanted to, but we knew nothing except her first name and that she was from a place no one ever heard of. And no one, except you, had even seen her."

"So what happened?"

"You grew up and forgot about her," her mother said. "Never mentioned her again."

"I guess the Big People never found out where she lived," Kaley said with a smile. But the name and the three-toe thing bothered her. And now that she thought about it, the woman she met never said where she was from.

Kaley took the last bite of her cake. "I gotta run. Gotta get me a TV in hopes Best Buy can install it before *The Good Wife* comes on next week. Have a fun birthday dinner tonight."

Kaley walked through Best Buy to the back of the store, where a dozen TVs were all showing the six o'clock news with no sound. She scanned the screens to see which would be the best size for her small living room.

"Can I answer any questions?" a young man asked. His badge said his name was Alan.

Kaley turned to him. "Yes, Alan," she said. "My couch is about nine feet from where my TV will go. What size screen would be best? I don't want one of those humungous ones."

Alan walked to a set in the middle of a row. The top half of Diane Sawyer's body filled the right side of the screen. To the left was a photo of a planet with a headline, "New Planet Discovered."

"This one looks about the right size for your room," Alan said. "And it's made by Samsung, a reliable manufacturer."

"I like the picture quality. May I hear the sound?" Kaley asked.

Alan searched for the control and turned up the sound. Diane's voice rang loud and clear: "Scientists have discovered a new planet that revolves around the sun."

Kaley listened, intent on both the quality of sound and the program. "Sounds good. What's the cost for delivery and setup?"

Alan went off to check while Kaley continued to watch the TV.

"The planet is 60 million miles from the earth and is located between Venus and Mars."

Two students in Cal Poly T-shirts joined Kaley in front of the TVs. "Cool!" one said. "This'll blow Prof. Steinberg's mind."

When Alan returned with the price, Kaley asked, "Can you have it delivered by next week?"

"Let me check," he said, heading to a computer.

Diane said, "Scientists call the planet Arcadium, a name derived by use of an ancient algorithm."

Kaley's ears perked at the name.

Diane continued. "Research is being done on the possibility of life on Arcadium. When Dr. Stewart Barrymore of NASA was asked what he speculated, he replied, 'Anything is possible.'"

"Awesome!" the students said.

Kaley's mind spun. Alan returned to her. "We can have it installed in three days. Will you be home between 9 AM and noon?"

"Absolutely," she said, her gaze locked on the screen.

Diane said, "Dr. Barrymore believes Arcadium is one of the oldest planets. Its orbit is such that scientists here on earth did not have the sophisticated equipment we have now to discover it."

"I'll need your credit card," Alan said.

Kaley extracted a card from her wallet and gave it to him, her eyes still on the TV.

"This is your library card," Alan said, handing it back.

"Oh, sorry." Kaley looked away from the screen to find her Visa card. "Here."

Alan took it. "You'll have to come with me to sign."

"Sure," she said, following him, but her mind wasn't on the transaction.

What had she just heard on the TV? What did it all mean?

Alan ran her card through the machine and Kaley signed her name. "Here's your receipt and your card," Alan said. "We'll see you in three days."

Kaley took both and wandered out of the store in a daze, trying to make sense of it all. The events of the day ran into each other. Finally, she pulled out her cell and punched the button for her parents' home phone. Her mother answered.

Kaley cleared her throat. "Turn on your TV, Mom. The Big People have found out where Silica lives."

# Candace Sargent

Candace Sargent is a member of the California Central Coast Sisters in Crime and is delighted to be numbered among so many of their more seasoned authors. She is a retired teacher from a private school in Los Osos and began writing short stories for her students and about her family—who always had enough "character" of their own to fill a library!

"A SLO Death" is Book 2 in the "Kate Henderson-Detective Series" as well as the second to have been accepted for the Sisters' anthology.

"A SLO Death" is based on the 1991 San Luis Obispo cold-case of Marina Ruggiero—who came to San Luis Obispo for a wedding and was found stabbed to death in her motel room. Police reports showed Ruggiero was grabbed from behind and a rag was used to gag her. An attorney for Ruggiero's family believes the killer was waiting inside the room when she arrived.

The investigation is reviewed annually.

# A SLO DEATH

by

## Candace Sargent

### CHAPTER ONE

I hate L.A. traffic!" Kate groaned as yet another car sliced in front of her. "Gil, you owe me big time!"

Two weeks ago Gil's father was admitted to the hospital in Newport Beach and Gil took a leave of absence to be with his parents. Now that his father was improving, Gil was ready to come home and Kate offered to drive out and pick him up—in order to save the cost of another airplane ticket, or so she said. Of course, in reality, her offer was for purely selfish reasons.

She needed his help. It had nothing at all to do with how empty her car felt when he wasn't sitting in the passenger seat or the number of times she walked toward his office only to turn around when she suddenly remembered he wasn't there; and yes it was more than just a little embarrassing when the captain caught her leaving the break room carrying a coffee cup in each hand. She made up some feeble excuse about caseload and saving time, but she knew he didn't buy it. She could tell by the expression in his eyes as he walked past her.

She needed her partner back and that was that! Her newest case just wasn't going right—for which she solely blamed Gil. He wasn't there to be her extra pair of eyes and ears. Besides, there was absolutely no one else that she could trust to bounce her thoughts off of. Gil understood her. He understood how her thought processes worked.

Kate's hands tightened around the steering wheel. When she suggested picking him up, she thought it would be a great idea: drive down to Newport, collect Gil and then basically pick his brain all the way home. It seemed simple enough. Kate looked at the long line of cars in front of her and sighed. Now she just wished she could take it all back.

Kate glanced at the Tom Tom Navigator sitting quietly beside her. "Say something! Anything!" She dared it. The machine remained silent. "Arrgh!" She growled. "Stupid machine!"

Kate continued to inch down the highway. Stop, go; stop, go; then sit for a while. If she'd been able to convince the Captain that this would actually be a duty run, her trusty bubble light would have come in handy right about now.

"Well that would be stupid," she snorted. "Even if it was flashing up there, where would I go?" Traffic was too packed in for her to move even the slightest out of her lane.

A few minutes passed and the traffic finally started to show signs of thinning as cars wrestled for position into one of the exit lanes leading to LAX. Kate felt her shoulders relax. Okay, now things should go a little more smoothly, she hoped. It's only another hour and I'll be there. "He is so driving home," Kate growled.

Just then, the voice phone announced a call from Gil. "Hey Gil!" Kate mustered up her happy voice.

"Oh-Oh, you're using your happy voice. Am I in trouble?"

"Let's just say that I realized too late what a bad idea this was."

"So I'm guessing you're stuck in traffic. Where are you now?"

"Actually, it's thinning out now that I'm finally past LAX. I'll see you in a bit. And, by the way, dinner's on you." Kate pushed the hang up button before he could answer. A smile played across her face. That felt so good.

* * *

"Don't get me wrong," Kate said as they began their drive home. "I'm really happy that your Dad is better...."

"I hear a 'but' coming up, right?"

"No." Kate interrupted. "Well, yeah. It's just that I'm also really relieved that you're finally home."

"Oh?" Gil glanced in her direction. "Aww. I'm flattered. You actually missed me." He smiled and wiggled his eyebrows.

Kate smacked his arm. "Not like that! It's just that I'm getting nowhere on this case I picked up a couple of days ago and I need your help..."

"....so you missed me *and* you need me? That's so sweet, Kate... *ow!*" He winced as she punched his arm. "Hey, if you keep this up I'm going to be black and blue!"

"It'll be your own fault!" Kate turned and glared at him.

"Alright already!" Gil chuckled. "I missed you too, okay?" He cringed as she raised her fist. "And before you punch me again, tell me about the case we picked up."

"*We* picked up?" Kate smiled.

"Let's just say I had a hunch that there was something behind your offer to drive me home."

"Very intuitive," she agreed. "Now, here it is in a nutshell. A young woman is a bridesmaid at her cousin's wedding. She agrees to meet her family at Mama's Tavern for drinks after she goes back to her hotel to change into less formal clothing. Three hours later, she's still a no-show, so her family goes to the hotel and finds her on the bed covered in blood. Paramedics were called and she was taken to Sierra Madre hospital. She didn't make it."

"Possible robbery?"

"Could be. We did find pry marks on the door to her room, but..."

"... you're not convinced," Gil interrupted.

"No. I just don't buy it."

"Yeah, let me guess. It just doesn't feel right?"

"No. Well, I mean yeah." Kate let out a heavy sigh. "And before you ask, there is absolutely no evidence that supports any scenario other than a burglary gone south." She shrugged her shoulders, "I just don't think it's the case here and I can't sign off on it until I'm sure. I have to feel inside here," she placed her hand over her heart, "that I've done everything I could for her. I can't leave it like this; leave her like this when my gut tells me there's more to her death than the obvious."

Gil was silent for a few moments. Kate's gut feelings were usually right on the mark. So what was the big problem? They just needed to do what they always did: dig a little deeper, interview a little harder...

When he first came on as detective he probably would have closed the case as is. Ever since he partnered with Kate, he began to see things in a different way. When before it was just a case, now he fought, as Kate did, for the rights of their clients—the victims who could no longer fight for themselves. Kate taught him that. Her clients always deserved peace and she never rested until she told their whole story.

He stole a side glance in her direction and sighed. "Okay, I'm in."

Kate smiled. It was so good to have him back—to have her partner back.

"So," Gil asked. "What exactly is it that your 'gut' is telling you?"

"Okay, since you asked. There a few things that just don't add up. First, if the victim had walked in on someone, my experience says that the burglar's first thought would have been to flee the scene, right?"

"Yeah." Gil nodded. "That makes more sense to me, too. Maybe shove her down or push her into a wall just to get her out of the way."

"Then, there was the fact that there were designer clothes and shoes in the closet, expensive jewelry on the dresser."

"So the burglar was picky? Was there anything missing that you know of?"

"We're not sure. The mother is going through her daughter's things now. Hopefully we'll know soon."

"So, third..."

"Third," Kate continued, "there were multiple stab wounds. Why add murder to a burglary charge when he could have just slammed her down onto the bed and made a run for it. It doesn't make sense."

"So you're thinking...?"

"The way it plays in my head is that whoever it was just wanted to get in and get out, but the victim came back unexpectedly and suddenly the whole scenario changed. The knife that was used to pry open the door was handy and in a moment of panic...." She stopped and shrugged. "Well, you get the picture."

Gil remained silent for a few moments. "Okay, so catch me up on what else you have so far. You went to all this trouble to get me here, a captive audience so-to-speak. Let's just see what we can come up with between here and home, shall we?"

Kate shot him a broad grin.

"What's that for?" Gil laughed. "Do I have broccoli in my teeth or something?"

"No," Kate chuckled. "I'm just happy to have the team back together. With both of us on the case, I know that Amanda will get the closure she deserves. Thanks, Gil."

"Well, two heads are always better than one. Besides, I was going stir-crazy with nothing to do all day. So, shoot. I'm all ears." He wrapped his fingers around the steering wheel. "By the way, tell me again why I'm driving home?"

"That's just the way it worked out." Kate shrugged.

## CHAPTER 2

Kate took out her legal pad and began reading aloud.

"Amanda Willis, a 27 year old female. At 8:30 p.m. Saturday evening, when she didn't meet her family at Mama's Tavern, they went to her hotel room and found her dead. She suffered multiple stab wounds—Doc says 12 in all. The weapon was not on the scene. I arrived on the scene at approximately 9:15 p.m."

"Witnesses?"

Kate shook her head. "No one saw or heard anything. Family said the only people they saw were the usual night staff."

She turned the page in her note pad. "The victim arrived in town the day before the wedding. She spent the whole day at the hotel spa with the bride and the rest of the bridal party. A limo picked them up from there and transported them to the rehearsal. After the rehearsal, limos took everyone to "The Bayside Restaurant" for the rehearsal dinner and then delivered them back to the hotel—where they were all staying."

"Man, that must have cost a pretty penny; the Spa, a limo, and then dinner at the Bayside."

"The bride's parents own one of the top wineries in the area. Cost doesn't seem to be an issue. Anyway," she continued, "the scene was pretty well tossed—a real mess. Drawers pulled out and emptied; the contents of her jewelry box were dumped on top of the dresser. Whoever it was wanted something in particular.

The voice phone announced a call from Doc, and Gil pushed the call button.

"Hey, Doc, how's it going?"

"Why hello, Gil, it's good to hear your voice. I hope that your father is improving."

"Yup. He's back to his ornery self. Ordering nurses around and complaining about the food. I know they'll be glad to see him leave in the morning," Gil chuckled. "So, what have you got for us?"

"Well not much that we didn't already know. The victim sustained repeated punctures—12 wounds in all. However, I did find one thing that was not expected. A small burn on the nape of her neck, just below the hairline. I have deduced that it was inflicted post-mortem."

Gil looked puzzled. "Wait, Doc, are you saying she was burned?"

"Not in that sense of the word, Gil. It's more like an abrasion similar to a rope burn—only on a much smaller scale."

"Do you have any idea what caused it, Doc?" Kate queried.

"Nothing solid as yet, but the victim's mother did stop by. She mentioned that there was a small locket missing in her daughter's personal effects."

"A locket? Is she sure?"

"Yes, quite sure, Detective. Apparently, her daughter never took it off. It could account for the wound on the back of her neck."

Kate thought for a moment. "So the killer must have yanked it off. Were there any signs of a struggle? I mean, did she try to fight off her attacker?"

"No. I believe that the killer's first attacks came much too swiftly—from behind. There were also several wounds on her chest and arms as well as around her collarbone. The fatal blows were to the left chest area puncturing the heart and severing the left anterior descending coronary artery. After that, death came swiftly. Due to the location of the chest wounds, I would venture to guess that your murderer was right-handed." Doc paused for just a moment. "I'll have my full report ready for you upon your return."

"Thanks Doc." Kate leaned forward and pushed 'end call'. "A locket. Sounds like we may know what the murderer was looking for."

"So what was so important about it?" Gil asked.

"Not sure." Kate took out her cell phone. "But I'm going to see if I can find out."

The phone rang over the car speaker.

"Hello?" A woman answered.

"Mrs. Willis, this is Detective Henderson. I'm the lead on your daughter's case."

"Yes, Detective, I remember you. Is there something I can do for you? I'm on my way to the mortuary. I know you can't release Amanda yet, but I had hoped to get... the arrangements started."

"I understand, Mrs. Willis. This will only take a moment. I just got off the phone with our Medical Examiner and he mentioned that you told him something was missing in your daughter's personal effects."

"Yes, her locket." She answered slowly. "Were you able to locate it?"

"I'm afraid not Mrs. Willis. It's my belief that the locket was taken from her during the, uh... robbery."

"I don't understand, Detective. That locket wasn't of any value."

"Mrs. Willis, I understand that this is hard for you, but you said yourself that Amanda never took it off. It was obviously valuable to her. Could you tell me why?"

"The photos inside," Mrs. Willis replied. "Those were special to her." She took a long shaky breath. "Amanda was given that locket by someone who was very close to her. I just can't imagine what a total stranger would want with it."

"I'm not sure, either, but that's the only lead we have so far. Who were the photos of?"

"Amanda and Brett." Mrs. Willis sighed. "I had hoped that since Amanda came to the wedding that any ill feelings had been resolved."

"Ill feelings?"

"Yes." She paused for a moment. "I guess there's no reason not to tell you. You see, Amanda and Brett were dating... Amanda was in love. When Brett suggested they move in together she jumped at the chance. I begged her to reconsider and just continue the way they were for a while, you know, to see if he was as committed to the relationship as she was. But, she just laughed and said that living together would be the best way to 'test the waters.' Then Brett met Marie." Her voice became unsteady. "Amanda was devastated when he moved out. He told Amanda it had been fun but this was something he had to do. She came home, here, for a while and I was there to pick up the pieces." She took a deep breath before continuing. "Detective, Amanda had found her one true love—Brett. That was why she never took the locket off. She still loved him."

Kate flipped quickly through her notes and found what she was looking for.

Bride: Marie Jennes—cousin to Amanda,

Groom: Brett Michaels

"So, Mrs. Willis, you're saying that Marie and Brett are the same Marie and Brett who just got married?"

"Yes, Detective. Marie is... was... Amanda's cousin.When she invited Amanda to be her bridesmaid, I just naturally assumed that they had mended fences and moved on. But when I saw Amanda wearing the locket at the rehearsal—and the way Marie looked at her, I knew that Amanda had accepted the invitation just to fan the flames. When I asked her to take the locket off—just for the wedding —she refused at first. She called it 'payback'. When she arrived for the ceremony the next morning, she put the locket in her purse. Said she just wanted to let it all go and she'd wait to wear it until after she left. She said that Brett and Marie had enough problems and she didn't want to bring them additional pain. Even so, there was still a lot of tension between them. I was relieved when Brett and Marie left the reception early."

Kate wrote down notes as Mrs. Willis spoke. "What time did the bride and groom leave?"

"Let me think. The wedding began at 2:00 and the reception started immediately after that. They left early; I'd say it was probably around 3:30... right after they cut the cake. They reserved a cabin in Big Sur... Glen Oaks, and they didn't want to drive up Highway 1 in the dark."

"Thank you, so much, Mrs. Willis. You've been a tremendous help. I'll be in touch with you." Kate ended the call and sat for a moment.

"Penny for your thoughts." She glanced over to Gil.

"So, you're not thinking those two lovebirds could have...."

"I won't know for sure until I talk to them, but I think it's a good place to start and worth digging into. They had motive and opportunity and Mrs. Willis said there was tension between them and Amanda."

"Why do I get the feeling that we're driving up to Big Sur in the morning?" Gil groaned.

Kate turned toward him and grinned. "I guess that's because you know me all too well, partner."

## CHAPTER THREE

At 8:00 a.m. Kate pulled into Gil's driveway, armed with donuts and coffee. She waved when she saw him walk out the door

"Good Morning!" Gil chirped as he got in and buckled up. "I see *you're* driving this time."

Kate forced a tight-lipped smile. It was definitely nice to have him back as her partner, but sometimes—especially before coffee—he could be downright irritating.

"Yeah looks like," she grumbled. "I brought coffee and donuts." Kate never understood how anyone could be so chipper this early in the morning. "You can have some if it'll stop you from talking." She glared.

Gil chuckled. "I see you're your usual perky self this morning. By the way, I did some research last night on our love birds... seems the groom isn't all snowy white."

Kate took a sip from her cup ad enjoyed the feeling of the hot liquid as it coursed down her throat. "So, spill," she growled.

"Well, for starters, I dug up what I could on the Michaels family—with a particular interest in their oldest son, Brett. Gil read from the notes on his legal pad. "Jonathan Brett Michaels, age 28. Attended Cuesta college right after high school and went from there to Cal Poly as a business major. He was the captain of the wrestling team, and was pretty good. They won the NCAA four years in a row—which was directly attributed to his skill and leadership abilities. Following in his father's footsteps, he joined the Delta Sigmas. GPA was around 3.8 during most of his terms. However, when I dug a little deeper, I found something a little juicier. He has a record with us."

Kate turned to look at him. "Okay. Now we're getting somewhere!"

"Thought that might draw your attention." Gil smiled broadly. "He and a fellow Delta got into it during Mardi Gras—supposedly over a girl. He was arrested and the other guy was hospitalized with bruises and lacerations. Brett became an overnight guest of the County; but here's the weird thing, he was charged with assault, but never served time. Didn't even appear in court. Apparently "Daddy" had more in his pocket than loose change, if you catch my drift?"

Kate nodded. Why was it that money and power always seemed to go hand-in-hand? Of course, Brett didn't do time.

"Not surprising," she said aloud. "Brett's dad is a powerful man. So what was the weapon of choice?"

"That's the good part," Gil leaned back in his seat. "It was a Navy Seal Ka-Bar. They're routinely issued to Seals when they graduate. Pretty unique weapon. On one side it has the Seal logo. The name of a fallen Seal is engraved on the other side."

"How did he get that? Was he a Seal?"

Gil shook his head. "Nope, but his brother Michael is."

"Whatever happened to it?"

"Not sure; probably returned to Brett along with all of his other personal items when he was released from custody. Definitely something we need to ask him. You drive and I'll just keep plying you with donuts and coffee."

Kate smiled to herself. He definitely understood her. Maybe the coffee was kicking in, because at this moment Gil seemed almost tolerable. She snuck a sidelong glance at him and suddenly realized how much she'd really missed him— missed this—when he was gone.

They arrived at Glen Oaks Resort almost four hours later and—after a short "official" chat at the front desk—were now on their way to "The Big Sur" cabin located across from Big Sur River.

Brett opened the door. His hair was a mess; his eyes were bloodshot and he only wore sweat bottoms.

"What?" he barked. "My wife and I chose this cabin because it was secluded and private. Who the hell are you and what do you want?"

Kate smiled. "Good afternoon, Mr. Michaels. I'm Detective Henderson and this is my partner Detective Baker." They both flashed their badges. "We're investigating the murder of Amanda Willis. May we talk to you?"

Brett stood for a moment holding the door. "Can't this wait until next week? We're on our honeymoon... had a bit of a late night," he smiled. "My wife is still sleeping."

"I'm afraid it can't wait, Mr. Michaels."Gil answered. "We only have a few questions and your answers just might help us put this case to bed. We would really appreciate your cooperation."

Brett raked his fingers through his hair and quickly glanced back over his shoulder. "Yeah, okay," he whispered. "Just let me get a shirt on and we can talk outside." Leaving the door ajar, he tiptoed back to the bedroom and reappeared a few moments later. "We can talk over there," he walked over to a picnic table located a few feet away and straddled the bench. "So what questions do you have?"

Gil flipped some pages of his legal pad. "Mr. Michaels, how well did you know the victim, Amanda Willis?"

"Very well, actually—we both did. It was a real blow when we learned she'd been killed." He took a deep breath and blew it out. "She and I were an item for a while. Then I met Marie and I realized that Amanda just wasn't what I was looking for. Marie was. Amanda took it pretty hard."

"Mr. Michaels," Kate started. "Did you give her a locket?"

Brett nodded. "I did, when we decided to move-in together. You know, trying to sweeten the pot in my favor." He smiled.

Kate decided to ignore the urge she had to punch him in the face. "Can you describe it for us?"

"Sure, but she never took it off. Wasn't it on her... you know?"

"No, it wasn't on her body. Your description will be helpful."

"Oh, wow. Are you telling me that some stranger is walking around with my picture? Oh, man. If he recognizes who I am it might be disastrous." He wiped his face with his hands. "Yeah, okay, detective. I understand. It was a small heart-shaped, silver locket on a chain. It had a diamond chip on the front, and a rose engraved on the back. Oh, and I had our initials engraved under it, J.B.M. +A.W."

"Sounds nice."

"Yeah. Well, I was young then and still believed in... well, a lot of things. In the end, my Dad was right. I had to grow up and take my responsibilities seriously. You know, for the family."

Kate flashed to her own childhood and understood exactly what he meant about having dreams but eventually having to face the reality of life.

"Thank you, Mr. Michaels. One more question, though. Do you still have the Ka-Bar? We'd like to see it, if possible."

Brett's eyes flashed for just a second. "Uh, no. You see, when I was in college, I kinda borrowed it. You know, just for show. Unluckily, I got in a little bit of trouble with it and my father took it from me. I have no idea what he did with it; probably gave it back to Michael. I didn't really care at the time."

Gil stood up. "Thank you, Mr. Michaels. I think you've given us the information we needed." The two men shook hands and Gil started to walk off with Kate trailing behind him. "If we need anything else, we can always find you," Gil called over his shoulder.

"What was that all about?" Kate demanded as they walked back to the car. "That was a long road trip for nothing! There's so much more we—"

"—You're not the only one with gut feelings, Kate." Gil interrupted. "And mine are telling me he didn't do it. Didn't you hear him? He married because of family obligation, not love. He loved Amanda. He couldn't have hurt her.

"Okay. So what if he did still love her?"

"Think about it. Who convinced him and why?"

Suddenly, Kate smiled. "I get it! We need to follow the money!" She tossed the keys at him. "But you're driving."

## CHAPTER FOUR

The next morning, Jarrett Michaels paced the length of the interrogation room and back again. This was ludicrous. It was bad enough to be pulled away from an important meeting with the Mayor—and the Deputy Chief, no less— but he'd been waiting here for what seemed like hours. He checked his watch and wondered why his lawyer hadn't arrived yet. His secretary should have called the firm an hour ago. He looked at the two-way mirror. Were they all back there just watching him?

"Hey! If you're back there show yourselves!" He had a right to be angry. After all, he had a company to run. "I'm a busy man!" He growled and approached closer to the mirror. "I have no time for childish mind-games," he snarled.

When the door clicked open, a satisfied smile played across his face. "Well it's about time," he huffed.

Kate sat down in one of the chairs at the table and motioned for him to take the seat across from her.

"Record on. Detective Kate Henderson. Monday, June 5th at 6:30 p.m. Ongoing investigation; Willis case; Interview with Mr. Jarrett Michaels." She looked at the man who stood across the table from her. "I apologize for the inconvenience, Mr. Michaels. We were waiting for a key piece of evidence and I guess I just lost track of time. Please have a seat." She motioned, for the second time.

Mr. Michaels pulled the chair out and sat. "Well then, let's get on with this. The sooner we get started, the sooner I can get back to—"

"—Absolutely, Mr. Michaels." Kate smiled as she took out her legal pad and pen. "I just have a few loose ends that need to be cleared up before we can close the case. I'll try to get this done as swiftly as possible."

Mr. Michaels looked directly at her. "What can I do to help you, Detective?"

"Now, Mr. Michaels, where were you between the hours of 6:00 pm and 8:30 pm on Saturday, June 3rd?"

"I was at my son's wedding all day. I didn't leave until late. I'd say around 8:30 or 9:00."

"Alright." Kate jotted down his answer. "Do you recall what time your son and his wife left?"

"Right around 3:30... Highway 1 is treacherous enough in the daylight."

"Yes, I know. Do you recall seeing the victim, Amanda Willis?"

"Of course I do. She was part of Marie's bridal party." Can we get on with this, Detective?

"Of course Mr. Michaels. Just a couple more questions and I'll have you on your way." She looked at her notes. "Mr. Michaels, do you recall seeing Miss Willis leave?"

"Actually, I don't. There was some sort of mix up with the caterers and I offered to take care of it. Marie's Father had so much he'd already done, so it was the least I could do to help out. It took quite a while to resolve the issue."

"And at what time did you do that?"

"5:30 or 6:00. I honestly can't recall exactly. There was so much going on. When I returned, Amanda and her family were already gone."

"Hmm, I see." Kate looked over her notes when she heard a knock at the door. "I'm so sorry, Mr. Michaels This will only take a moment, I promise." She rose and opened the door for Gil. "Is that it?" she asked excitedly.

"Yup." Gil replied. "Found it right where Michael said it was."

"Michael?" Mr. Michaels stood up abruptly. "What's this about Michael?" Then he saw the object in the evidence bag. "Where did you get that?" he demanded. "That's Michael's Ka-Bar. He got that after he graduated from Seal training. You don't suspect Michael, do you?"

"Actually, he was a suspect until we found *this* knife." Gil held up the bag. "This isn't Michael's." Gil sat down in the chair Kate had occupied and laid the evidence bag with the knife on the table. "This is a replica. But you should know that already. After all, you were the one who had it made. An exact duplicate of your son's; superb craftsmanship, I might add." Gil picked the bag up and began turning it around. "Powerful weapon, don't you think? I mean, it gives you a feeling of power just holding it, doesn't it, Mr. Michaels?"

"I don't know what you're talking about."

"Hmm. Well, Michael was very enlightening—and, by the way, I'd believe a Navy Seal over a CEO anytime. You see, he was packing his bag and can you imagine his surprise when he found this mixed in with his belongings. It looks like his knife except for one thing. Michael had 2 small slashes on the handle just below the hilt. I think he said they were tally marks. Anyway," Gil took the knife out of the bag. "You can see that there are no marks on this one. We tested it and guess what we found?"

Mr. Michaels remained silent.

Gil smiled. "So glad you asked. We found paint residue embedded in the leather wrappings of the handle that matched the door to Miss Willis' hotel room. There were also faint traces of blood under the hilt as well. Funny isn't it? People cleaning their knives forget about cleaning down to the bottom of the blade. Except for Seals, that is. Their knives are always kept in pristine condition."

Gil produced another bag with a blood soaked rag inside. "Anyway, I'm guessing this was used to wipe the blood off the knife. It seems that most people don't know this, but just wiping blood off the blade doesn't clean it completely. There's always some residue leftover. It didn't take long before our forensics team had a match." He put the bag next to the knife. "As I'm sure you already know, the blood on the blade matched that of the victim."

"Why would I know that?" Jarrett snapped. "I've never seen that knife before and I didn't kill Amanda Willis."

Kate stepped forward and leaned down next to Gil's ear. "You know, I just hate it when people beat me to the punch line."

"Yeah, me too," Gil agreed. "Kinda rude, don't you think?"

"It's a shame about your tux, Mr. Michaels." Gil reached into his satchel and brought out a piece of paper. "You reported it stolen, and charged the full price to your credit card." Gil moved the paper closer to Mr. Michaels. "See? This is the charge receipt for it. Since you made the transaction over the phone, you didn't get a receipt. Men's Wearhouse was only too happy to print out a copy of the sale for us."

Jarrett stared at the piece of paper. "I don't know what you're talking about. I wore my tux all day!"

"Really?" Kate pulled a chair up next to Gil. "Well, I suppose it's possible that someone used your credit card. Maybe, whoever it was, wanted to frame you?" She looked at Gil who nodded.

"I guess it's possible, all right. However..." Gil reached down to his satchel once more, brought out another evidence bag and pushed it across the table. "We believe this may be Amanda's locket."

"That's not her locket." Mr. Michaels pronounced after closer inspection. "Hers had a diamond chip on the front."

"Oh?" Gil picked up the bag and looked more closely at the locket. "Detective Henderson, do you have your notes from your conversation with Brett this morning?"

"Just happened to bring them along." She answered and began flipping pages. "No. No diamond chip here," she lied.

Mr. Michaels became visibly irritated. "Yes, yes it did. I saw it at the ceremony! She was wearing it through the whole thing!"

Kate leaned across the table and looked directly at him. "No, sir, she did not."

"But she did." Jarrett insisted and pounded his fist on the table. "I saw it on her! I remember because I thought how brazen of her to do something like that! But what do you expect from trash like that? She was *nothing* but trash, you know. No breeding, no culture, and no real family name. I could never allow my son to marry someone like that— someone so obviously beneath his station."

"Mr. Michaels, her mother told us that Amanda took the necklace off and put it in her purse before the ceremony began and didn't put it back on until she left the reception."

"She's lying!" He shouted. "Those types of people always lie. I know Amanda had it on all day!"

"Well, I would believe you, Mr. Michaels, except for these photographs." Kate looked at Gil as she took a small stack of photos from her satchel and laid them out on the table.

"Mr. Michaels, did you know that your photographer used a digital camera?"

"Yes, of course. Marie wanted the photos available as soon as possible."

"Well, I'll have to remember to thank her later," Kate smiled. "Anyway, if you look closely," she continued, pointing to each photo as she spoke. "No necklace. Not during the ceremony; not during the reception; not even during the pre-ceremony shots or the formal photos. She did wear it during the spa day and even at the rehearsal. See it, here?" Kate pointed to the photos. "Oh, and look..." Kate leaned forward. "There you are at the rehearsal. You're staring at Amanda. You don't look very happy, Mr. Michaels."

Kate sat back in her chair before continuing.

"On the day of the wedding, Amanda told her mother that Brett and Marie had been through enough. They didn't need her to add to their problems. Were *you* one of their problems, Mr. Michaels?" she asked as she picked up one last photo. "Oh, I forgot to show you this one." She slid it over in front of him. "It's a photo of you. Not from the wedding. It's actually from the hotel's security camera. See?" She pointed. "There you are, in your car, exiting the parking lot and see the time stamp? It says 7:30 p.m. You're not wearing your jacket. What exactly happened to your jacket, Mr. Michaels?"

Jarrett remained silent and sat back in the chair. "Nicely played, Detective." He smiled smugly. "I will not be saying another word until I talk to my lawyer."

"That's fine, Mr. Michaels, because Detective Baker has something to say to you."

Gil took out a pair of cuffs and walked around the table. "Mr. Michaels, please stand up with your hands behind your back." He locked the cuffs securely around Jarret's wrists. "Mr. Jarrett Michaels, you're under arrest for the murder of Amanda Willis." He opened the door to admit the two officers who were standing in the hallway. "Officers, please escort Mr. Michaels to lock-up, and don't forget to read him his rights."

"Oh, by the way, Mr. Michaels," Kate said as she stood up. "Your lawyer just arrived and is on his way up. Who would have thought that traffic could be such a bitch in this city?"

# Susan Tuttle

Susan Tuttle is a professional editor, writing teacher and the slightly twisted, award-winning author of the suspense novels *Tangled Webs, Piece By Piece* and *Sins of the Past,* the newly released historical suspense novel, *A Matter of Identity,* the indieB.R.A.G. Medallion-awarded paranormal suspense novel, *Proof of Identity,* a short story collection, *Death in the Valley,* and the comprehensive 6-volume *Write It Right: Exercises to Unlock the Writer in Everyone* workbook series based on her writing classes, for fiction writers of all levels. Her work has also appeared in anthologies for SLO NightWriters and Central Coast Sisters in Crime, in Tolosa Press and various literary journals.

Susan, a past president of SLO NightWriters and the Central Coast Chapter of Sisters in Crime and presently the newsletter editor for both organizations, is hard at work on her paranormal Skylark detective series, and two YA fantasy series.

"Figment" was written for the SLO NightWriters Short Story contest. The judges didn't seem to like it but I believed in it, so, after changing only the first line (the NW contest gave a pre-selected opening line), I sent it to the Mind Prints Literary Journal's contest, where it won first place. The judge's comment: "I can't believe how much plot there is in only two pages." Paul Alan Fahey features it in his new book, *The Short and Long of It,* where he says *"Figment* is a master class in writing tight short fiction... a fast read with an emotional center... and a philosophical ending that knocks you out. *Figment* is what great flash is all about."

# FIGMENT

by

## Susan Tuttle

The police car squeals to a stop; officers race up the steps, through the doorway. I watch them bend over Andrew. The light in his eyes is dimming; scissors stick up from his chest. Not bad work for someone who's invisible.

A suited detective calls for an ambulance.

"Don't bother. He'll be dead before it gets here," I tell her. But she doesn't see or hear me.

I've been invisible for years. In the beforetime I was real, but Andrew ended that. Once the ring was on my finger, he denied me existence. At first, I was invisible only to him. Then other people started losing sight of me. Now, no one can see or hear me. It's an interesting way to live.

"She... she..." Andrew struggles. The detective bends lower.

"A woman did this?" she asks. Andrew nods. "Who?"

"My... wife." Andrew whispers. Then he dies.

"Canvas the neighborhood," the detective orders. "Find out what anyone heard, or saw. And find this wife!"

She walks over to the desk, to our wedding picture, searches for something more recent. She won't find it; the invisible don't photograph well. People come and leave, taking Andrew with them. A patrolman tows in Andrew's friend, Mitch, and his wife, Sarah. Mourning, they extol his virtues. Naturally; Andrew was kind to everyone but me.

Mitch frowns an answer. "He wasn't married."

"He didn't need to be," Sarah adds. "He was so... domestic, on his own."

Right. If they only knew.

They look at the wedding picture and shake their heads, puzzled. They have never seen me. The detective thanks them and they leave. She again scrutinizes the scene, then turns to the window, almost bumping into me. She stops, frowns, peers in my direction. Then she blinks and shakes her head. She stares out the window until a sound in the hallway turns her around. She gasps, startled, and takes a step back.

"Who are you?" She looks at the blood on my hands.

"The wife."

"You can see me?" I ask.

"Shouldn't I?"

"I'm invisible. At least, I used to be. Strange." I look at where Andrew fell. Did he recreate me by dying? It seems so, but I doubt he intended it.

The detective looks at the wedding picture. "You haven't changed much. Why did you kill him?"

"I didn't mean to," I say. "It was an experiment. I was trying to make him see me."

She gives me a look, half disgusted, half fascinated. "We searched the house. Where were you?"

I smile. "I've been here all along. Right beside you."

"Yeahhhh..." she says, rolling her eyes. "What a nutcase."

She calls the uniforms. They handcuff me, put me in a squad car. But I've learned from Andrew. I bend my head and focus my mind. One by one they will all wink out of existence. It's easy; if you don't give control to someone else, you can create your own reality. Invisible or not.

# Paul Alan Fahey

Paul Alan Fahey is the author of the writing book, *The Short and Long Of It*, and the *Lovers and Liars* gay wartime romance series. He is the editor of two nonfiction anthologies, *The Other Man: 21 Writers Speak Candidly About Sex, Love, Infidelity, & Moving On*, and *Equality: What Do You Think About When You Think Of Equality?* His short fiction has appeared in *Byline, Palo Alto Review, Long Story Short, African American Review, The MacGuffin, Thema, Gertrude, Kaleidoscope*, and in various anthologies from *Cup of Comfort, My Mom's My Hero*, to *The Best of SLO NightWriters in Tolosa Press 2009-2013*, and *Somewhere in Crime*. He lives on the California Central Coast with his husband, Robert Franks, and a gaggle of shelties.

How "Mistaken Identity" came about: Most of us growing up in the late 1940s and 50's watched the great post war black and white thrillers of that era on TV. Many come to mind: *The Third Man, D.O.A, Scarlet Street, The Stranger,* and *Detour.* Television also offered dark and exciting weekly episodes of *Alfred Hitchcock Presents, Perry Mason, The Lineup,* and *Mickey Spillane's' Mike Hammer.*

During the 1950s, Hollywood probed the mysterious depths of the mind with films like *The Cobweb, Lizzie, The Three Faces of Eve,* and later in the 1960's with *Psycho, Homicidal, Marnie,* and *Lilith.* It's no wonder that this environment would influence a child raised during this period of post war disillusionment and preoccupation with the "why" of human behavior. My short story, *Mistaken Identity*, is an example of the confluence of these two popular film and television genres.

# Mistaken Identity
by
Paul Alan Fahey

Late at night, the wind blows west from the Santa Lucias, shaking windows and rattling doors, then sweeps across the arroyo to the edge of the mesa. Sometimes, the dry, hot air lingers in town, roams Main Street, and sails over the three-story Victorian with the rounded glass turret and white picket fence.

Near a moonlit grove, the wind picks up the scent of eucalyptus mixed with pine and pauses by a garden in front of a white stucco house. Inside the cottage, which is the last one on the road leading out of town, a woman stands by a window watching the fog drift over the bluff to the sea.

One hundred eighty miles south, a hospital languishes in the Santa Monica hills, a cement building with an iron gate and a twisting drive. From her bed, a woman with no name stares at her reflection in the window. She is a victim of senseless brutality and has no memory of her life before the assault. The woman listens to the doctors talk about her as if she isn't there. Without an identity, maybe she isn't.

\* \* \*

## Diane

Miguel, the evening orderly, arrives with my medication. I take the pills he offers and wash them down with a few sips of juice. My gaze is riveted to the TV, a film from the early 1940s, the mystery *Laura*. Later, in a dream, the movie unspools in my mind. It isn't the film script, but a different version of *Laura* with my own personal spin and point of view. I become the murder victim. Her name is Diane Redfern. I wake when I hear the doorbell. I turn on the bedside lamp and put on Laura's robe and slippers. The apartment is dark, but I know the way as I often stay over when Laura's out of town; Laura, who understands me, who knows the difficulty of making ends meet, especially for a young model new to the business. She offers me the key to her apartment, and I become her friend. Her good friend.

Not thinking to check the peephole, I open the door.

I see a shotgun muzzle, hear a sudden blast.

I reel backward into the darkness, my face no longer recognizable. It is an act of senseless violence and mistaken identity. The killer thought I was Laura.

I open my eyes. Diane Redfern. I repeat the name aloud. I feel empathy for the celluloid Diane who, like me, was left alone to die. I like the name. It's mine now. I'll tell Dr. Macias tomorrow. It'll make her day. Anything's better than Jane Doe, or ma'am, as they call me around here.

Macias says I'm smart, that I remember dates, places, literature, and art. She knows this from all the tests they've given me. "What is this picture? What's twelve times twelve divided by two? Who was JFK?" I ask her, if I'm smart, why can't I remember my own name, my past life? She smiles but doesn't answer. Psychiatrists do that, I've learned.

The next morning, I pad in bare feet to the bathroom I share with another patient, Selma. I don't know Selma's last name. They don't allow last names here. I can tell Selma's recently taken a shower since the glass is misted over. I pick up a damp towel thrown over the tub and run it across the mirror in sections, top to bottom. I'm fifty-ish—so they tell me—with a round face, short-cropped hair, and blue eyes. I turn sideways and notice the beginning of jowls. I move my head up and down, work my jaw, try to make the bags of fat under my neck disappear. Newsflash: They don't.

Later, near the end of my therapy session, I stop pressuring myself to remember and decide to give Macias what she wants. Poor thing, she's tried for weeks to restore my memory and failed miserably. I guess I feel sorry for her.

The doctor clasps her hands, drops them in her lap, and leans forward. "You've got to do better, Diane." Macias loves my new name. I thought she would. "Don't you want to get well?"

"Of course I do." I hope I sound sincere.

"Then try a little harder. You have to trust me."

My roommate, Selma , failed the trust test. We were sitting in the solarium one day, having a cup of coffee, and she opened up, told me about her surgery, the double mastectomy, and the middle-aged technician with the stringy blond hair who took her blood. Selma watched the woman pump red fluid from her veins and listened to her go on about the hopelessness of her situation.

"They always drop some cells, Selma," she said, "no matter how small. Microscopic traces that continue to grow. Nothing you can do about it."

Selma became my friend, and I trusted her until the morning I opened the bathroom door and saw her sitting naked on the john, applying a foamy cream to her sagging breasts, rubbing it over them, unaware of my presence. I think trust doesn't mean much to me anymore.

So today I give Macias what she wants. I look up at the painting, the one hanging on the wall behind her, the one she said she bought on a trip north to Santa Maria. I study the brown mountains Macias calls the Santa Lucias and the mesa below, something you'd expect to see in New Mexico or Arizona but not in California. I learned all this from Macias, who seems to know everything.

Like the detective in *Laura*, I dive into the painting and begin my daydream. "I see a windswept plain dotted with oak trees. High, sandy mountains rise above a dry riverbed. An arroyo, I think it's called."

"Yes, this is a good start."

I continue on. "There's a white stucco house with a red tile roof, kind of Spanish-looking. A woman is working in a garden." I pause here for effect. "No, she's not in her garden. She's inside the small cottage watching me from a window."

Macias gives me a smile of beautiful white-capped teeth, then a nod of approval. "Go on."

"I think it could be my mother or maybe a sister." I take a deep breath and smile triumphantly. Macias might remember the painting when she goes over her notes, but for now I'm safe from the endless questions.

"Wonderful! I think we've had a breakthrough." Macias looks at her watch. "Same time tomorrow?"

At least one of us is happy.

On my last day at the hospital, I stroll to the solarium. On the road below, a bus rounds a bend, and people with maps and cameras angle for the best photos. I think only in Southern California could a mental hospital or a cemetery be a tourist attraction. Not much difference between the two that I can see.

I pour myself a cup of coffee from an urn set out for visitors. I check my mood, a little exercise Macias has taught me, and decide I feel like someone who's just seen the Prize Patrol stop at her driveway, note the address, and accelerate on down the street.

I sit in my usual spot, a comfortable, rattan chair opposite a flowery painting. A few ferns and a creeping

Charlie dangle from pots on either side of a large bay window. A neglected palm dies quietly in a corner. I walk over to the tree, run my fingers over a brown-edged frond, and snap it off, then drop it into a pink plastic wastebasket. It's the dead weight that kills you. It has to go.

Macias is late this morning, and I wonder what's keeping her? Would she miss me if I split?

\* \* \*

## Dr. Macias' Log

I was surprised the patient—current name Diane—left without seeing me, without being formally discharged. I'd been detained on the ward, but this often happened and she knew to wait. It wasn't like I'd forgotten her. It's upsetting because we've invested so much staff time and hospital resources in her care over the past weeks.

I really thought we were making progress. I asked Nurse Wiggins, and she said she'd looked in on Diane earlier this morning and heard her showering through the closed bathroom door. Wiggins reported her clothes were neatly laid out on the bed, things she planned on wearing when she was released this morning to the group home in town. Something must have happened. I wouldn't have predicted she'd walk out before our last therapy session.

We had a breakthrough the other day. The patient initially resisted my efforts, but I think lately she was trying harder, beginning to remember. I can only hope she'll return.

\* \* \*

## Diane

I find myself outside, carrying a large white plastic bag and walking a crowded street without any idea how I got here. I stop, look inside the bag, and find most of my clothes.

Blouses, skirts, two cotton dresses, a sweater, some socks, and underwear, all donations from a local benevolent society.

I fish out my purse, then flip through the wallet. The hospital social worker gave me some cash, money they set aside for hardship cases like mine. Not much, just under two hundred bucks.

A dry wind warms my face and I visualize the painting in Macias' office. I focus my thoughts and energy on a cloudless sky, the bluish-black outline of the Santa Lucias, a mesa dotted with pine and eucalyptus. For some odd reason, they trusted me to get to the group home on my own. "Just a few blocks," Macias said. "It isn't far."

Forget it. I know where I'm headed.

A long train ride and several hours later, I'm walking past an orchard with rows of orange and lemon trees. I hear traffic sounds in the distance. On my left, a collapsing barn squats in a parched field. A windblown cypress leans toward a tired oak. A few cattle graze by a wire fence while the mountains tower above me.

I've already seen what passes for a town center: a barbershop with a hitching post and a faded striped pole, a hay and feed, a liquor store, an automotive repair shop, and a small white church across from a Victorian with a bed and breakfast sign out front.

I cup a hand over my eyes and follow the pot-holed road as it winds through a grove of eucalyptus, travels up a hill, then disappears. The only sign of life is a woman working in the garden of a white stucco house with a red tile roof.

I walk up to the gate and peer through the iron latticework.

I study the woman inside, who wears jeans and a plaid shirt. She looks familiar. The blond hair, parted in the middle and pulled back in a bun, accentuates an oval face. I remember I've seen someone like her. Macias called it art therapy.

"Look through this book," she said. "Maybe it will jog your memory." And so I flipped though the pages until I came upon a sour-faced woman standing by a man. He was holding a pitchfork. The woman in the garden glances up at me, and I see she's nothing like the spinster daughter in the painting. She has creamy skin with no lines or wrinkles, and she's smiling. She appears younger than me, in her thirties or early forties, but I can't be sure. Along with my memory, I've lost the ability to judge age.

\* \* \*

## Hope

"I'm sorry. I didn't mean to intrude," the woman says, then she turns away from my gate.

"Come back here a minute! Please."

"It's just your garden," she says.

"What about it?"

"It's lovely. Prettiest thing I've seen in a long time."

I get up and brush some dirt from my jeans. "You gotta be kidding, honey. It's nothing but an overgrown jungle."

I hear the grandfather clock in the hall strike the hour, and Grover begins his routine, the barking and running, the sound of his toenails scratching the hardwood floor.

"He's disabled," I tell her. "Noise sensitive."

Just then a blur of brown and white, one ear up, one down, leaps from the porch, and before I can warn the woman, she sticks her hand inside and pets him. I'll be darned if he doesn't spread his teeth in a big grin. "Some watchdog, my baby."

This lady bends down, stares into Grover's eyes, then tells him the old cliché about barks being worse than bites, and, of course, he's a goner.

"Speaking of jungles and wild animals," I say, "meet Grover. He's pretty harmless, but you've guessed that. Wouldn't know what to do with an intruder if he caught one.".

I look down at the white bag she's dropped at her feet. "Lady, where'd you
come from?"

She says she's from L.A. and looking for a place to stay. I tell her good luck. "Not much in hotels around here. Why not stop a while, have a cup of tea?"

"Yes, I'd like that." She tells me about a Victorian bed and breakfast she passed up the road, near the church. We don't have anything as quaint as a B & B and nothing you'd label Victorian, but I let it slide. She must have a good ten years on me, and given the weather, I think maybe she's had too much sun. I say it's pretty hot for early spring, and she just stares at me with a kind of bewildered look that makes me a little uncomfortable when my words, "I'm Hope," just lay in the languid air between us.

I open the gate and offer my hand. "Last name's Diamond. Parents had a sense of humor."

"Hope Diamond. Sounds like they had high expectations, too." The woman laughs and shakes my hand. "I'm Diane. Diane Redfern."

"Red Fern. Now there's an unusual name. Nice and lush like a rain forest." I motion for her to sit on the front stoop. "I've got a set of perfectly good lawn furniture stored in the garage, but we've had some windstorms lately, lots of dust and sand, so I just got tired of wiping everything off and put it all away."

Diane sits on the porch step and strokes Grover's fur. He glances up at her lovingly, then lays his head in her lap.

I tell her he's a good little dog, though the running and barking get to me sometimes.

"But he's not a threat to intruders," she says, and I

sense I've hurt her feelings.

"I'm sorry, I didn't mean it to come out that way. I say what's on my mind and usually get in trouble. Plenty of it."

"There's no place to stay in town," she says, in a low, whispery kind of voice like she's talking to herself, thinking out loud.

"No. Nothing for a good ten miles." I point down the road toward the Bakersfield cutoff. "If I were you, I'd take a bus into Arroyo or Pismo. Lots of motels, some right off the freeway. But it's too late for today. Last local left around three. I'd drive you, but my car's in the shop, the one you passed in town." I study the angle of the sun. "I'd say it's after four."

"You can do that?" she asks.

"Do what?"

"Tell time just by looking."

"Yep. One of my hidden talents." I pick up the pot, pour some tea, then feel the sides of her cup. "It's cold. I'll make some fresh. Stay put, honey. Just relax with your new pal."

A few minutes later, I return and offer her a steaming cup and a platter of cookies. She inhales two gingersnaps and starts in on an oatmeal. "You must be starved."

"Guess I am a little."

"Didn't you eat today?"

"I had a sandwich on the train from Los Angeles. It was a beautiful ride."

Her growling stomach tells me different.

I can't resist being a nosy busybody, so I jump right in. "Tell me, and I mean this kindly, what's a woman your age doing walking around the mesa in the heat of the day?"

"I love it here, don't you?"

I tell her I was born and raised in this climate and decide she's a pretty good subject jumper. I try again. "What brings you here?"

"Oh, this and that, I suppose."

I'm rot about to let her off easy. "What this and what that?"

"It's a long story. I'm making a change in my life. I've wanted to do it for some time, and here's where I wound up."

"I guess it's never too late," I say, and drop the interrogation. It's none of my business, and she's a stranger to me. I'm just making conversation, being polite, that's all. Still, when I turn from her, suddenly distracted by the siren of an emergency vehicle on 101, I have this funny sensation I've imagined this woman, conjured her up from my dreams. How many days and nights have I waited for a new friend to come into my life, to walk down this road, and stop at my gate? Too many.

\* \* \*

**Diane**

Hope is nice and seems a decent sort, very down to earth. I can tell from the short time I've spent with her, but I need to be careful, watch what I say and do. This feeling of people talking behind my back is hard to shake. Someday, I'll take control of my life like this woman has. I'll own a home with a red tile roof, tend a garden, and play with a little dog of my own. But for now, I don't want people to think I'm a loony who's been locked up.

\* \* \*

**Hope**

I tell Diane she can stay the night. "Grover and I have plenty of room, don't we, honey?" Then the clock strikes, and my little neurotic is off and running in tight circles around our feet, barking like a seal at a clambake.

Diane says she can't stay. "I've just walked into your life. You don't know me."

I tell her I know what I know. "We've become shut-ins, Grover and me. Look at it this way, you'd be doing us a favor by being our company." Then she gives me that dazed look again, and I figure this is Diane's way of saying okay. Who knows? Maybe I've made a friend.

\* \* \*

## Diane

That night in Hope's cottage, I sit on the edge of the living room sofa she's made into a bed. I hear the wind rattle windows and shake the front door and, after a while, decide this is a friendly sound, not something I should fear.

In the morning, I wake to unfamiliar surroundings, to a bed in a white room with a white door. My possessions are scattered across the top of a beat-up chest of drawers, and nothing from the previous day remains other than the echo in my mind of a little dog running in circles, barking at the chimes of a grandfather clock.

\* \* \*

## Dr. Macias' Log

I was surprised when the patient reappeared at the hospital after a seven-month absence. Nurse Jenkins discovered her in the solarium, sitting quietly by the palm tree, her hand moving back and forth over her empty lap. When Jenkins questioned her, the patient said she was petting her dog, Grover.

Physical examination has proved unremarkable. Patient's hair is longer and dyed blond. She parts it in the middle and pulls it back in a bun. She no longer answers to

Diane and wishes to be called Hope. She doesn't initiate conversation and is mostly unresponsive during our sessions. She has the pallor of someone who has spent her time indoors, yet on one of her better days, she spoke of living on a windy, sun-drenched mesa in Central California.

Given the patient's initial diagnosis of dissociative identity disorder, exacerbated by physical assault, it would appear a fourth personality, Hope, has emerged. We had previously documented three separate identities: the emotionally scared, nameless woman we admitted last year, then Selma, followed by Diane. I believe we can still make significant progress and integrate the separate personas into a stable, central consciousness, but for now, only time will tell.

# Judythe Guarnera

Editor of the SLO NightWriter column in Tolosa Press for five years and editor of the *SLO NightWriter Anthology*, Judythe has been published in local publications and in six anthologies (including *Chicken Soup for the Soul*). She has been a frequent winner in the Lilian Dean Contest at the Central Coast Writers Conference and a finalist in the SLO NightWriters Golden Quill Contest. She is a Mentor Mediator, which gives her more opportunity to connect, as she seeks to do through her writing.

My daughter-in-law, Julie, was puzzled by a dream she experienced, a dream that bordered on fantasy. I was inspired to see if I could weave a mystery around her dream, which would leave the reader puzzled. The result: *Little White Pills*.

# LITTLE WHITE PILLS

by
Judythe Guarnera

This damn hole I live in gets deeper every day. Pretty soon I'll need a ladder to climb out. I open the cabinet and pull out the bottle of little white pills I keep stashed behind the toothpaste.

No! I promised Mom. With a trembling hand I stuff them back.

\* \* \*

The alarm chirps. I slap the off button and bury myself under the covers—until nature's call forces me out of bed.

"This isn't working," I mutter, careful to avoid the bathroom mirror. I can't bear to see the brown hair that straggles around the gaunt-looking face; the eyelids that droop and almost merge with the bags under my eyes; the lines at the corners of my frown that resemble punctuation marks for my dark state of mind.

\* \* \*

I don't know if it was Karma, or not, but a year ago, I found the perfect house in Shell Beach, the heart of the Central Coast of California. I've always felt connected to the energy of the ocean and still regularly pinch myself to see if I'm dreaming when I wake up to the roar of the sea.

Anxious to meet people and enjoy local activities, I dropped in at the Pismo Beach Chamber of Commerce. I talked with Briana, who volunteered there. We hit it off and began to surf and hang out together, quickly becoming best friends.

Then everything changed.

Brianna always rode her bike home from the chamber, even in the summer when she worked until 9:30 at night. We had recurring debates about whether that was safe or not.

"Bree, all those vacationing drunks are slithering off their bar stools and heading to their hotels or camping spots at the same time you bike home. You're a frickin' target out there. Let me pick you up."

"Don't be silly. Have you seen the size of my bike reflectors? Not to mention my florescent green jacket."

"Silly? Me silly?" I kick the table leg. "Damn, what if something happens to you? How can I be your Maid of Honor if you're dead?"

"You're such a drama queen."

My chest tightens. Bree is the most independent, stubborn person I know.

\* \* \*

I slam my fist on the table; the coffee in my cup splatters its contents onto the floor. Why did I have to be right? I had to push myself to go to her funeral. I was so angry.

The phone rings; my heart lurches. Maybe it's Victoria. Maybe she's changed her mind. The ringing stops.

A week ago Victoria, my girlfriend, calls. "Shelena . . . sorry . . . uh . . . oh shit, I've found my soulmate. I'm sorry," and she hangs up.

Soul mates—what the hell was I—the practice round? And I thought I didn't have any tears left.

\* \* \*

I get to work on Monday and my boss demotes me. Cites poor job performance, but what he really means to say is he's sick of me dragging my sorry ass around and dragging everybody down with me.

\* \* \*

My phone vibrates against the wooden nightstand. It's Mom. Her sixth sense kicks in whenever I travel the road of depression. Says she birthed me and it's her job to keep me alive. Especially after my first adventure with the little white pills. Then I was glad she arrived in time to call an ambulance. Now, I wish she hadn't.

"Hi, Mom. Shower's running. Can I call you back?"

"You okay, Honey?"

"Been better, but I'm okay. Each day's a little easier."

Liar, liar, pants on fire.

"You sound kinda—you know—squeaky. Like when you're—you know . . ."

"Can't get anything past you, can I? To be honest, sometimes I think I'll never be okay. Like you always say, though, it takes time. Gotta go. I'll be late for work."

\* \* \*

After working another miserable eight hours in my demoted position, I stop for a sub sandwich on the way home. I won't eat it, but it fulfills another promise I made to Mom—to keep food in the house.

I dump it in the fridge and plunk down in front of the TV. I fiddle with the remote, but nothing interests me. After a hot bath, I climb into bed. I know sleep will elude me.

The bed creaks and shakes me awake. I sit up. The shaking stops, but the noise underneath intensifies. A form takes shape at the foot of the bed. I hide behind my pillow—as if it could protect me.

"Shelena," the voice quavers in the stillness.

"B...buh...Briana, is that you?"

"It is. I'm worried about you, Shel."

"Worried? About me?"

"Be honest. You're miserable since I died. And then Victoria dumps you . . . and I know about the demotion."

Now it's really quiet. All I hear is my heart thumping and the compelling voice.

"I have a proposition for you. I wasn't ready to die. We can change places."

"What? Switch? You mean you alive and me dead?"

"Yes, will you do that—for me—for us?"

"You know I love, uh, loved you, but . . ."

"Remember last time—the relief you felt—how the pain disappeared? Then your mom showed up and all the pain came back. I can stop your pain—right this minute." She shakes a bottle of little white pills; they sound like a death rattle.

"Bree, you know Mom needs me to live . . ." My lips tremble. "No, damn it, I need me to live. Leave—now." I watch my friend, now a specter, fade, like Morro Rock as it's engulfed in the marine layer.

I slide out of bed and stumble into the bathroom. I have to throw away those damn pills. I open the medicine chest and pull out the toothpaste. The space behind is empty.

# Sue McGinty

With little more than an urge to live at the beach, write mystery novels, and mollify a cat who'd never ridden in a car before, Sue McGinty left Los Angeles June 17, 1994, the same day OJ Simpson took his famous ride. Unlike OJ, Sue had a destination in mind: the Central Coast hamlet of Los Osos. Not the Cabot Cove of "Murder She Wrote," but close.

Her Bella Kowalski Central Coast mysteries include *Murder in Los Lobos, Murder at Cuyamaca Beach, Murder in Mariposa Bay*, and the forthcoming *Murder in a Safe Haven*. Her short fiction has been featured in four other Sisters in Crime Central Coast Chapter anthologies.

"Metaphor for Murder" combines some of my favorite things and people: World War II history, films, Hearst Castle and Winston Churchill.

# Metaphor For Murder

by

Sue McGinty

I was just seventeen in 1938, the first time I visited Lorna's Castle, radio commentator Louis Labrador's memorial to his late wife. Alas poor Lorna—former heiress, former child star, dead too soon. Of natural causes they said.

As my grandfather and I made our way up the Cabrillo Highway, Lorna's Castle rose majestically from the fog on California's Central Coast, a faux antebellum mansion, the place to go for a wicked weekend party. The Hollywood elite might not agree with Louis Labrador's right wing politics, but they loved his free food and wine.

So how did I wangle an invitation? Simple. I had connections. My grandfather was character actor Josef von Strasser. He wanted to unwind after the wrap of his latest film, and asked if I would like to see real movie stars at play.

I would indeed. After watching him die in the leading lady's arms sixteen times on the set Thursday afternoon, I was ready for some real excitement, not just the fake stuff.

It was now Friday night and as winter's first storm raged outside, I stood apart from the others in Lorna's gathering room. Alice in Wonderland meets *Gone With the Wind*, green drapes puddling on the floor and all. Floor-to-ceiling bookcases flanked a hearth big enough to roast an ox, and the pine smell of crackling logs filled the air. I stood with my back to the fire, allowing fingers of warmth to caress that spot just below my shoulders where silver sequins ended and bare skin began.

A silver-foxed woman approached waving an ivory cigarette holder in one hand and a cocktail in the other. "Some shindig, eh?" Without waiting for an answer, she swiveled, hips first, and moved toward more important prey.

Fingering the wave in my newly-bobbed hair. I counted seventeen other perfectly coifed heads. Men in tuxedoes and tails swaggered like penguins. Women in bright satin inspected each other for sagging necks. Grandfather huddled with three men in a corner. Several people gathered around a man playing Gershwin on a baby grand. They included Anna Gatesby and Beau Calhoun, Hollywood's newest beautiful couple.

A man in a white ten-gallon hat spoke earnestly to the hot new reporter from *Movie Fan* magazine. Her fellow journalist and chief rival, the veteran Amanda Pickle, lurked nearby. Glaring at them. Miss Pickle stood by a table caressing an old sword. That is, until a man in a dark suit jogged over and whispered in her ear. The hand fell to her side.

"Cocktail, Miss?"

"Uh..." I hesitated, saw Grandfather's averted gaze, and chose a Martini from the proffered tray. "Thank you."

I held up the glass. The drink matched my blue-white diamond ring exactly. The stone caught the firelight and my palm began to itch. The diamond was so large, so.. so not mine. I would think about *that* on Monday.

The first gulp of raw alcohol burned my throat and produced both tears and coughing. Through a haze of running mascara, I peered down the hall to see an older man lumber through the massive oak front door. He was dressed all in black and shaped like an egg. He shook rain from his umbrella onto the entryway's marble floor. In a flash, the man who'd whispered to Amanda Pickle jogged toward him.

They conferred briefly, and the older man walked back out into the storm. I'd seen that egg-shaped man somewhere, and not long ago.

*Oh-oh.* With waiter in tow, Grandfather approached. He removed the glass from my hand, set it on the waiter's tray, and waved him off.

"Come, Zelda. Allow me to introduce you to Beau and Anna," Grandfather said in his precise, measured tones. He gestured to the mustachioed man and blonde woman standing by the piano.

As Grandfather and I moved across the room, people stared at the tall gentleman of the old school and his petite young companion. Though his name wasn't a household word, Josef von Strasser had played critical roles in many important films. With Hitler poised to sweep across Europe, Grandfather worried that it might soon be hard for a German actor, even a skilled one, to find work.

"Beau, Anna." They tore eyes from each other and focused klieg light smiles on Grandfather. "I would like you to meet to Zelda, my granddaughter. She is visiting from Tucson, Arizona."

"Tucson, you say? How quaint," Anna sniffed.

"Yes," Grandfather said. "After we came here from the old country, my son moved to Arizona, while I remained here."

"Lucky for you."

"Yes, Hollywood has been good to me." Grandfather ignored Anna's barb. "I have even arranged a screen test for Zelda on Monday."

"What am I, invisible or something?" Beau reached over and pulled my hand into both of his. "Hi ya, kid." His hands were warm and smelled like lemon pie. "I'll bet you have a contract by Monday afternoon."

At that moment I found out hearts really do stand still.

Anna removed my hand from Beau's and placed it in her own, which felt cold and dry. "So, your name's Zelda von Strasser?" I nodded.

"I'm sure the studio moguls will change that moniker in a hurry. What with all the Nazis—Ouch!" Beau elbowed her in the ribs, as Grandfather's eyes narrowed.

James, Mr. Labrador's new secretary, picked that exact moment to enter the gathering room. He had shown us to our quarters earlier. He adjusted round, tortoise shell specs, held up pale hands, and waved for attention.

"Ladies and gentlemen," he said in clipped, British tones, "Mr. Labrador has just rung up from his broadcast studio in Los Angeles. He has been detained by the storm." The guests groaned and James waved for silence. "Please enjoy your dinner. He'll join you for the cinema afterwards." He made a sweeping gesture. "Dinner is now served in the dining hall. I'll be around if you have questions."

"Zelda, please allow me." Beau held out his arm. As the four of us glided down the corridor, I felt a chill and looked over my shoulder. Once again the egg-shaped man stood in the entryway. This time it was James who moved toward him.

In the dining hall. I forgot about the egg-shaped man as my eyes took in the three enormous crystal chandeliers suspended from a ceiling at least twelve feet high. "Like those?" Beau asked.

"They're beautiful."

He whispered, "Fake. Like everything else." I struggled not to fan the air. Beau's hands might smell like lemon, but his breath reeked of garlic.

A long, narrow table with eighteen gold chairs dominated the center of the room. On the rose damask tablecloth a king's ransom in fine silver refracted the firelight from yet another enormous hearth. *Silver.* Surely that was real. My palm itched again. I glanced at Grandfather, who warned me with his eyes.

Using place cards by each plate, we found our seats. Grandfather and I sat across from each other; Beau and Anna found themselves at the far end of the table, close to the fireplace, the "hot seat," according to Beau.

The first course arrived; raw oysters, looking like...well, I couldn't say in polite company. I ignored the slimy things and turned to the man on my right. Without his ten-gallon hat, he was cute, with straw colored hair and intense blue eyes.

"Wolf Montana," he said in an "aw-shucks" accent, sticking out a large paw. He wore a silver and turquoise cuff-style bracelet.

"Pleased to meet you." I shook his hand, extending my fingers to brush the bracelet's dappled stones. My father designed jewelry and unless I missed my guess, Wolf's bracelet had been hand-crafted by the Navajo.

"Wolf is Century Studio's new cowboy actor," Grandfather said and turned to the woman next to him. "And this is Dora Golightly, a reporter for *Movie Fan*."

"Pleased, I'm sure," Dora said, and turned to a nearby waiter. "May I have the catsup, please?"

Amanda Pickle, on my left, eyed the Heinz bottle, quickly set before Dora. "There you go, darling, 57 varieties, just like you. Stuff yourself," she purred.

"Well, I never—" huffed Dora. She poured catsup over her oysters until they resembled a nosebleed.

"Heard tonight's movie is *Saratoga*," Wolf said, probably to change the subject. "Too bad about Miz Jean Harlow."

"Yes, it's interesting to see the scenes where they used a double," Dora said between mouthfuls. "Throws the studio into a tizzy when a star dies in mid-picture. Why I remember when Lorna Labrador died..." She left the sentence unfinished.

With nothing to contribute, I moved my oysters from one side of the glass plate to the other.

Wolf lost interest in shop talk when the main course arrived. He piled curried chicken, peas, and rice on the back of his fork, patted them into a tidy mound with his knife, and with a rolling motion, popped the fork, upside down, into his mouth. Grandfather ate that way and I was always afraid he'd stab his tongue.

"Wolf, where are you from?" I asked.

Wolf wiped each corner of his mouth with a napkin. "Butte."

"Butte?"

"Yup, capital of Montana." Seeing my puzzled expression, he asked, "Get it? Montana, that's the surname my agent gave me."

I got it all right. What I didn't get was why a man from Montana wouldn't know the state capital was Helena. The nuns at Santa Clarita hadn't taught me much, but I did know the 48 state capitals. A movement under the table caught my eye. I looked down just in time to see Dora's pointed toe make solid contact with Wolf's boot.

Interesting. Something was definitely rotten and it wasn't the oysters.

Or was it? Suddenly, Dora set her fork down and stared at the plate, her face green as the curry on it. One waiter whisked it away as another placed in front of her pie ala mode. Cherry juice swirled into pale ice cream, like blood on snow. She rose unsteadily, resting red-lacquered fingertips on rose damask. "Sick. *So sick.* Excuse me," She fled the room, a hand over her mouth. With narrowed eyes, Amanda Pickle watched her departure.

\* \* \*

I scrunched down in my seat in the theater and checked my tiny, jeweled wristwatch. Almost eleven, time for the film. Amanda Pickle had said that Mr. Labrador usually screened his late wife's childhood movies for weekend guests. Tonight was an exception. *Saratoga* had created a sensation last year, largely because of the untimely death of its star, Jean Harlow. A strange choice for a grieving man, but then Mr. Labrador wasn't here.

"Sit here, Grandfather." I patted the seat beside me, gazing at the chintz covered, floral walls. Tacky.

"Thank you, Zelda my dear." He took my hand. "Did you enjoy your dinner?"

"It was okay."

"Well, are you having a good time?"

"Of course." The truth was, I hated this place. Telling myself not to be a goose, I put my other hand over my grandfather's and smiled into his gray eyes.

"Can we sit with you?" Beau and Anna stood beside us in the aisle.

"Of course, of course," Grandfather said, a bit too heartily. "But I reserve the right to sit next to my granddaughter." Was I wrong or did he give Beau a "hands off" look?

While Beau and Anna settled in, I turned around. People clustered in small groups throughout the theater. Behind us, Amanda Pickle joined a couple of journalists in animated conversation. Wolf sat in the back—a lone cowboy. I hoped Dora was okay. Lights dimmed and we settled in to watch the film.

Soon after the short subjects began, a door opened at the back of the theater. I looked around to see a man backlit by the hall lamp. I couldn't make out his face, but there was no mistaking that build. The egg-shaped man took an aisle seat in the last row.

I blinked when the lights came back on, yawned, and stretched both arms over my head. My watch said 1:00 a.m. How did all that time go by? I must have dropped off.

"So Zelda, what did you think?" Beau asked. He had scooted over next to me when Grandfather, whispering that he wasn't feeling well, had excused himself midway through the film.

I chewed my lip for a second. "It was okay, for a horse racing movie. I thought it was really obvious when they used a double for Jean."

"I agree," Anna said. "Too bad she couldn't have gone out on a high note."

"Yeah," Beau sighed. "I'm gonna' miss that little filly." He looked sad for a moment, then slapped his knee. "Hey, how about we all take a midnight swim?"

"In this weather?" Even the thought gave me goose bumps.

Anna laughed. "The pool's indoors, silly, right under this theater."

"I need to check on my grandfather." I was already feeling guilty for not leaving when he did.

"We understand, kid," Anna said, cuffing me on the arm. She turned to Beau. "First one in gets to skinny dip."

Anna tore up the aisle, with Beau in hot pursuit. Upon reaching the last row, she stopped dead and let out a shriek they probably heard in San Francisco. Beau rushed to her side; others soon followed. Without knowing how I got there, I found myself among them. The egg-shaped man still sat in his aisle seat, his black vest slashed across the chest. With unseeing eyes, he stared at the ceiling. I still remember the blood.

"My God," a journalist exclaimed, "Someone's murdered Winston Churchill!"

\* \* \*

Around three a.m., I fought relentless wind and rain on the walkway from the main house to Grandfather's room in the two-story guest house. Feeling like Rapunzel, I'd spent a restless two hours my loft bedroom listening to rain pummel the glass. Listening and thinking of what had happened. I'd seen Winston Churchill in newsreels. That's why he looked familiar. He had warned of the danger Hitler presented to Europe and even the United States. But why was Winston Churchill in California, here at Lorna of all places?

I just wanted to go home. That was impossible. The highway had washed out above Santa Barbara and there was major flooding on the lower road leading to the mansion. Also, the telephones were dead.

We learned this when James appeared in the theater, just after Anna found the body. The main gate was locked, as were all the others. He ordered us to remain in our rooms, prisoners on this hillside. A major political figure had been killed. One of us was his murderer.

James hadn't mentioned guards, but they must be out there. Still, no one stopped me when I dressed in dark clothes, sneaked out of my room, crept downstairs, and let myself out the front door into the storm. I'd worry about getting myself back in later. Right now, I had to see if Grandfather was all right.

I opened the door of the guest house and stepped inside the dimly lit foyer. Thank God, the electricity was still on. The guest house seemed eerily quiet after the furor outside.

*That's funny*, I thought. *Grandfather said his was the only room on this floor*. But there were several closed doors. At the far end, one stood ajar. Grandfather's, I hoped.

As I opened the door, a lightning bolt lit the room like a scene from hell, but I had to go in. I groped my way to a lamp on the nightstand and switched it on. Wolf's bracelet lay beside the lamp. Why would he go off and leave his door ajar, with his bracelet in plain sight and a murderer on the loose?

Still, a bracelet was a bracelet. I slipped it over my wrist. Nice. Very nice. My palm itched.

I heard voices in the hall. Heart pounding, I froze. A man and a woman. Wolf and a woman. Wolf and Dora! Frantically, I looked around. They mustn't find me here.

*Hide, Zelda.*

The closet? There didn't seem to be one. The bathroom? Too exposed. At the last possible moment before the door opened, I switched off the light and dove under the bed. The duvet was too short to provide much protection, but it would have to do. I lay on my stomach, arms splayed in front of me. I was still wearing the bracelet.

"Strange. One of the servants must have closed the door," Dora said. "I can't believe you'd go off and leave it ajar. You mustn't be so careless, honey."

"You are too tense, my darling. Do not worry so much. These stupid Americans." Wolf's "aw-shucks" accent had become chillingly Teutonic.

Two pairs of feet appeared beside the bed, dripping puddles on the floor. "I'm freezing. Why did you insist we take that stupid walk?" Dora whined. "And I feel sick again."

"You needed the air, my dear. A person who covers good oysters with American catsup deserves to be ill."

"Very funny, Wolf."

Wolf laughed. "I thought Frau Pickle poisoned you."

At the word *Frau*, my foot jerked back in surprise. An object under the bed clattered on the bare floor.

"What was that?" Dora leaned over, lifting the duvet. I shrank back in terror as her arm appeared.

"It is nothing. Relax, my darling." Wolf said and Dora's arm disappeared. Lightning again filled the room. I could see the bones in their feet, like those x-ray machines that showed your toes in the shoe stores.

I reached back and grabbed the fallen object. Was it? No, it couldn't be. It *was*. The sword. The murder weapon? I began to shiver.

"I hate storms," Dora cried as thunder rolled across the sky. "Wolf, I know you have a flask of brandy. Please honey, give me just a little nip for my nerves." She fell back across the bed. Wolf sat beside her, his feet on the floor, and began rummaging around in the nightstand drawer. Would he notice the bracelet was gone?

"Turn on the light, honey," Dora begged.

"No, I like the darkness. Here," Wolf said finally. "Drink this."

"That's better." I heard swallowing, then, "Hold me, Wolf baby, I'm so scared."

Bodies moved above me and the mattress began to jiggle. *Oh no*, I breathed. *Not here, not now.* Thankfully, the mattress stopped and after a few seconds of silence, Dora sighed, "I feel better now. I'm going back to my room and try to catch forty winks."

"That's an excellent idea," Wolf said.

The door shut softly and Wolf settled back down. I'd have to stay put until he fell asleep. *If* he fell asleep.

In a few minutes, I heard loud snoring. Time to make my escape and tell someone—anyone—what I'd seen and heard. But what was my excuse for being under Wolf's bed? If I was accused of snooping—or worse, stealing a guest's bracelet—my movie career would be over before it began. And I'd shame Grandfather.

*Wait a minute, Zelda. We're talking about murder here.*

I wiggled out from under the bed and paused, taking stock. My heart skipped a beat when the snoring ceased and Wolf began to thrash around. I wiggled back, kicking the dagger again in my haste. Sugar! But I got lucky and the snoring swelled to a crescendo.

I was halfway to the door before I remembered. *The bracelet.* I crept back toward the bed and was just placing it near the lamp, when I heard, "*What?*"

I whirled around. Another lighting bolt electrified the room. Wolf sat upright, staring at me. Staring, I soon realized, with blind eyes. He sighed, sank back and began to snore again. I tugged the door open and sprinted toward the foyer like Jesse Owens in the '36 Olympics. Straight into the arms of James.

* * *

"Baskerville, British security," James announced to the guests hastily summoned to the gathering room. Now everyone was dressed in night clothes. Again satin predominated, the men in black robes with long lapels, the women shivering in light peignoirs.

A journalist said, "Then you're not Mr. Labrador's new secretary?"

James shook his head. "Unfortunately, no. This murder is a tragedy, not only for England, but for the United States as well. Mr. Churchill seems, that is, *seemed,* to be one of the few politicians on either side of the Pond who understands what Hitler is up to."

"But why was he here?" the man persisted.

James turned to me. "Miss von Strasser has a most extraordinary story to tell. I would like you to hear it from her."

I stepped forward and looked at the faces, all eyes on me. James stood to one side, watching the guests. I took a deep breath. "I know who killed Winston Churchill." Everyone gasped. Well, I'd jumped off the dock. Now I'd have to swim to shore.

I pointed at Wolf. "He did it."

"That's flat ridiculous, little lady," Wolf said, putting a hand on his chest. "Why would I kill a British diplomat? I'm just a cowboy from Montana."

"No, you're not," I said. "You're a Nazi spy."

"Why do you think that, little lady?" Wolf was a better actor than spy.

"Because you don't eat like an American, you eat like a Continental, and you don't know the capital of Montana for starters," I answered. "And one minute you talk like a cowboy and the next you sound like Hitler."

"That's mighty flimsy evidence, Miss *von Strasser*," Wolf said. He looked around the room for support, and several people nodded.

"I was under your bed and I heard you and Dora talking." Dora's gasp could be heard above the others.

"What were you doing there?" Wolf asked, looking at Dora.

Dora answered for me. "I know what she was doing. I saw her eye your bracelet at dinner. She came to steal it."

At that point one of the bookcases swung back and a man literally materialized out of the woodwork. Beyond the opening I saw a circular stairway. This undoubtedly lead to Mr. Labrador's private quarters. Leaving the bookcase ajar, the man handed James a towel-wrapped bundle. James unwrapped the bundle and cradled the sword in the towel, being careful not to touch it. On cue, the crowd gasped. The sword was covered with dried blood.

Wolf's eyes narrowed. "It was you, von Strasser," he shouted at my grandfather, who sat across the room, pale and shaken. "You left the film early."

"And you're his accomplice!" Dora shrieked, pointing a red talon at me. "I'd bet a dollar to a donut your fingerprints are on that sword." She rose from her chair and started for me, claws extended. I jumped to one side.

"Just a minute, young lady," James grabbed Dora by the arm and lead her back to the chair.

"Wait. It could have been Amanda." Dora shouted, desperate now. "I saw her with the sword earlier."

"Be serious, darling," Amanda Pickle said. "Why would I kill Winston Churchill when you present such a tempting target?"

None of us saw it coming. Wolf jumped up, grabbing me and the sword in one fluid motion. Standing behind me, he put an arm around my neck, grasped the sword by the blade, and held it to the side of my throat. "One false move and the Fraulein dies," he shouted. Dragging a reluctant and terrified me along by my heels, he backed up toward the open bookcase.

We were almost out of the room now. The others seemed to be looking beyond me. Wolf took one last step back—straight into the arms of the egg-shaped man.

"What the hell?" Wolf spat.

With surprising agility the man wrestled the sword away from Wolf and handed it to James. Wolf and Dora sagged against the bookcase. Men in black poured through the front door, surrounded the couple, and led them off.

"Second rate spies," the man said, dusting his palms together. He looked around at the open mouths, then bowed slightly. "Winston Churchill, the *real* Winston Churchill, at your service."

"But you're dead!" Anna Gatesby said.

Churchill leaned toward Anna, inviting her to pinch his chubby cheek. She did and he winced. "As you can see, I'm quite healthy. Unfortunately, the man who acts as my double on official missions is not." He shook his head. "Morse always did have a weakness for Anna Gatesby. It was his undoing."

"What are you doing here?" I asked.

"That's official business and none of yours, young lady," James snapped.

Mr. Churchill waved his hand. "No, that's quite all right. I don't mind telling you, but it must go no farther than this room. At the behest of His Majesty, I'm here to persuade Mr. Labrador to soften his isolationist position regarding the Nazis."

"And Mr. Labrador, unfortunately, is stranded in Los Angeles," James added.

Churchill nodded. "It's becoming evident England is going to need American help if she's to resist Hitler. I'm asking you, as people of honor and good citizens, to let your knowledge of this night's affair stay in this room." He looked around, his eyes coming to rest on Amanda Pickle. Amanda blinked.

"Okay, I'll admit Wolf had motive," Beau said, "but what about means and opportunity? Don't forget there were at least seventeen other people in that theater."

"Think about it," James said, smiling, "and tell me what you think happened."

Beau fingered his mustache for a few seconds. "I've got it! At least I think so. Wolf sat in back, then picked his time and popped out into the hall. Several people came and went during the film, so he wasn't noticed. Dora waited close by with the sword she'd grabbed from the gathering room after that hasty exit at dinner. Wolf slipped into the theater, stood at the back, and offed the poor man during a loud part in the film. After all, it was a horse racing story. He just didn't figure on Churchill having a double."

"Like Jean Harlow in the film," I breathed.

"Exactly." James said. "I'm sure, when the road opens and the G-men arrive, Dora and Wolf will, as you Americans say, 'Spill the beans.'"

"G-men?" a journalist asked. "The phones are dead."

"There's a short-wave radio in Mr. Labrador's personal quarters," James said, gesturing toward the open bookcase and the staircase beyond. "After all, this is a very isolated spot. And we had a tip. That's why Mr. Churchill brought his double. Too bad about Morse. Sorry to lose him. He was a good man and he has a wife and young son at home."

"If you had a tip, why didn't you arrest Wolf and Dora right away?" Anna asked.

"A tip is just that, my dear, a tip. Besides, we were told the threat came from a German man and his American accomplice." He gestured towards Grandfather and me. We suspected von Strasser here and his granddaughter. We thought that if we gave you two enough rope...But things got out of hand. Sorry 'bout that, old chap."

"These things happen," Grandfather said.

"I saw the egg-shaped—I mean, Mr. Churchill—I mean, Mr. Morse, twice. Once during cocktails and again as we were going into dinner."

"Actually, you saw Morse once and me once," Churchill said. "We both love a good party and we were anxious to join you, despite being told to stay out of sight." He sighed. "Unfortunately, we didn't coordinate that awfully well, I'm afraid."

"It doesn't matter in the end," James said. He turned to me. "Zelda, I'm not going to ask why you were in Wolf's bedroom, because the fact that you were, changed history." He looked toward Churchill, his eyes shining. "I can't imagine the consequences if this man had really been killed."

He faced the others. "My men and I will stay here and guard the prisoners. I suggest the rest of you call it a night." He consulted his pocket watch. "Or should I say, morning?"

In the half light I walked Grandfather back to his guest house. His room was one floor below Wolf's. I'd gotten turned around in the storm.

It was a new day at Lorna, where nothing was what it seemed, where everything was illusion, imitation, a misplaced metaphor. The storm had spent itself, moved on. The mansion road was open, telephones worked, and the highway was being repaired. Mr. Labrador would be here by lunch time. Too late. The party was over. Through the mist, we saw headlights from several cars ascending the hill.

"Probably G-men."

"Undoubtedly." Grandfather answered.

"Grandfather, why were you and Dora both sick?"

He smiled. "It may actually have been the oysters."

"I'm glad I didn't eat them."

We walked a few more steps, then Grandfather stopped and turned to face me. "Zelda, our friend Dora was right about one thing. You were going to steal Wolf's bracelet." He turned my face toward his. "Weren't you?"

"I just wanted to try it on."

Grandfather shook his head. "Granddaughter, you have a decision to make. You can be a film star or you can be a thief, but you cannot be both. Think about what you want."

I slipped the diamond off my finger, taking just a moment to caress its faceted surface. I'd stolen it from his leading lady's dressing room while they were filming those endless takes. Hard to believe that was less than twenty-four hours ago. "Will you return it for me, Grandfather?"

"Of course," he said, pocketing the diamond. "It's fake anyway."

# Ruth Cowne

Ruth Cowne is a SLO NightWriter who loves reading and 'riting but not 'rithmetic. Will worry about the last when I sell my first novel.

# A MURDER SO FOWL
## by
### Ruth Cowne

It was the fourth Thursday in November when Henny Penny burst into my office looking like a Grade A chick with a problem.

"I've been expecting you," I said. "Let me guess. Your Tom flew the coop."

"Yes," she answered in her sultry, clucky voice. "How did you know, Sam?"

Before answering her, I let my eyes feast on the feathered outfit she wore. It was short enough to expose her curvy drum-stick legs.

"Because you've come to me five times before, always the last week in November."

Tears filled her eyes. I gave her my hanky. "It's happened again. Please help me."

I wanted to grab her and give her a big smackaroo on her regal beak, but I controlled myself. This wasn't the time. She was upset. The bones of her previous Toms had been found discarded in a trash can, always in late November. I was determined to solve this mystery or my name wasn't Sam, Private Eye.

"When did you last see Tom?"

"Last night. But he was gone when Farmer Dell came to the barn this morning. I've looked everywhere for him."

Her eyes grew large; she put her delicate feathered hand over her beak and said, "Oh, no, do you think he's dead?" She began to run around in circles, like a chicken with her head cut off. I grabbed her and held on until she calmed down—well maybe a little longer.

"Can it be that Farmer Dell is behind all of this?" she asked.

"Maybe, but I need proof and this time I won't stop until I know what happened."

"Oh, Sam, I'll be forever grateful."

I seriously doubted her sincerity. Penny was at the top of the pecking order when it came to Farmer Dell's chickens. She was a spring chicken and could have any Tom she wanted but I would never be included in that list.

Just as I suspected, I found Tom's stiff carcass in the overturned trashcan by Mrs. Dell's back door. And just like the other Toms, the wishbone was missing—perhaps a macabre souvenir the murderer decided to keep?

*Then I saw it.* The perpetrator of this fowl crime had left a clue. I picked it up and examined it carefully. I knew who the murderer was and I could prove it.

I called for a chicken coop caucus. When everyone was roosting, I said, "I know who killed Tom but it wasn't Farmer Dell as I suspected. The Dell family always eats ham the last week in November." Then I walked over to Henny

Penny, looked straight into her beady eyes and said, "It was you, Henny Penny."

The hens began to cluck; but Henny Penny gasped and ruffled her feathers, "Why would I kill Tom?"

"Because you wanted one more Tom before your Grade A status was downgraded." I turned to the other hens and continued. "Henny Penny ran to Tom and squawked, 'The sky is falling, the sky is falling' and when he looked up, Henny Penny viciously hen-pecked him to death. She buried most of Tom's remains but left the bones in Mrs. Dell's trash can."

"You don't have any proof." she said.

"Yes, I do. This feather belongs to you. It's an exact match. I found it at the scene of the crime." I shoved her off the nest and six wish bones fell to the ground.

As they took her away, I said, "Henny Penny, when you get out of jail, marry a Dick or a Harry. Not a Tom."

# Susan Tuttle

"Murder Under the Oaks" is an amalgam of two inspirations. One of the employees at my local grocery who I've gotten to know told me she had never read her name in a book or story, so I promised her I'd use it in one of mine. That started the thought train chugging along.

Then the Central Coast Chapter of SinC put out a call for stories set on the California Coast, using our series characters if we wanted, and suddenly the whole story of "Murder" burst into my head.

I planned this story to be the introduction of my psychic detective, Skylark; her debut, as it were. At this point, she's been on her own for five years, and is keeping her psychic abilities—she considers them a curse—to herself, though they are referred to in the story.

That was the plan, anyway. Now another even earlier adventure is knocking on my door, so I guess her "official" debut is still in the offing. I'm just about finished with two novellas that take place after "Murder" and feature her time travel adventures, and there are three other full-length novels of the series that are at least planned or started.

Each Skylark story is as much an adventure for me as it is for readers. I learn more and more about her with each manuscript—her unraveling backstory keeps me enthralled. I hope you love her as much as I do.

# Murder Under the Oaks

by

## Susan Tuttle

"You!"

The word reverberated off the walls. I looked up, startled, from where I sat pecking away at a tardy report to see God's curse on female private investigators—or at least this female P.I.—standing on the other side of my desk: SLO County Sheriff's Detective Carrick Dunwitty. I couldn't believe that this behemoth of a man, who usually stomped his way through life, had actually tiptoed into my office and caught me unawares. Of course, that was the only way he'd ever catch me, and well he knew it. Hence, the sneaky feet.

I raised my brows in query and pointed at myself. Dunwitty growled as he stomped around my antique mahogany banker's desk. The huge piece took up half the floor space of my less-than-roomy office and served as a reliable barrier to most people. But this was Dunwitty, whose long arms reached for me before he even rounded the end of the desk. I shoved back my chair, scrambling to get out of his way.

*What the hell's his problem?* I wondered. I hadn't done anything—not this time, at least. I'd finished my last cases well over a week ago, two tame embezzlement inquiries that I'd wrapped up without even leaving my office Both of which, I might add, were out of Dunwitty's jurisdiction, as the companies were headquartered in Santa Barbara County.

I was heading out for Ojai in a couple of days to follow an errant spouse, which excited me so much I'd been putting it off for at least three days. Hadn't killed, or almost been killed by, anyone in a good month. So what was the bane of my existence doing here being a bane in my ass?

I didn't move quite fast enough. Dunwitty made it to my side of the desk, clamped his meaty paw on my arm and yanked me out of my chair, which flew back and smacked into the wall. He was so gonna pay for any damage.

"What the hell are you doing?" I twisted in his grip. "Let me go!"

"Shut up, Skylark. You're coming with me."

Dunwitty turned and began dragging me toward the door. I dug in my heels and grabbed onto the corner of the desk to stop our forward momentum.

"Why? Where?"

"The station. Shut up and move."

He jerked me hard and my hand slipped from the wood. We continued toward the door, me squirming all the way. Not that it slowed him down any.

"Are you arresting me?"

"Do I need to?"

"I didn't *do* anything," I insisted as I looked around for another handhold. Dunwitty manhandled my five-feet-ten-and-three-quarter-inches as though I weighed a mere few ounces instead of the hundred forty-five my scale told me about this morning. Okay, one-fifty-five, and I'm giving up eating chocolate cheesecake for midnight snacks. Promise.

"Never said you did," he muttered in his usual garrulous way. "Got someone you need to meet."

"What? Who?"

He didn't answer, just towed me out of my office and into the tiny deserted reception area.

"Damn it, what the hell is your problem?" I yelled.

"You."

Holy shit. I'd be dammed if his growl didn't roll like thunder from the foyer walls.

"Hold on!" I grabbed the outside doorframe and held on for dear life. "At least let me get my purse."

"And that fancy Glock of yours?" He snorted. "I think not."

He increased the pressure and I could feel my grip slipping.

"Damn it! Ease up, I have to lock the door, you imbecile."

"Why?" His supreme unconcern flowed over me like a smothering blanket. "This is Los Osos, not LA. Your office will be fine."

He smirked, gave me a sharp wrench and I lost the doorframe.

"And if it's not, I'll sue you and the department for everything you have!" I cried as he hustled me across the sidewalk toward a waiting car, opened the back door and shoved me in.

"Promises, promises," he muttered, settling himself behind the steering wheel and firing up the engine. I slammed my hands against the wire barrier that separated the front and back seats, wishing it were his head.

"You have no right to do this, you jackass!" I screeched as he swung out into Los Osos Valley Road traffic. I kept battering the wire cage. "Let me out of here! Now!"

He stood on the brakes and stopped in the middle of an intersection. Then he turned and skewered me with his most menacing glare.

"Do I need to cuff you?" he growled.

We stared at each other with car horns blaring around us until I finally backed down and subsided against the seat, knowing full well he did not threaten idly. I crossed my arms and returned his glare, my teeth clenched so tight my jaw hurt. Dunwitty nodded. He gave me his snarky self-satisfied grin—the one he reserved for perps he was about to ruin for life—then turned around and began driving again, leaving me stewing in the back seat. This was so going down as one of the worst mornings of my life. Which figured, given the day it was.

Did I mention it was a Monday? I hate Mondays. Bad things happen to good people on Mondays: the start of the workweek, paperwork to finish, phones to answer, bills to pay, duties to perform. Being dragged to the cop shop by a Neanderthal masquerading as a detective is never a good thing, but on a Monday morning it truly presages disaster. Not that Dunwitty could actually ruin my entire life—worse jerks than him have tried and failed—but he could definitely put the rest of my week in the toilet.

I didn't say another word to him for the two whole minutes it took to reach the Sheriff's substation on 10th Street. In fact, I didn't even look at him, not even when he oh-so-politely opened the door and jerked me out, then escorted me into the station, uncompromising fingers clamped tight on my arm. He hustled me past reception and the snide grins of other on-duty officers, then down the dim corridor to the interrogation room. When he pulled me to a stop he leaned down and shook a thick finger in my face.

"You believe in all this woo-woo shit, Skylark, not me. So you handle this." He hitched a thumb sideways toward a closed door. "Make it go away, you hear me? If not, I'll lock you both up and throw away the keys."

"What? What do you mean, woo-woo shit?" I said.

My mind leapt around like a cat in a room full of snakes. Dunwitty didn't enlighten me, he just spun around and was halfway down the corridor before I could take a breath. I blinked at his back a few moments, then turned to the door he'd indicated. I wondered what—who—I'd find in there. I wondered if Dunwitty somehow knew my deep dark secret, though I couldn't see how. He might be a detective, but he wasn't *that* good. And I wondered why he couldn't have simply called on the phone like a normal person and asked me to come in to talk to whomever, instead of dragging me in like a criminal. Then I remembered—this was Dunwitty. He was nothing if not an abnormal creature wearing human clothing. Normal didn't register on his radar.

I sighed, rubbed my bruised arm—maybe I would sue, after all—and opened the door.

She looked like a lost, scared little waif, though she wasn't little by any means. I estimated maybe five-five or five-six, though it was a loose estimate at best since she was sitting down. Slender, reedy almost, with full breasts and a long torso. And what looked to be even longer legs angled under the chair. She had gorgeous hair the color of ripe wheat fields. It curled softly down past her shoulders and shimmered in the harsh overhead lighting. I felt a momentary stab of jealousy; I was pretty sure that hair had never seen a drop of coloring in its life, and I doubted it turned nasty when fog clamped around the town. She sat in profile to me, her deep forehead covered with bangs, her nose straight, lower lip slightly fuller than the upper one, chin well-defined and strong. I knew, before she turned to look at me, that her cheekbones would be a photographer's dream. She'd be damned easy to hate.

I noted the moment she realized someone had stepped into the room. The knuckles of her clasped hands whitered, her shoulders hunched and she drew in a deep breath. Then she swiveled her head, her eyes—dark as a stormy ocean—widened and she gasped.

"It's you!" she said, her voice a low alto. "Oh, my God, I don't believe it. Please," she reached out a hand to me, "stay away from the oaks. He's going to kill you there, I saw it. He wants to kill you under the oaks."

"Huh?" I said—sometimes I'm so intelligent it scares me—then blood began gushing from her nose, her eyes rolled back and she slid unconscious from the chair. Gracefully, of course.

I stared at her a moment, at the blood dripping onto the cracked linoleum, then opened the door behind me.

"Hey!" I shouted into the corridor. "Dunwitty! Get an ambulance here, quick!"

*This should be interesting,* I thought as I turned back into the room and glanced at the two-way mirror behind which I was sure Dunwitty had been watching the drama. At least until our little waif took her nose dive. I wondered who else was in there with him, and how many cats would be set loose before this was over. *Shit, why me?* I grabbed a handful of tissues from the box on the table and crouched beside the bleeding woman.

"You okay?" I asked when her eyes fluttered open. I ignored Dunwitty who'd erupted into the room and now stood behind me, excoriating my efforts to handle the situation. "Don't move, we've got an ambulance coming."

"No, please." The tissues muffled her voice and I had to lean closer to hear. "I don't want an ambulance. I'm fine, really."

Since she seemed coherent and could wield the tissue wad without help, I looked up at Dunwitty and shrugged.

"You heard her. Go cancel it."

He snarled at me, but turned and left the room. I wondered if he'd come back, or simply lurk in the observation room where he could roll his eyes in peace as I continued to probe into what he termed "woo-woo shit."

I helped her back into her chair, then sat across from her and waited for her to give me some kind of explanation. Silence is a great tool; most people simply can't abide it. Patience really is its own reward, at least for me.

"I'm sorry," she said, giving her nose one last wipe and checking to make sure the bleeding had stopped. "I didn't expect this to happen, it usually doesn't anymore. Mr. Fish said eventually it will stop altogether, once my body gets fully acclimated."

"Mr. Fish?"

"My mentor. Bass Ehrler." She gave me a half grin. "I call him Mr. Fish because of his name. Bass?"

I might have found that amusing—and did, somewhat later—but the shock that shot through me at the sound of that name wiped out all rational thought. It had to be the same person, no two people on the face of the Earth—or any other planet—could possibly have that ridiculous moniker. Bass Ehrler, that grand ectoplasmic pain in the ass, had mentored me when my abilities first reared their ugly heads. He still popped in at the most awkward times to check on me and my "progress," as he called it. I finally found my voice.

"How do you know Ehrler?"

I knew by the way her eyes widened that I hadn't disguised the danger in my tone. I stared on at her, willing her to talk. Fast.

"I-I don't really *know* know him. I've never met him, not in person. I mean, he... he..."

She started twisting the soiled tissues, so I let her off the hook. *Sotto voce.*

"He astral travels into your, what? Living room? Or maybe bedroom? Sitting in an armchair, wine in hand, right?"

She froze and stared at me. The storm had left her eyes, which were now a lovely deep blue.

"You know him? How?"

"That's for later," I murmured with a shake of my head. No way were Dunwitty and his cop shop pals going to be privy to *that* conversation. "Tell me what you know. And how you know it. Who's going to kill me under what oaks?"

Her name was Kayla Menna, and she'd been under Ehrler's "guidance" since the visions began three months before. When she'd had this latest one—a tall, black-haired gypsy look-alike being strangled on a hill under a bunch of trees—Ehrler sent her to Dunwitty who, after hearing the vic's description, beelined right to my doorstep. I was so gonna figure out how to knock ectoplasm into another dimension. A very nasty one.

I gave Dunwitty the old "she's-nuttier-than-a-squirrel's-winter-hoard-no-woo-woo-shit-here" song and dance and razzle-dazzled Kayla out of the cop shop.

\* \* \*

I had no business letting Kayla get close to me. And I certainly didn't intend it. But she had a way of sneaking up on a person. At least that's what I told myself.

I'd not let anyone matter to me, not since my then foster father had crawled into my bed when I was ten. After that, I closed myself off. I kept my life on an arm's-length-only basis and it worked just fine. But Kayla... Somehow she left me wanting more.

At lunch that Monday, after she gave me the full details of the vision that had put storms in her eyes, she asked how I knew Bass Ehrler. I dismissed instincts that screamed at me to run and clued her in on my own reluctant association with our astral-projecting, self-styled mentor and my own psychic curse. I sometimes see the past superimposed over the present and, if I consciously look for them, connections between people show up as glowing lines of light. She seemed awed by what for me was an inconvenient nuisance.

We met twice more that week and three times the week after, sharing both woo-woo shit and our mutual lack of family ties. She'd lost her parents when she was three; I'd never known mine at all. She grew up shuffled from one cold, distant relative to another and I'd survived—after a fashion—Children and Family Services Hell. It wasn't the same, and yet it was.

Each time we met she wormed her way a little deeper into me. Her sweet, elfin air tugged at my heartstrings in a way that made me supremely uncomfortable, but I stupidly came back for more. Maybe because I had no one else I could talk to about Ehrler and psychic curses. I ignored my gut and went to a place I'd sworn I'd never again go. She was smaller than my estimate, only five-three, which made me close to a full head taller. It lent me a big sister vibe I just couldn't resist.

The last time we met, we stood in the brilliant late-afternoon sunshine outside Starbucks. Early home-goers whizzed past on Los Osos Valley Road. Kayla laid her hard on my arm and looked up into my eyes.

"Thanks, Skylark. For making this seem somewhat normal. I think I can handle it now, because you do. But please, be careful. Don't let him kill you."

"Ain't gonna happen," I told her.

I gave her a grin, patted her shoulder and sent her home with another lunch promise for next Tuesday. I had work to do, and as much as Kayla wanted to watch me do it, I never let civilians into my world. Besides, my spidey sense had been tingling ever since she described the figure in her death vision. Tall and lean, she'd said, in dark clothing. She hadn't seen his face, but she'd caught a hawk nose and jutting chin limned in moonlight. Lips that curled up at the outer corners.

And a bird, tweeting away in an overhead tree.

At night.

In the dark.

It reminded me of something, but the something wouldn't come clear no matter how I scratched at it. So I gave it room. Set it aside. I made detailed notes, picking out the salient points of her vision for further study. I put off that wandering husband case yet again, and further distracted myself by spending long hours in the gym and rearranging closets and files, but it didn't help me unearth what lurked below the surface of my mind. It hung there, niggling, not even letting me sleep. By Sunday night I was running on empty and nature took over. I pretty much passed out around one-thirty in the morning, so when my cell shattered the oblivion three hours later I wasn't exactly in a sociable mood.

"This better be good," I growled into the phone, eyes still closed, doing my damnedest to keep from waking fully. A deep scratchy voice reverberated into my head.

"I'm in your office. Get over here."

"Dunwitty?" I sat up, heart pounding. "Why the hell are you in my office?"

"Just get here. Now."

The phone went dead. I stared at it a moment, then launched myself out of bed, snatched up whatever clothing I could find and was out the door in about ninety seconds, still blinking sleep from my eyes. In less than five minutes I pulled up to where cop lights flashed a macabre red-and-white carnival outside my office. Did I mention how big a town Los Osos isn't?

The building sat adjacent to Starbucks, cater-corner across the parking lot, facing Fairchild Way. Long and low, it housed a wide variety of businesses from a pizza parlor to a real estate firm. My office stood near the center, a tiny niche sandwiched between larger offerings. I'd moved in eighteen months before and so far it served me better than the corner of my minuscule living room had. Definitely easier to meet clients in a private office than in a public coffee shop or my own house.

I stopped at the shattered glass entry door. Dunwitty's massive form blocked my view of the interior.

"Jaime Arroyo," he rolled the r's and hitched a thumb toward the corner restaurant that served a breakfast pizza, "saw the broken glass when he arrived to start his dough. Called 9-1-1. Who's got it in for you, Skylark?"

"Besides you? No one I can think of."

Dunwitty grinned and tipped his head to the left. Then he moved aside and gestured me into total chaos.

Whoever had trashed the place had done a Nobel Prize-worthy job. Furniture, lamps, picture frames smashed, file drawers jimmied open, papers shredded and scattered everywhere, paint splashed on walls and carpet. Nothing left untouched; I stood staring at the gouges in my beautiful antique desk, jaw tight, hands clenched, resisting the urge to pull out my Glock and shoot the CSI team that arrived to add their black-powdered signature to the disaster.

Dunwitty wandered around, poking and prying, then came to stand beside me.

"This is way more than drunk kids," he said. "Someone really hates you."

I took in a steadying breath and kept my gaze on the ruined desktop.

"Is that a confession?"

"Don't shoot the messenger, Skylark."

"I'd rather shoot the doers," I gestured at the destruction, "but sometimes you have to settle for second best."

"True." Dunwitty nodded, then sighed. "Once we're done, you need to see if anything's missing."

"*Thank* you." I didn't even attempt to keep the snark out of my tone. "*Never* would have thought of *that*."

"Skylark—"

"Don't." I held up my hand. I could feel my eyes burn when I looked up at him. "Just find them before I do."

He stared at me a long moment, then nodded.

"Don't do anything stupid, Skylark."

"Don't worry." I gave him a tight grin and turned away. "I'll leave that up to you."

It was early evening when I finally dragged myself home, exhausted both physically and emotionally from hours of sifting through debris, dealing with a recalcitrant insurance company and an irate landlord, and enduring Dunwitty's obnoxious presence. I was so tired I didn't notice anything wrong until I hit my bedroom and reached for the lamp that sat on the dresser just inside the door.

It wasn't there. I stared at the dresser in the dim light spilling in from the hall, my weary mind refusing to process what my eyes were seeing. The lamp stood on the far side of the dresser, having switched places with the jewelry box that now sat beside the bedroom door. Heart thudding, I pulled my Glock and scanned the rest of the room. Everything was neat but out of place, just as the things on the dresser were. My book and alarm clock had swapped nightstands. The curtain tiebacks were missing. Even the pictures on the walls had changed places.

I inched through the rest of the small house, gun in hand. If I didn't know where things were suppose to be, I'd never have known someone had been in there. Everything was pin-neat, organized and wrong—except for the kitchen table, which was gouged like my desk had been. I stared at the looping scars while rage built, and decided not to call Dunwitty. Nothing had been taken that I could see, and given the care with which the intrusion had been done I doubted fingerprints—or any other evidence—had been left behind. I inspected both front and back entries, but could detect no scratches or other damage. Both had been locked when I arrived home. How had they gotten in?

Then it hit me. I kept a spare set of keys—unmarked—at the office. I hadn't found them in the debris, hadn't even thought of them. That meant the office had been a diversion. Whoever had done this knew that the mess on Fairchild would keep me away from home for hours, long enough for them to mess with my private space. What were they after? What else had they taken?

I checked everything I could think of, but found nothing obvious missing. The safe I'd secreted behind a false fuse box panel didn't appear disturbed. The thumb drives that held copies of my files were all still there. It seemed that all they'd done was simply paw through my possessions. I stood in my living room, hands and jaw clenched, feeling vulnerable and violated. My vision misted red when at last I called Dunwitty.

"They did take something," I told him when he answered, my voice strangling with fury. "The keys to my house."

"I'll be right there."

"Don't bother," I said, but he'd already hung up.

I hadn't wanted him to investigate, I'd just wanted him to know what had happened. I could have called back and insisted he not come, but I knew it wouldn't do any good. Dunwitty did what he did, regardless of what anyone else said or wanted.

He set up the CSI dusters then took me to the cop shop for his squirrelly version of debriefing. When I finally got home my house didn't seem like mine anymore. Nothing was where it should be. Black grit coated every surface without even a tape mark to show where a print had been lifted. None were found—big surprise. It was nine-thirty in the morning, I'd been running for over thirty hours on less than 3 hours sleep, my eyes wouldn't focus and my head throbbed. So I chose to ignore my life and plunged back into oblivion after making sure both doors were deadbolted from the inside.

The scream of my cell phone dragged me up into life again at the ungodly hour of 2:12 in the afternoon.

"If it's not an atomic bomb, I don't want to know about it," I growled.

"Skylark?" The voice, breathy with fear, shivered into me. "He's coming!"

"What?" I struggled to shove sleep out of my brain as I sat up. "Kayla? Who?"

I heard a sniff and the crumple of soft paper and figured she'd had another nose-bleed-inducing vision. I opened my mouth but she stepped on my words.

"Don't look for me. That's what he wants, Skylark. But I don't count. You do. Don't let him—"

A loud crash reverberated from the phone. I heard a scream, the sharp smack of a palm on flesh, then a sharper crack as her phone hit the floor. I shouted into mine, but within seconds all went silent.

My heart thudding like a runaway train, I leapt from the bed and threw on jeans, a long sleeve tee and my leather jacket. I grabbed my gun, strapped a knife to my ankle and was in the car in about ninety seconds.

Kayla lived on the far side of town, up in the hills that overlook the estuary, about five minutes from my house on Palomino. I broke every speed record ever made, ran both of the town's red lights, and made it in two and a half. The sun beamed its honeyed blessings onto the land. Cicadas trilled in the empty field across the street, and out in nearby Montana de Oro State Park a solitary coyote yipped a lonesome call. Driveways sat deserted, houses shut up for the workday. Except Kayla's. Her front door stood wide open. A monarch butterfly danced across the lintel as I watched.

It was a small house. It didn't take me long to search its one story. There were signs of a struggle and a disturbing trail of blood leading from the front door toward a room in the back. I stepped carefully alongside the blood, eyes and ears alert, until I stood just inside the kitchen archway.

There, centered on Kayla's kitchen table, held down by the mug that had been on my office desk, a mug my foster grandfather had given me when I earned my license—*I'm not nosy, I'm a P.I.*—was a folded sheet of paper with my name printed on it. I pulled it out and flipped it open with my fingertips. My breath caught in my throat as I read the manic printing inside.

It's Game Time!
Come play as we hide, she's yours to seek
This sweet young thing so luscious and meek.
High on a hill overlooking the road
The pain from my knife will make her explode.
Hung from the rafters or nailed to the barn,
Buried alive or drowned in the tarn;
Come seek her by day or in the night's dark
Do you really think you can save her, Skylark?
P.S. No cops!

\*    \*    \*

*No cops.*

I thought about Dunwitty as I searched the rest of Kayla's house for other clues and knew there was no way I'd call him even if Kayla's abductor hadn't made it clear. All I needed was that ignorant bulldog bursting his way into this case. First I'd find Kayla and get her to safety, then I'd call the detective and let him take it from there.

Maybe.

But Kayla's house gave up no other clues than the demented poetic note that had been left for me. Trusting it—trusting Kayla—to Dunwitty wasn't an option, not for me. So I stewed over the note as I drove home again, which took twice as long as getting to Kayla's since this time I navigated without the lead foot. And stopped for the red lights. It was clear that Kayla'd been right—it was me he was after. That he'd take and harm an innocent young woman to get to me boiled my insides. What a coward.

I read the note over and over as I paced around my house: *it's game time; she's yours to seek; by day or night; do you think you can save her?*

How the hell did he expect me to find her if he left no other clues than a stupid poem that pointed me nowhere? If this was "Game Time," where was the board? The dice? The clues? I paced the house, my stomach in knots, hands and teeth clenched. Down the hall past my bedroom, the guest room, back into the living room, past the kitchen and around again. Ignoring the neat rearrangement of my possessions and the black dust, catching the injured kitchen table from the corner of my eye every time I stalked by it, my mind a jumble of disconnected thoughts as the minutes, then hours, elapsed and I worried about what he was doing to Kayla. Because of me.

And then, on the two-hundredth—or maybe two-thousandth—pass, it stopped me. I stared at the kitchen table, my fingers tracing the seemingly random gouges in the lovely burled maple. It seemed familiar, the way the scars curved and jogged. *Damn*, I thought, *this is not random.* I got my Los Osos street map from the desk in the guest room/office and spread it out on the table beside the gouges. It took no more than thirty seconds to find it; the same arching curve, the same jog, the same loop around to join Los Osos Valley Road. I stabbed my finger on the map.

Turri Road.

He'd gouged the game board into my table top  And, if I remembered right, into my office desktop, too. The juncture of Los Osos Valley Road and South Bay Boulevard, joined by the meandering curve of Turri Road. With an erratic loop in the middle around, if I wasn't mistaken, the old Alfaro homestead. What I needed had been staring me in the face all along. And I'd wasted hours in futile pacing.

*Kayla...*

The westering sun threw long shadows as I armed up, left the house and headed for Turri Road. Eight forty-three p.m. The air had cooled, bringing with it the dense fog that, during the day, had hung far out over the ocean. It rolled onto the land as dusk fell, an undulating misty curtain that devoured roads, grass and bushes, and created isolated islands out of hilltops. I drove through an increasingly obscured landscape, almost missing the turn onto Turri from South Bay Boulevard. The rising fog kept pace with the elevation of the road, enmeshing me in eerie mist as the sky above continued to darken.

I parked below the hill on top of which the half dozen abandoned Alfaro farm buildings stood. The old compound had been deserted for about twenty years; a faded For Sale sign hung lopsided beside the drive's entry posts. The chain that usually blocked the narrow winding driveway lay slack along the ground.

I ignored the blatant invitation—that was a trap just waiting to be sprung—and scaled the steep hillside about twenty feet west of the drive. The thickening fog veiled obstacles and slickened the ground. By the time I broke into clear night air about fifteen feet below the hill's crest, I was shivering with cold and my bruises had bruises.

As I gained the hilltop I pulled my Glock and thumbed off the safety, then crept around the nearest outbuildings, searching for Kayla, alert for any sound or movement. The half moon, riding in a clear sky, shed its luminescence onto the rolling fog that enisled the hilltop; it felt like I paced along a landship that floated on an undulating, phosphorescent sea. Silence clamped down, an absence of sound so profound it felt solid. I found no sign that anyone had been near the old Alfaro homestead until I rounded the left side of the original farmhouse and caught a glimpse of movement to the right in my peripheral vision.

She'd been beaten bloody and tied to the broken porch railing, arms spread wide. I wasn't sure she was alive at first. I stood still, watching, scanning the area, until she moved again. Then I went to her. She'd been bound at the wrists, neck and waist with my missing tiebacks. I worked at the bloodied knots with one hand, keeping the Glock ready in the other. I neither saw nor heard anything other than Kayla's soft moans, not that I believed for an instant that whoever had taken her and lured me here wasn't around somewhere. Somewhere close, I was sure. So I didn't let down my guard even though it took twice as long to free her.

She could barely stand, much less walk without support. I couldn't dare try to take her down the steep, slippery hillside. By default we had to risk the driveway, the only somewhat stable route to the road. I wrapped my right arm around her waist, my right hand still clutching the Glock, and pulled my cell from my pocket with my left. Then I inched her down the long drive, the rambling buildings to our left, a steep drop-off on our right. I thumbed up Dunwitty's number and hit 'send' just as Kayla spoke.

"You shouldn't have come." It came out as a choked whisper.

"And let you have all the fun?" I said, only half listening to her. Where the hell was this creep? Surely he wasn't about to let us just walk out of here.

Kayla stumbled, pulling me off balance, and I lost the cell. It flipped through the air and bounced into the darkness of the drop-off. I thought I heard Dunwitty answer the call, but Kayla's gasp overrode the tinny sound.

"Skylark!" she screamed. "No!"

I felt him behind me, but I had Kayla in my arms I couldn't bring my gun up and around fast enough. Something hard slammed into my head; fireworks burst across my vision and I dropped into a deep, dark hole.

\* \* \*

I woke wishing I hadn't. My body felt like an ice cube and a pile driver had taken up residence in my head. My stomach kept crawling up into my throat. I fought the good fight, but a thousand years of agony later I gave in, turned on my side and let my stomach spew out of my mouth. Then, shivering, I rolled onto my back and tried to figure out what had happened to me.

I longed to press my fingers against my throbbing temples, but I couldn't. My wrists were taped—in front, not in back, which surprised me. It took a few hundred years of lying completely still, barely breathing, before memories started trickling in.

Driving. Fog. A hill. I'd had my gun out. Something, someone, had hit me. Hard. From behind. I'd been walking —no, stumbling—down a trail, no, a driveway, with something, someone in my arms—

*Kayla!*

Adrenaline shot through me, which started up the sledge hammer once again. I pressed my bound hands against my forehead as I waited it out, not that it helped much. I was still alive but that didn't give me much comfort. The fact he hadn't killed me outright only meant the creepazoid had much nastier plans in store for me. *And Kayla?* I moaned at the thought.

When things settled and held still for what I guessed was about five eternal minutes, I let my eyes drift open. I hoped I'd see a way out and not Poetry Boy grinning at me. But all I saw at first was darkness. Solid. Black. Like a boulder pressing down on me. I tested the extent of my injury by slowly rolling my head to the left while I scanned for some clue as to where I was. My stomach lurched a few times but stayed south of my throat.

Progress.

I turned my head back to the right, grimacing as I rolled over an excruciatingly painful spot, and caught a glimpse of red a few feet away. About the size of a half dollar, it seemed to pulsate a bit. I locked my gaze on it, rolled to my side and struggled onto all fours. I couldn't kneel upright, there was a ceiling not three feet above me. I raised my hands and felt around.

Wood. Rough and splintery. I gave it a tentative knock. It sounded solid. Thick.

Where the hell was I? Stuffed in some crawl space below one of the outbuildings? Or had he taken me somewhere else?

The red light beckoned, the only thing visible in my Stygian prison. I shuffled toward it on my knees. The dirt floor gritted into my legs and I realized why I was so cold. All I had on were my panties and the t-shirt. Jeans, jacket and boots all gone. As were my Glock and the knife I'd strapped to my ankle. Pretty hard not to feel vulnerable and helpless when you're stuffed into an overgrown, coffin-like ink-dark space unarmed and half naked. What else had the asswipe done while I lay unconscious? And what had he done with Kayla? Rage began to build, a slowly rising fire that radiated out from my core and heated my body. *Someone is gonna die tonight,* I vowed, *and it isn't gonna be me. Or Kayla.*

It took me a minute to figure out the light. It came from a smooth, round glass nob set into the splintery wall. I passed my hands over it twice before it hit me. A camera, infrared, filming my every move. He'd been watching me all along.

"Damn you," I growled, spotting two other red knobs on adjacent walls—he had the place covered, nowhere to hide—there I began shuffling along the wall, feeling with the sides of my hands, seeking a way out. I winced as splinters wormed under my skin, but didn't stop until something long and sharp ripped out a deep gouge. I huddled, panting, until the pain eased, hoping Poetry Boy was enjoying the show. Then I raised my hands again and carefully felt along the wood for whatever had impaled me.

A nail, protruding about half an inch. I used it to rip apart the tape on my wrists, even knowing it would cause further injury But I needed my hands free if I was to have any chance at all to escape whatever my captor had in mind.

It took maybe five minutes of work until the tape tore apart. Blood dripped off my fingers from a dozen or more cuts on my hands and wrists, but at least I was free. I wiped as much of the blood on my shirt as I could and prayed I'd be able to hold whatever I could find to use as a weapon once I got out of this place.

I started to crawl, again seeking a way out. I'd not gone five feet before an eerie whisper echoed around me.

"Time to play, Skylark. Come out, come out, wherever you are."

The darkness began to lighten. In a moment I could make out the limits of the space. It was about the size of a one-car garage—in width and breadth if not height—the low ceiling making it feel like an overgrown coffin, indeed. Pinpricks of brightness sparked from the far narrow wall, poking through breaks in boards nailed criss-cross over an obvious exit. I crawled to them and began to work. The eerie whisper still echoed around me, shivering down into my core. By the time I'd pried the boards loose, my fingers looked like raw ground beef and my nerves felt shredded.

I crawled out into the light and it vanished, leaving me blinded in darkness once again. A bird call reverberated on the clear night air, the sharp whistle of a Northern Cardinal, a bird not native to California. It underscored the evil that surrounded this place. The recognition that had earlier eluded me burst within me like a bomb blast.

Pietr Kaiser!

The Whistling Predator.

But it couldn't be. I'd run afoul of him four years earlier during one of my first solo cases. I'd thought Melissa was a runaway. I tracked her by her light line connection with her parents—that "curse" of mine that lets me see connections between people as glowing ropes of light—to the San Gabriel Mountains and found what little Kaiser had left of her. Then he found me. I still had nightmares about that battle, what I'd been forced to do to survive. But he was dead; I'd watched them haul his shattered, shredded body out of the ravine.

So who the hell was whistling Kaiser's death song at me?

I lurched to my feet, leaned against the building at my back, and waited for the world to stop revolving. My eyes slowly adjusted to the night. My body shuddered from the damp chill. Wisps of fog coiled tendrils around me; above arched a star-studded sky. Spreading out from the building were eight-foot-high walls made of unstable-looking piles of rubble and trash that must have taken months to gather and stack. If I wanted freedom I had no choice but to follow the narrow trail between the walls.

I took a deep breath and, still dizzy, inched along, unable to see the ground through the billowing fog. Sharp stones and other objects jabbed into my bare feet, throwing me off balance. Twice I fell against one of the walls, only to have it come crashing down on top of me. The second time I dug myself out, I found a three-foot-long metal rod that was pointed on one end—maybe an old fence pale. It felt rough and pitted, probably with rust, and I didn't know how strong it was, but it was at least a semblance of a weapon. So I ignored the way the gritty surface cut into my injured hands and kept it at the ready as I continued down the Kaiser-wannabe-designed path. Above me, the manic whistle continued.

I used the rod to keep my balance and to probe both directions at each corner and thereby avoided a few dead ends and more burials in garbage. By the time I reached the end of the maze my head was swimming, a deep gash on my right thigh made my leg a bit unreliable, and I could barely hobble on my cut, abused feet. But the psycho still had Kayla out there somewhere, doing God knows what to her, and that kept me going.

I stepped out from between the teetering walls to find myself facing a clearing filled with undulating tendrils of fog. The farm buildings sat on my right; the driveway carted somewhere off to my left, hidden in darkness. Twenty yards ahead a cluster of tall oaks fanned out above the steep drop-off. Beneath them Kayla stood on a huge boulder, head bowed, eyes closed. I couldn't tell if she was conscious or not. A man, half hidden behind her—Poetry Boy, I figured—held her upright. The moon shed an incandescence over them, as though a heavenly spotlight showered blessings from above. I limped toward them, using the rod as a cane. The man holding Kayla lifted his head and shot another Cardinal whistle into the air. I stopped about five feet from the boulder and stared into his dark eyes. He held one arm around Kayla's shoulders. The other hovered a broad, sharp knife near her abdomen.

"You're not Kaiser," I said.

He laughed.

"Not Pietr, no." His tone held triumph, contempt and hatred. "I'm Damon. His brother. Well," he shrugged, "half-brother."

That startled me. I hadn't known Pietr had a brother of any kind. Things were starting to make sense.

"So, that's what this is about? Revenge? Or are you just looking to prove you're man enough to beat down defenseless women?"

He laughed again and shook his head.

"I like you, Skylark. You've got spirit. Not many could have made it through my game alive. Or still standing." He tilted his head and studied me. My skin began to crawl. "I could change my mind. We'd make a sensational couple."

"Not even in your dreams."

He raised his brows and shrugged.

"It was worth a try. I have no problem killing you. In fact, I prefer it. Shall we begin?"

He tightened his grip on Kayla. She moaned and her lids fluttered. My heart stuttered in my chest.

"Look," I said, "you've got what you want. I'm here, right where you want me. Let Kayla go."

"No, I don't think so," he said, pursing his lips and glancing down at her. The knife moved closer to her body. I limped a step closer to the rock.

"Don't. You've got me, you can do whatever you want to me. I won't fight you. Or I will," I added when he scowled, "whatever you want. You have me. You don't need her."

He stood quiet, staring at me. Far in the distance, a siren softly ululated. A second joined it. He looked again at Kayla, then smiled at me.

"You're right. I don't need her."

He stared me in the eyes as he drove the knife into Kayla's stomach, then yanked it up, raising her to her toes.

Kayla's eyes flew open. She gasped in an agonized breath. Her arms spasmed and her hands splayed.

"No!" My scream echoed out over the hillside.

Damon Kaiser widened his grin. He gave the knife a vicious twist then yanked it out and threw Kayla off the rock, over the drop-off. As I watched her vanish from sight he turned, lifted the dripping blade, aimed, and threw it at me. Then he leapt off the boulder, arms outstretched.

I twisted to the side. Pain shot through my leg; it buckled and I fell. Burning seared across my forehead as the knife slashed past me. Blood flooded into my eyes. The night turned red. I smashed onto my back and the breath left my lungs. I heard a strangled gurgle close above me and blinked my eyes semi-clear.

Damon Kaiser hung over me, impaled mid-torso on the iron rod I'd been clutching as I fell. His legs draped over mine, a heavy weight pinning me to the ground. His body warmth flooded over my legs and I shuddered.

"Now...we...both...die!" he growled.

He clasped his hands on the iron rod and pulled himself down it, lips stretched in a pained grimace. Hot blood flooded over my stomach, soaking my shirt. His body suspended inches above me, he let go of the rod, clamped his fingers around my neck, and squeezed.

Even dying, he was wicked strong. Agony shot into my head, down into my body. Blood pounded behind my face. My lungs shuddered, screaming for air. I clawed at his hands to no avail, my stare locked on his grinning visage mere inches above me, on the red halo that surrounded his head and the joy that flooded his face as I lost my fight for life. Black spots swam across my vision. The night darkened and my strength failed. My arms fell to the ground. I felt my body shudder as blackness swooped in to claim me.

Then the light died in his eyes. His head bowed. His hands loosened just enough for me to pull in a trickle of air. I lay there for what seemed hours, gathering enough strength to pull his hands from my neck, shove him off me and kick his legs away from mine. Blood still tapped at my eardrums, joined by the sound of the sirens, closer now. I gasped more air through my burning throat then turned onto my side and pulled myself toward the drop off and Kayla. It seemed to take forever to climb onto the boulder, but I forced my battered body to move and somehow found myself lying on its crest, staring down at the wild grasses lining the steep hillside that undulated down to Los Osos Valley Road far below.

And there she lay, Kayla, on a ledge just below the boulder, like a broken rag doll, legs twisted, arms flung out from her sides, eyes open and unseeing on the star-studded heavens above. The moon illuminated her hair into a glowing halo swirling around her head. Feathers of fog, tinged red by the blood still dripping into my eyes, wafted out from beneath her shoulders. A fallen angel, dead because of me.

I reached out to her, though I knew she was too far away to touch. Tears flooded my eyes, clogged in my tortured throat. The sirens screamed, very close now; I heard tires crunch gravel, doors open and slam shut. Male voices called out; I recognized Dunwitty's deep bellow.

"Skylark? Where the hell...? Here! She's over here!"

"I'm so sorry," I managed to whisper to Kayla before I gave in to the darkness that had waited so long for my surrender.

\* \* \*

My hands shook and vodka spilled onto the counter. I added a generous splash of vermouth to the pitcher, praying my bandaged fingers wouldn't drop the bottle. The room spun around me when I reached for the jar of olives and I hung onto the countertop, teeth clenched, until it stopped. Then I added a healthy swig of olive juice and about ten olives to the lovely swirling mixture. It took me two trips to get it all, pitcher, remaining olives and martini glass, into the living room. I allowed myself a sardonic grin when I only slopped about half a glass worth on the way.

I'd limped out of the hospital about three hours before, although the medical staff wanted me to stay a few days for "observation." Seems along with a multitude of sprains, contusions and stitches, Kaiser's blow to the head had caused a fairly severe concussion. The kindly doctor had kept the cops—namely Dunwitty—away from me during his ministrations, then I took advantage of a lull in supervision to absent myself. I didn't feel the least bit guilty about stealing a set of scrubs in which to abscond.

I poured the cold libation into the glass, added two olives, then closed my eyes to stem the tears that threatened. I saw him in my peripheral when again I lifted my lids. Bass Ehrler. In his red velvet armchair, black twill-clad legs crossed, gray smoking jacket open to reveal an oatmeal colored turtleneck. Wine glass in hand, my front drapes visible through his semi-transparent body.

"Go. Away," I said.

"You shouldn't drink alone," was his answer.

I didn't bother to look at him.

"That's my choice."

We sat in silence while I gulped down my drink and poured a second. He sipped at his wine and studied me and I wished I could knock his ectoplasmic ass into some other county. He was as bad as Dunwitty, and I hated them both. I was halfway through the second martini when he spoke again, his voice filled with pain and regret.

"I'm sorry about Kayla. I liked her, she was a sweet girl."

"Really?" Rage shot through me and I turned burning eyes to him. "You liked her? Then why did you send her to me? Why did you give her those damned visions?"

"Skylark, you know—"

"She's dead because of *you!*" I screamed. "*You* did this! *You!* Go away, leave me alone!"

We stared at each other and I tried my best to ignore the pain that flitted across his aristocratic features. He looked old, worn and tired, but I felt worse. I was the one who had watched Kayla die, not him. He'd only sent her there.

I looked away first and topped up my glass. Ehrler cleared his throat.

"It doesn't work that way, Skylark, and you know it. I don't give my proteges their gifts, I only help them manage them."

"And a stellar job you did with Kayla." I saluted him with my glass. He shook his head.

"This isn't my fault."

"No," I agreed, tears again choking me. "It's mine. She's dead because of me."

"No, not because of you. Because of Damon Kaiser."

"No, it started with me, when I killed Pietr. If I hadn't..."

"If you hadn't, he'd have killed you, and gone on killing. How would that have helped all the people you've saved since that day? And those you're still to save?"

I bit my lip as the dam broke. Tears cascaded down my face, darkened the blue scrub top I still wore.

"Mourn her, Skylark," Ehrler said. "Drink to her, celebrate her, remember her. And move on. It's what she would want you to do."

I knew he was right. It just hurt so much. I'd finally opened up after so long alone, and now she was gone. I let the tears fall until they finally dried up, then finished the second drink and poured a third. I had just lifted it when a loud bang rattled the front door.

"Skylark! I know you're in there. Open up!"

Two more bangs, a heavy fist thumping against the wood. I sighed. Dunwitty, pissed as hell that I'd ducked out without being debriefed.

"Perhaps you should see to that," Erhler suggested, his dry tone scraping down my nerves like nails on a chalkboard. I sighed again and looked at the door.

"He sure as hell won't go away," I said. "Don't you dare leave me alone with him."

I turned and stared. Ehrler had faded back into whatever ether he'd popped out of.

"Coward," I muttered.

I heard his ghostly laughter as I stood up and weaved my way to the door, each hobbling step accompanied by another of Dunwitty's sharp bangs. I swung the door open and caught him with fist raised; he almost whacked me in the face, which would have done wonders to the stitches in my forehead. We stared at each other a long moment, then I handed him the martini.

"Mr. Fish says I shouldn't drink alone," I told him, turning away and limping into the kitchen for another glass. "You might as well come in and join me."

# Cora Ramos

Cora Ramos is an award winning author of stories of mystery and suspense that straddle the edge, whether that edge is the paranormal, a deadly decision or the place where science ends and magic resides.

A collection of her short stories can be found in the anthology, *Valley Fever, Where Murder is Contagious. Dance the Dream Awake,* her first novel, a paranormal romantic suspense, dips into a Mayan past life. *Haiku Dance,* a spicy historical romantic suspense, is set in ancient Heian Japan.

She is currently working on *Dance the Edge,* a follow-up to *Dance the Dream Awake.* Find Cora on her website (www.coraramos.com); follow her blog (coraramos-cora.blogspot.com); on Facebook (CoraJRamos.Author); and find her books on Amazon.

The inspiration for the story: On one of my visits to the Pacific Coastal town of Carmel, I was out one night wandering up and down the deserted streets, glancing in the spotlighted windows of closed art galleries. I came across one with an door open. Inside was a young man wearing a black cowboy hat, sitting on a folding chair and playing Hendrix licks on a guitar. All around him were large expressionist type paintings in bold colors. I took a video of this scene which became the inspiration for my story.

# Pushed Down and Tucked Away

by
## Cora J. Ramos

In the closed art gallery, the reds and blacks of Stanley's abstract paintings hanging on the walls around him gnashed out like rapacious jaws seeking his soul. He squeezed out the screaming Hendrix chords on his electric guitar, squashing the troubled thoughts trying to worm their way into his conscious mind.

He didn't see it coming. He never saw it coming, but they always left—just gone.

No sales. No woman. No place to be tonight. He was free. But that freedom was empty. He'd rather be tied down and happy than free and alone.

The high-pitched licks that rang out into the night repressed uncomfortable feelings, leaving him empty and numb. Empty was good. He played for himself—whether he was alone or in front of a crowd, always canceling out everything but the moment.

Five women had walked into and disappeared out of his life in the past six years, he was none the wiser as to why. What was he missing?

Another headache was starting. Would there be another blackout moment? He abruptly swung the guitar off his knee and set it in its case, snapping the lid shut. He stood and stretched out his back and rubbed his arms. Why were they so sore tonight?

He needed a drink.

After switching off the lights and locking up the gallery, he stepped out into the quiet Carmel night.

A few tourists on the near empty streets of the beach town strolled past. They browsed the lighted storefront windows up and down the street. Golden Baroque frames gave the plebeian art more cachet than his unframed art. He was in the wrong place to sell art like his. The California Central Coast was for tourists and tourist tastes—paintings to take back home and talk to their neighbors about— neighbors who did not understand the bigger picture, the deeper meanings—the darker themes of *avant garde* art—like his.

That his work didn't sell troubled him, sure—but was only a distraction from the other feelings trying to surface. He turned down the alley and headed to his favorite bar. Inside, he nodded at an old man swaying on the stool at the far end. The refrains of the mediocre trio that played in their own little world swirled around the clientele.

"So what brings you in tonight, sonny? You look beat. Come, sit by me and let's chat." The old man swayed so far over the bar stool, Stanley reached out to grab him to keep him from falling over, but the old man recovered and caught himself. He raised his beer mug and pronounced, "To all you young 'uns." He swung his mug in a circle in the air to include Stanley and the four other customers.

The couple dirty dancing in front of the trio ignored him, the woman squirming in the embrace of the man feeling her up, lost in their lust-induced haze. The other two at the table in the corner were deeply involved with whispering onto each other's necks with breathy sighs.

*A romantic evening,* Stanley thought sarcastically as he rubbed his temples, trying to wipe out the headache dancing around the edges.

"See them there couples?" The old man leaned close to Stanley. "I think they gonna be leaving soon—you know, before they do it right there on the floor." He laughed at his own joke and took another swig.

Dark amorphous images he couldn't quite grasp flitted through Stanley's mind. He rubbed his temples. Why was he getting these headaches?

The old guy squinted. "You know, I have some advice for you, sonny. The minute you came in, I said to myself, now there's a guy with troubles. *Real* troubles."

Stanley told the bartender to set up a double scotch. He needed something strong to be able to listen to the old guy. As soon as the bartender set the drink in front of him, Stanley upended it, bracing himself for the huge swallow that would burn all the way down.

The old guy leaned in and glanced down at Stanley's guitar case. "Been off somewhere getting lost in the music, eh? I used to play myself. I know how it is. I even wrote a few songs."

Stanley nodded, half listening. The painting he'd completed earlier in the day flashed to mind, expressing all that was buried deep. He always painted like that—spurting it out—ridding himself of the pain—probably why no one wanted to buy his art. Too much pain. He needed to change that—lighten up if he ever hoped to sell anything. But how can one change those painful feelings pushed down and tucked away?

"Know what the title of my last song was?"

Stanley shook his head, humoring the old man as some thought tried to niggle its way into his consciousness.

"My song was *Cut to the Heart.* A love-gone-wrong song—heh, heh, don't love always—go wrong, that is?"

Stanley wanted to retch. Bile rose in his throat, surprising him. He downed the remaining scotch, willing his stomach to settle. The headache was affecting his gut.

"Yeah, it was pretty popular when I sang it in bars like this." His gravelly voice belted out the lines,

> *"I loved her but she cut me right to the heart.*
> *Opening my soul to despair.*
> *If you tell me, 'don't be in pain'*
> *I'll know you've never been there."*

Stanley smiled at him. Yeah, he knew pain.

The old guy set his glass down like a confidant preparing to sympathize. "So tell me about the woman who done you wrong." He indicated to the bartender to bring Stanley another double.

Stanley wanted to escape, but he couldn't move. He was tired. Tired of fighting these feelings, tired of being alone and tired of his paintings failing to sell. Tired of the headaches. He grabbed the drink when the bartender set it down, and swallowed it in two gulps. The pain finally began to ease. And then his thoughts went to Janine. He remembered that last fight. It got loud and angry and he'd snapped when she'd said 'momma's boy.'

*He'd snapped? What did he do? He couldn't remember.*

Suddenly, the dam broke and images came rushing in. The slashes of red like his paintings—slashes to her body and blood—all jumbled together. He jumped off the stool, ran outside and threw up. He retched until he thought his insides would come out.

*Oh, god, what have I done? Where is she? Is she in the hospital?* He couldn't remember. His head ached; the jagged visuals of a migraine had started.

The old man was at his side handing him a handful of cocktail napkins and putting his arm around Stanley. "Hey, sit down here for a minute." He indicated the brick flower bed in front of the bar.

Stanley couldn't stem the images—they spun out of his subconscious mind. Sand—piles and piles of sand below cliffs on some hard-to-reach beach. It was coming back to him.

"You okay, sonny?" The old man looked worried and Stanley could see in his eyes that he sensed something very wrong.

"I'll be okay, just give me a minute." He tried to recover. "Can you get me some water?"

When the old guy went inside, Stanley took off. He ran back down the street and reopened the gallery. He flicked on the lights. The full horror hit him. He hadn't just murdered Janine—not just *one* murder. He saw it all over the walls. It was all four women who he'd thought had 'left' him. He'd killed them all before they could leave him. They were all out there, cut to the heart and buried in the sand.

# Victoria Heckman
# and
# Sue McGinty

Victoria Heckman's first *Hawai'i mystery series* features officer Katrina Ogden, K.O., of the Honolulu Police Department. The newest K.O. book, *K.O.'d at Banzai Pipeline* , sends K.O. to the big surf contests of O'ahu's North Shore. Her second series, *Coconut Man mysteries of Ancient Hawai'i* begins with *Kapu-Sacred*. Her third mystery series (*Burn Out & Wet Work*) starring animal communicator Elizabeth Murphy is set on California's Central Coast. Stand alone mystery, *Pearl Harbor Blues,* begins on Dec. 7, 1941 and uncovers a dynasty of corporate intrigue. Victoria is a member of Sisters in Crime-Central Coast Chapter. Her books are available in print and various e-formats online and from your favorite book dealer.

(See Sue McGinty's bio on page 53)

Since we both write series set in the same town, we thought it would be fun to have our characters meet. We'd been chatting off and on about it for a couple years, and this was the perfect opportunity for us to do it! Also, in our town we have a little old lady dog walker who takes her pup out in a stroller and we just had to make something sinister out of it. The time frame is somewhere between 2012 and 2015.

# The Canine Caper

## by
## Victoria Heckman
## and Sue McGinty

"What's the matter, Sam? You look like you lost your best friend."

Bella Kowalski's old golden Lab stood the side yard looking... hangdog, was the only way to describe it. Sam's young Corgi friend used to drop by every day, but they hadn't seen him in almost a week. Maybe that had something to do with it.

Bella knew that Corgi's person lived at the Los Lobos Bayside Residence Hotel, a mega senior residence adjacent to her windmill home. It sported both warm and cool pools, a spa, workout room, a library, and craft room. Even a gourmet restaurant with fine wine, and a guy with a key around his neck to serve it, catered to clients.

Unlike most places of similar ilk, the hotel welcomed and encouraged small pets. Hence their large population of yappy dogs, cats, parakeets and even an illegal ferret across the way—though this was a rumor.

"Sam is everything okay over there?" Bella asked, pointing to the complex. Considering that all the residents were up in years...*Don't go there Bella, you're no spring chicken,* she reminded herself.

Sam pawed the ground listlessly. Not a good sign.

Bella would often see the mostly female residents in the morning and at dusk walking small dogs. After years of having few neighbors, her "hood" had become a busy place. She could do worse she decided. At least there were no late night partiers and souped-up cars to keep her awake. With the divorce from her husband Mike in the works, she wasn't sleeping too well.

From her bedroom window Bella often saw a woman, head completely covered by a scarf, walking the road. The woman pushed a baby stroller also completely covered. Perhaps, Bella thought, a fussy baby took comfort in the salty aroma of the sea. Or maybe Mom just liked the view of the sand spit and open ocean beyond it.

She forced her thoughts back to the present, stroking Sam's bony back. He lifted his head; sad eyes met hers. "Come on, old man, I'll make you a veggie burger."

When Bella set his favorite meal before him a few minutes later, he sniffed and walked away. "Okay Sam, that's it," she called after him. "We're going to see Doctor Irene."

\* \* \*

"Everything checks out fine physically with our friend here," said Doctor Irene, fondling Sam's ears, his favorite thing. The vet paused and ran a hand through her graying hair. "You know, he seems depressed about something."

Bella nodded. "I think so too. This little Corgi used to come over from the Bayside. We haven't seen him lately."

"You don't think his owner . . .?" The vet's voice trailed off. "You know, I've worked with an animal communicator before in similar cases. I'll bet Sam would tell her what's wrong. Her name is—"

"Elizabeth Murphy," Bella finished. "Sam was supposed to see her while in I was in Michigan recently. My house sitter thought he had separation anxiety. But when I came home unexpectedly, he perked right up. I cancelled the appointment."

"Time to rebook," Doctor Irene said. "Do you still have the number?" Bella nodded.

\*     \*     \*

Elizabeth Murphy finished scritching Teddy's chin, to his satisfaction, apparently. Her chubby tabby cat stretched. *That felt so good. How about something to eat?*

"Okay, but only a little of your diet food. Dr. Irene says you have to—"

*I know, I know. I'll just have to get a mouse later,* he mumbled.

"I heard that. I'll have to ask doc how many calories are in a mouse," Elizabeth said.

*I don't think very many,* Edward's sweet voice added. *I am very thin,* he added somewhat smugly.

"All right you two. Enough. Edward, you know you are thinner because that is just the way you're built. Maybe some Siamese in there." Elizabeth picked up the svelte black cat and snuggled him close. He went boneless and purred. "Not due to any sense of virtue."

*Still,* Edward started.

*Mom said enough,* Teddy reminded and waddled, sway stomached, out the back door to the koi pond.

Elizabeth diced some tofu into her hand and followed. The koi loved tofu. Just as she'd tossed the last cubes in, with watery thanks from the fish, the phone rang.

"Hello?"

"Hello. Dr. Irene suggested I call. I'm concerned about my Lab, Sam. She said he was in good health for a senior dog, but something still seems not quite right. Do you think you could see him?"

Elizabeth could tell the woman wasn't totally comfortable with the topic of animal communication. She was used to that and reassured her.

"Of course. Start by telling me your name and where you'd like me to meet Sam."

"Oh, of course. I guess I wasn't ready for this 'animal communicator' thing to be real. I'm Bella Kowalski."

"Where do I know your name? We haven't met, have we?"

"No, but I do the obituary column in the paper. Maybe from there?"

"That's probably it." It always helped to find common ground with a new client. "Can you email me a picture of Sam? I am happy to come out for a visit, but I like to try and establish communication early. It helps if I know what your pet looks like."

"Will do." They set a time for later that day. Elizabeth wanted to keep her day full. Her fire fighter husband, Tig, was on his 24 hour shift and it always seemed longer and more lonely than a regular day.

\* \* \*

"Okay Sam, come here I need a photo of you." The golden loved to have his picture taken and perked right up. "You need to look more dejected. Elizabeth Murphy's going to think you're faking." She'd just gotten her first ever smart phone and fooled around, finding getting an acceptable shot. After several more minutes of fiddley-farting, she managed to send it to Elizabeth's phone along with an e-mail inviting her to the house. She thought Sam would do better on his home turf.

\* \* \*

Shortly after, Elizabeth received a picture of a handsome, elderly Lab. He had the soulful eyes of the breed, but she detected a little rascally spark.

Because of her remote-contact ability, she was able to sit in her mediation chair at her front window, ground herself quickly—an extension of her daily morning mediation—and get in touch with Sam. He was surprised to be "spoken" to that way, but domestic animals adapted quickly. Wild animals were much harder, as she'd discovered. Sam was quite content to chat. His relationship with his 'mom' Bella was stable and long-term. Bella understood most of Sam's attempts at training her, but his newest concerns he had not been able to convey. He was thrilled to express himself.

*Hi Sam. My name is Elizabeth. Your mom asked me to talk to you.* Elizabeth sent a picture of herself at the same time she pictured Sam getting it. He was receptive.

*Hi. Are you a new friend? For me?*

*Sort of. Your mom is worried about you, but Doc Irene says you're healthy. Is it okay if I check that out? You might feel a warmth, like maybe I'm petting you, but I promise it doesn't hurt.*

*Sure!* He was happy to receive even virtual petting.

Elizabeth moved carefully through Sam, checking his fur and skin, organs, bones, nerves, and brain. Other than some mild arthritis, he was in excellent health. He had a slight vision reduction, normal in an animal his age, and he vainly compensated with his senses of smell and hearing. Elizabeth understood he felt a great sense of responsibility for Bella.

*Well, you look great. Do you feel okay?*

*I feel fine, except I miss my friend. He used to visit all the time.* Sam sent a picture of a Corgi romping with him, coming from a large property adjacent to his home.

*What is that place?* Elizabeth asked.

*I don't know. A lot of old people live there, but they have a lot of dogs! I want to visit and make some friends. Chuck used to visit all the time, or sometimes I'd sneak over, don't tell mom. We played a lot.*

*How do you know the folks are old?*

*Different smell.* His response was borne of wisdom and a lifetime of gauging the world by smell.

*Why doesn't your Chuck visit anymore?*

*I don't know. We would play every day and now he's just gone.*

*Do you think he was sick? Maybe died?*

*No.* Sam was adamant. *He did not smell like that.*

*What about cars? Can the dogs get to the street? Los Lobos Valley Road has a lot of high speed traffic. Could he have made it that far? Maybe gotten hurt?*

*I don't think so.*

*Okay, Sam. I'm going to visit you today, okay? I'd like to meet you and maybe we can walk over to the dog place. Would you like that? Maybe we can find Chuck.*

*Yes yes yes.*

*Sam, I don't want to upset you, but you know, we live very close to the wilderness at the state park. You know there are predators. A lot of small dogs and cats disappear and are never found. Do you know why?*

Sam didn't know the word, but he flashed her a picture of a coyote, so clearly he was aware. He also sent her the sound the coyotes make when they've trapped prey. Elizabeth heard it often enough as their property bounded the same 25,000 acre state park. It always gave her the willies, and she figured she wasn't the only one.

*Okay, Sam. I'll be over soon. Thank you for talking to me.*

*Yes yes yes!* Sam was looking forward to the visit.

Elizabeth made sure her own starving kitties—Teddy, verging on obese, and Edward, slim and slinky—had sufficient crunchies to survive the couple hours she'd be gone.

She drove west on Los Lobos Valley Road, looking for the landmark windmill house on the right. She had gone past it so often and wondered about it, and now she'd been invited inside. And, have a new client to boot.

After negotiating the winding driveway, she parked by the front steps and took a moment to study the house. White paddles, brown clapboard exterior and a widow's walk gave it a timeless—almost mystical—air. A great place to communicate.

She told Sam she was here and while she waited for Bella, she spied the Bayside Residence Hotel both Bella and Sam referenced. The senior residence was huge, the grounds vast and lushly landscaped. On her quick scan before the door opened, she noted that it would be easy for a wild animal to be on the property and not be seen. Also, it would be easy for a dog to play or hide in the eucalyptus leaf litter and tall grasses bordering the lot.

Bella opened the door with Sam poking his nose next to her knee to get to Elizabeth.

"I wondered who this might be since Sam didn't bark at all, which isn't really like him." Bella gestured for Elizabeth to enter a long hall that led to a small living room on the left and a kitchen on the right. "Come on, let's go in here. This is Sam's favorite room. Closer to his food."

When they were seated at a cozy table that faced Bella's herb garden, with Sam looking on, Elizabeth said, "Why don't you tell me again what you've seen?"

"Well, pretty much just what I mentioned on the phone. Sam, who's usually the most easygoing of dogs, has not been himself lately. Depressed, not eating, not sleeping well either. That is definitely not Sam. Like me, he's a big nap person. I wonder if maybe the Corgi's owner passed and he has a new home. He used to come every day and we haven't seen him for a week."

"Let me talk to Sam," Elizabeth said. "It won't take long, but I might seem asleep, and I can't talk to you while I'm talking to Sam." Bella's eyebrows rose but she nodded and sipped her tea. Elizabeth flattened her feet on the floor, relaxed her hands in her lap and closed her eyes. Her connection was immediate, as if Sam had been waiting for her.

*Hi Sam. So nice to see you.*

*Yes! Are we going to look for Chuck now?*

*Soon. I have a couple more questions. You said you don't think he's dead, but that he is definitely not at the residence next door, right?*

*Yes!* Sam sent a picture of himself, looking around the property, sniffing shrubbery, avoiding detection by the staff. Other residents reached out to pet him and were familiar with his stealthy visits. He gave much comfort and joy even though he was on his own mission.

*Do you think Chuck's owner died? Could he have been placed at another home or given away?*

*No.* Sam showed her a picture of an elderly man in a wheelchair, wrapped in a beige well-loved cardigan, forlornly looking around the grounds.

*Is that Chuck's person?*

*Jim. Jim. Jim.*

*Okay, Jim. Why do you sound like that?*

*I like to say Jim. It sounds nice and makes me feel happy. It used to make Chuck happy, too. Now no one is happy.*

*What do you mean, no one is happy? You mean Chuck and Jim?*

*More than that. Ella Ella Ella.*

*Who's Ella?*

*Miss Kate's little black cheewa.*

*What?*

Sam sent a picture of a black Chihuahua, white frosting her nose like freckles.

*Oh, Chihuahua.*

*That's what I said. Cheewa.*

*Okay. Anybody else?*

*I think so. I think we should go look for them. But Chuck first. He is my friend and Jim Jim Jim needs him.* Elizabeth felt Sam's energy dancing in her mind, and when she brought herself back into her body at Bella's house, Sam, in fact, was panting and jigging his feet.

Elizabeth caught Bella up on the conversation.

"Did he say whether Prince Charles might be at the animal shelter?" Bella asked.

*"Prince Charles?"*

"Yes, the Corgi. That's what his tag said."

Elizabeth laughed. "That is so funny. Sam calls him Chuck, and I didn't even think about it, but it was a joke for him. He showed me the Corgi had sort of an attitude, and now I get it! Sam," she said to the Lab, "you are a funny guy." She rubbed his forehead.

*I know,* Sam said.

Elizabeth continued. "He doesn't know where he is. He's sure Chuck isn't dead, and that his person, Jim, is still with us as well. Something is fishy, because he specifically mentioned another dog is gone, and he doesn't think she's dead either. A black Chihuahua named Ella."

"Well," said Bella, draining her teacup, "I think the best thing to do is head over to the Bayside to talk to Jim. Do you have time now?"

"Of course," Elizabeth said, draining her cup as well. "And I promised Sam he could go, too. He might be able to tell me if any of the other dogs know anything."

\* \* \*

"Welcome to the Bayside Residence Hotel," said the receptionist, a hunky looking millennial whose name tag said Darrell. Bella decided Darrell probably caused heart palpations that weren't age-related. "What can I do for you ladies today?" He reached down to pat Sam's head, but Sam leaned out of reach.

Elizabeth indicated that Bella should explain. "Well, this is a bit odd, but Sam had a Corgi friend who used to come and visit every day at our windmill house next door. We haven't seen him in a while—"

Darrell nodded. "That would be Prince Charles. He's the only Corgi we had in residence."

"*Had?*" Elizabeth asked.

Darrell nodded solemnly. "Unfortunately he disappeared a few days ago. And he's not the first. Several of our residents' dogs have gone missing lately."

"Have they checked with the animal shelter?" Elizabeth said.

Another nod. "They have indeed. But you know, we have a lot of wildlife around—coyotes, mountain lions. You've seen the missing pet posters I'm sure. The animal owners are meeting now in the private dining room. Why don't you join them?" He gestured out the slider to a path that led to a dining room. "The private dining room is just to the left as you walk in."

"Can we take Sam?" Bella asked.

"Of course," said Darrell. "Guests of all species are welcome."

The three of them trooped down the path to the building ahead. On the left were two pools and a fitness center, and on the right, umbrella tables and a pit barbecue. *Sweet*, Bella thought. A baby carriage sat under one of the tables. *For grandkids*, Bella decided.

Elizabeth tuned herself to Sam, and then extended it to the animals she sensed on the grounds.

When they entered the room, several women and two men, including Jim Jim Jim, sat at one of the long tables. The mood of the room was glum. Elizabeth noted a shaggy dog under the table at the feet of one woman.

"Hello everyone. Sorry to intrude," Elizabeth began.

Heads of varying silver shades turned simultaneously. Sam immediately pulled away to join the shaggy dog under the table. Bella looked surprised at this, but let him go.

"I'm Elizabeth and this is Bella. We heard you're missing some animals and we want to help. May we join you?"

"Absolutely, of course, why not," came a chorus of assent.

Elizabeth and Bella sat together on one long side of the table. Sam had cuddled next to the other dog and they appeared deep in conversation.

"I see you brought Sam," said Jim. "That was swell of you."

"Yes, I did. He's very worried about Chu—um . . .Prince Charles."

"I am too." Jim gestured around the table. "All these folks, except Mellie," he pointed to a rotund woman also in a wheelchair, "have animals that have disappeared. We just don't know what to make of it."

"Mellie, is that your dog under the table?" Elizabeth asked.

"Yes. Ambrose is a sweetheart, but not young anymore. We were talking about coyotes when you walked in, but I think if coyotes got our dogs, they'd have gotten Ambrose there. He's pretty slow."

Another woman chimed in. "I'm Adele and I just can't see when our animals would have been loose and unsupervised. I know when we can't take them out ourselves, a staff member walks them, but five missing dogs? Really?"

"Maybe you can each tell us under what circumstances you noticed your dogs were missing. At night, or a particular time of day, when?" Bella said.

"I go to aqua aerobics every day and that's when my little Shih tzu disappeared," said a thin, well-coiffed woman.

"My little angel, a pure Pomeranian, was gone when I came back from my health check. They do it right here so we don't have to get on that awful old-people bus," a woman dressed head to toe in alarming pink said.

"I was going to arts and crafts, and Ella was gone when I came back to my room."

"You would be Kate?" Elizabeth asked.

The woman gave her a strange look. "Yes, I am. How do you know that?"

Bella started with, "Darrell said," at the same time Elizabeth said, "Maybe we'd better fess up, Bella."

Bella's expression told her she wasn't so sure this was a good idea, but she nodded. "Well, it started with Sam seeming depressed. I took him to Doctor Irene"—heads nodded around the room, everyone took their animals to her —"and he checked out okay physically. She suggested Elizabeth here, who's an animal communicator."

"What do you mean?" Mellie interrupted. "Like a pet psychic?" She arched a heavily penciled eyebrow.

Elizabeth was used to this misconception, but was quick to clarify. "No, I don't read minds, but I can share my thoughts with them, and if they are so inclined, they will respond." She noted varying degrees of skepticism. "It's true; Sam was in good physical health but was despondent. I'm sure you've all seen Sam visiting the grounds?" Heads nodded. A sideways glance at Bella told Elizabeth she was not aware of Sam's illicit visits. *Sorry, Sam,* Elizabeth told the

Lab. She only received happy energy. He knew she was helping.

"Sam loves to come and play with his friends, your animals, but especially Prince Charles, Jim's Corgi." At this, Jim perked up a little. "Sam has said he is sure that Chuck, as he likes to tease his friend, is alive. But he is not well. I tuned into Sam and Ambrose while they chatted." Mellie made a snorting sound but Elizabeth sent her a reassuring smile. "Ambrose was not taken because he is not 'special,' according to what he told Sam. The pictures he's sent indicate the dogs are being stolen because they are purebred and have a value."

Murmurs of assent around the table. *Poor Ambrose*, thought Elizabeth. *You are very special*, she told him. A tail thump said he heard, and Mellie reached down and fondled his ears. Elizabeth knew Mellie was grateful he was not 'special' enough.

Adele asked, "How can you steal a purebred dog and no one see you? This place is like Grand Central with all the crafty crap going on. They're going to kill us with all the classes and schedules!"

The other man who had thus far stayed silent nodded. "I go to the wood shop every day and it's too noisy so I don't take Spyder. He's a Lion-Crested dog and pretty valuable, I guess."

"That thing is not a dog. At least you got the name right," Mellie grumbled.

"Stop it, Mellie," Jim said. "Be kind. We're all after the same thing." He turned his attention back to Elizabeth. "What else? Is there anything we can do?"

"Ambrose mentioned a woman wearing a scarf pushing a bright red stroller with a black cover, you know, like sun shade for a baby. Did anyone else see her?"

"Yes, she's around the neighborhood. What about it?" Adele asked.

"Ambrose says there's no baby in there. He says it smells like dog. Each time he's seen her, he can tell it's a different dog. In itself, it's not a big red flag; a lot of folks push their older animals around, both for exercise for the owners and stimulation for the animal."

"I've seen her, too," Jim added.

Gradually all the group agreed they'd seen her just prior to each animal disappearing. It was never put together because the animals were gone from different sites around the complex, and different times of day. The Bayside had so many clients, staff, deliveries and visitors; it was easy for whomever to cover the thefts.

"You're sure, I mean, Ambrose is sure," Kate asked, "that they're all stolen? None of them were hit by cars or taken by coyotes?" A universal shudder at the mention of coyotes.

"We're supposed to take the word of a dog? I mean the word of someone we don't know who says she's speaking for a dog?" Mellie had her dander up.

"Now, Mellie," Jim said. "These nice ladies took a risk coming here to us, and no, we don't have to trust them, but what is their motive? Why offer to help?"

"Ransom!" Mellie said triumphantly.

Bella couldn't help it. She laughed. Elizabeth joined in. It was so ridiculous, but again, she was used to it.

"For Pete's sake Mellie, there's been no ransom request." Jim jumped in. "And if they were stealing the dogs, would they come here and tell us? You gotta stop watching so much *Law & Order*."

Mellie harrumphed but fell silent.

"You've all been so helpful, we'll do our best," Bella said.

"Ambrose has said which direction the stroller lady goes and between his directions and Sam's nose, we're going to check it out."

They took their leave and Elizabeth's heart broke a little at the despondent group, silent and immobile around the dining room table.

They headed back to reception and the main exit, but Darrell was on the phone, back turned to the room, so they didn't interrupt to thank him.

As they passed he snarled something about "delivering packages" into the receiver. Trouble with a shipper no doubt.

Elizabeth held the door for Bella and Sam and they re-entered the vast grounds.

"Where to, Sam? What did Ambrose show you?" Elizabeth asked. Sam showed her the stroller moving along a sheltered garden path and out a maintenance gate to the busy street. "Sam says to go that way on Los Lobos Valley Road. Ambrose was able to see the lady head that way for a while. I hope she didn't get in a car or we may never find those dogs," she told Bella.

They headed west toward large rural properties. Several minutes later Sam began to get very excited. Elizabeth tuned in.

*What's going on, Sam?*

*I smell her. I smell dogs, too. I'm not sure which ones. They are all kind of mixed together, but I definitely smell the bad lady.* He flashed her a picture that mostly likely came from Ambrose of a tall, thin woman, camo'd by a large scarf and sunglasses pushing an enclosed stroller. Elizabeth also got a whiff of cigarette smoke and some kind of medicinal smell. Maybe she was a nurse?

"Sam says we're going in the right direction" Elizabeth stopped. "Let me see if I can contact any of them now. I saw their pictures at the meeting, so that will help. I'm not sure why I couldn't reach them earlier."

"Okay," Bella said, and stood uncomfortably on the busy main drag while Elizabeth zoned out. Sam lay quietly by her feet, no longer wiggly or fretting.

For Bella, it was a very long time to do nothing but watch traffic eye her and her companion who might possibly be asleep standing up from the looks of it.

"I got them!" Elizabeth 'woke' up so suddenly that Bella jumped a little.

"Where? Are they okay?"

"Very close. Sam, you can smell the bad lady, right?" Sam wagged happily.

"The dogs are close. They've been drugged which is why I've had such a hard time getting in touch with them. They didn't see how they got where they are, but Sam definitely knows that scent. Prince Charles, the Corgi, is the most awake. I think she miscalculated his dose because of his size but he was able to give me the best information. We need to hurry. Some of them have been drugged since they were taken and are ill and dehydrated." She started along the sidewalk, Sam urging them along, nose to the ground.

"You'd think they'd take better care of them if they were going to ransom them or something," Bella said.

"I agree, but it doesn't seem to be a ransom thing. I got from bits of their conversation they were going to be sold off entirely. Black market purebred dogs. I gather it's been going on for a while. Someone else must be involved, but this woman provided transport and she fed them. I'm guessing the accomplice found a ready market and perhaps did the actual 'napping.'"

"I suppose she could do it alone," Bella said, "but you're right, it would be a lot harder."

They had topped a small incline with long dirt drives branching off both sides of the road. Sam unhesitatingly dragged them off to the ocean side down a drive leading to a large but somewhat ramshackle property. Bella noted a main house and several barns or storage shacks.

They didn't hear any barking. "Wait," Elizabeth said. "That's not good. Let me listen."

Bella knew that 'listen' didn't mean like anyone else listened, but she was enjoying her new friend's abilities and enthusiasm. Even Sam stood still; the only motion was his slowly wagging tail and hard-working nose.

"Prince Charles is awake and I told him not to bark, but to see if he can rouse any of the others. I'm very worried about that little black Chihuahua, Ella. She is out of it and not responding on even an unconscious level."

Elizabeth led them cautiously to an outbuilding. Prince Charles heard their footsteps and guided them. A door slam from the main house startled them and Bella dragged both Elizabeth and Sam into a clump of manzanita. Not comfy or very good cover, but the best at hand.

"I'll keep the dogs calm, you call the Sheriff," Elizabeth said. They crouched uncomfortably as Bella studied her phone.

Bella frowned trying to remember how to place a call. She never could get the navigation thing right. After a lot of pushing the screen one way and pulling it another, she got it right and dialed 9-1-1. "Hello," she began. Her finger slipped and the call ended. *Damn, damn, and double damn.*

Meanwhile, Elizabeth gasped when she saw a tall young woman, not an old one as described by the residents, pull a panel van out of the garage and back it up to the dogs' storage building.

"Hurry, Bella! What's taking so long? It looks like she's loading the dogs. Maybe she has a buyer or knows we're here!"

Fortunately the dog carriers were rather unwieldy and she had no easy task of moving them from one locale and into the back of the van.

Just then, Bella's cell rang. "Hello?"

"Dispatcher, Tolosa County Sheriff's Office. You called 9-1-1?"

Bella looked at the phone. How did they know? "I certainly did. Here's the deal..."

\* \* \*

Just as Elizabeth thought she was going to have to throw herself in front of the van to keep it from leaving, sirens wailed in the distance. This remote part of Los Lobos Valley Road led to the main entrance of the wilderness park —no exit for the dognapper.

Elizabeth almost cried with relief when Sheriff's vehicles pulled into the drive, blocking the van.

Bella must have felt the same because she knelt and gave Sam a huge hug. "Good boy, such a good boy," she repeated.

Elizabeth told Sam, *Good job, buddy. We couldn't have done it without you!*

*I know!* He pulled the lead from Bella's hand and raced toward the van's open doors where the deputies were trying to evaluate the dogs. The woman insisted they were hers and legally obtained.

Sam jumped right into the back while Bella and Elizabeth gave chase.

*Chuck! Where are you? Are you okay?* Elizabeth heard as Sam desperately looked for his friend while Bella tried to explain Sam to the deputies.

*Sam, my name is Prince Charles and I am of royal lineage,* said a surly voice from the van. But there was no mistaking the dog's relief at seeing Sam.

*Let's play!*

\* \* \*

The following week Bella invited Elizabeth, Jim Jim Jim and Prince Charles to an afternoon tea party to celebrate the return of the five dogs to their owners. Sam and Prince Charles lay under the table as the three humans drank Earl Grey and discussed the wrap-up of events.

"So Darrell and his girlfriend, Melody, are still in the slammer?" Jim asked, helping himself to a Lockhart's pumpkin donut.

Bella wiped her mouth on her napkin. "They couldn't make bail, and their place is about to be foreclosed on. Their plan to nap purebred pooches and resell them wasn't too well thought out."

Elizabeth added another sugar lump to her tea and stirred it with a tiny spoon. "They'd have to nap a lot of dogs to pay off a mortgage."

Jim chewed thoughtfully, then pick a crumb off his cardigan. "How did Darrell and Melody find out the jig was up?"

"Apparently Darrell became concerned after we left to meet with the owners," Elizabeth said. "He eavesdropped outside the dining room and learned we planned to scout the neighborhood using Sam."

*And my famous sense of smell,* Sam said from under the table.

*Yes, Sam, you are amazing,* Elizabeth agreed.

"Darrell called Melody to get the dogs out of there," Bella added. "We overheard him on the phone as we left. He mentioned 'packages.' I thought it was a beef with a delivery service."

Elizabeth reached for a chocolate croissant. "Is it true a deputy caught him sneaking out of the Bayside dressed as an old babushka woman?"

Jim snagged another muffin, lemon poppy seed this time. "Yup. Musta thought the disguise would protect him, but the deputies were wise to the scarf getup after nabbing

Melody." He broke the muffin in two and slipped one half under the table to Prince Charles.

Sam snorted. *What am I, chopped liver?*

"Shocking he would try to leave town and abandon his girlfriend to her fate," Bella said. "So much for that relationship." She turned to Elizabeth. "How did Darrell nab the dogs in broad daylight?"

Elizabeth said, "The dogs told me he had passkeys to all the apartments. He'd sneak in when the owner was gone, sedate the dog, and carry it out in a sheet. He also picked up the dirty laundry so no one thought anything of it."

"What then?" Bella and Jim asked at almost the same time.

"He put the pooch in the carriage, which was always in the office, and wheel it out to Melody down the street."

*Aha,* thought Bella, *the carriage was not for grandkids.*

Elizabeth wiped a smear of chocolate from her cheek. "She always wore a scarf over her head, a dark dress and covered the carriage with black netting. Their property was within walking distance from the Bayside. They kept the dogs sedated in their kennels so they wouldn't bark."

"The dogs are all okay now?" Bella asked with a frown.

"Yup, even little Ella," Elizabeth said. "I've talked to all of them. Being home and having lots of attention from their owners has done the trick."

Sam's chin lay on his crossed paws under the table. *Boring. Wanna play outside Chuck?*

*Sure, but I told you not to call me that.*

*Sorry. Sorry.*

*Tell you what. You can skip "Prince" and just call me "Charles."*

Sam shook his head, rattling the links of his collar. *This guy always had to have the last word.*

Elizabeth always had one 'ear' tuned to her animals and she laughed aloud at this exchange.

"What?" Bella asked.

"Sam is still teasing Prince Charles about his name."

Jim looked confused. "What about his name?"

"Sam says Chuck, as he refers to him, actually thinks he's a royal dog, and likes to give him a hard time about it."

Jim was distinctly uncomfortable. "That's my fault. I didn't realize he could understand me. I've never heard of anything like this. Like you." He indicated Elizabeth.

"What's your fault?" Bella asked.

"Prince Charles is actually descended from Queen Elizabeth's line of pet Corgi's. My cousin several times removed works at Buckingham Palace Mews."

"What's a mews?" Elizabeth asked. "Like cat mews?"

"No, it's where they keep the horses and hunting hawks, hounds and things. The queen's Corgi's visit there and my cousin was able to procure a descendant for me. I, uh, used to talk to Prince Charles about it when he was a pup. I've been alone a long time, even before I moved here and he was great company. So, we talked."

"Well, that's exciting!" Bella said. "Practically royalty right here!"

*See, I told you,* Prince Charles said smugly.

*I'll never hear the end of it now,* said Sam. *And he still got in the last word.*

Finis…. the End, that's all they wrote…

# Paul Alan Fahey

How "Jack's House" came about: Some time ago, Bob, my husband, and I, were driving the back roads on the Nipomo Mesa, when we passed a roadside memorial for a young man. There was a small sign with his name and the date of his birth and death; he was 21 years old. A small baseball cap with VONS stitched across the front was tied to a wooden stake. I wanted to know so many things. Who was this young man? How did he die? Who planted and tended his memorial? As I began asking questions, and with my background in working with adults with disabilities, I saw a woman and a man working through their grief over the loss of their son. Once I had the theme, *connecting to one's grief brings about healing*, I knew who the man was and why the woman was so reluctant to participate fully in the activity.

# JACK'S HOUSE
by
## Paul Alan Fahey

The old Ford pickup navigated the potholes in the two-lane road. Patches of mid-afternoon sunlight streaked through the eucalyptus and glanced off the windshield. The driver, a silver-haired man in his late fifties with a slim build, pulled the truck over to the shoulder and parked. The woman beside him, a Princess Grace look alike if the actress had lived into her sixties, waited for him to walk around and open her door.

Without talking, they emptied the truck bed of shovels, trowels, a rake, and a small flat of plants, and then walked to an area cleared of brush, a few feet from the roadside. The woman went to work almost immediately, digging her trowel into the hard, sandy soil. The man waited before beginning, perhaps assessing the situation as a surveyor might when evaluating a proposed construction site. When she motioned for him to get to work, he told her it was all in the planning. "Rome wasn't built in a day, Laurel."

"I can't abide clichés, Tom," she said, and then smiled. "Surely you can do better."

"I'll try." He laughed, shook his head, then grabbed a shovel and plunged it down into the earth, bringing up a mound of dirt mixed with sand—the life's blood of the Nipomo Mesa.

She continued to dig, dipping her trowel into the soil, stopping now and then to brush dirt from her red sweatshirt and off the tops of her gloves. "I hate getting messy."

"You need to get dirty here, Laurel. Touch the earth, sift it through your fingers. Connect your senses to what you're doing." He set his shovel aside and began pulling weeds around the hole he'd dug. "We want this to be a fitting memorial."

"For Samuel," she said.

"Yes."

She paused and watched him work the soil, mixing in the potting material, spreading it around the seedlings. He passed her the flat of plants, motioned for her to do the same.

Laurel grabbed two plants and unceremoniously stuck them in the ground.

"Whoa. They're too close," he said. "They need room to grow and develop. Take time and do this right, okay?"

She sighed and moved the young plants a few inches apart. She dipped her glove into the compost and tossed a handful around her charges, and then filled in the hole with surrounding soil. "I'm done."

"Not done," he said. "Far from it."

"What do you mean?" She stood and brushed the dirt off her jeans.

"Remember, Laurel, we want this to be the best it can be."

"Of course, Tom, I know. Maybe I'm just tired."

"Maybe."

When they'd worked for over an hour, she walked back to the truck and leaned against the hood. "Nice but... everything looks too small from here."

He walked up to her and then glanced back at the site. "Yep. It needs work. A lot more, but it's a start."

She reached up and touched his cheek. "You still have those Paul Newman eyes. So blue I get lost in them."

"Laurel, don't change the subject. We're talking about the memorial."

"I know," she said, a bit petulantly. "I understand what we're doing."

"Good," he said, "but you're absolutely right. It needs something, but what?"

She put her arm around his waist, rested her head against his shoulder. "Whatever it is, Tom, I can't see it."

"Of course you can't because it's not there," he said, and laughed.

She tapped him playfully on the chest. "You exasperate me sometimes."

"Why?"

"You keep at things. You never give up, never stop," she said. Then, "We should be going, don't you think?"

He glanced at his watch. "Give me a second." He walked a few feet down the road then returned. "Drivers will pass by without even noticing. What we need is more plants."

"No, Tom."

"Mature ones, bigger and flashier. This patch could also use some color." He waved his hands, encompassing the eucalyptus grove, the brush and hillside beyond. "Way too green. Our little plot needs to stand out."

"Tom, the soil is unforgiving, too much sand. Nothing will grow here."

"Native plants will," he said, "and tomorrow we're off to the nursery to buy some."

"Don't you think you're being a bit grandiose?" she said. "I thought we'd planned a small remembrance."

"We're just not finished. We want it to be—"

"The best it can be. Yes, so you've said."

He sighed heavily, went back to the site and started gathering their tools and supplies. Laurel took a deep breath, held it a moment then let it out. He was doing this mainly for her and she knew it. "You're right, Tom. We need color." She waited until he finished and went around to open her door.

\* \* \*

The next day they stopped at the nursery in the new Nipomo shopping center,, bought several native plants—those that would thrive in the sandy soil on the mesa—and then drove out to the site. An overcast sky and dark clouds hovered while they settled the "natives," as Laurel called them, into their new homes.

"That man at Blanchard's Nursery...what was his name?" he asked.

"Harvey." She was spreading mulch around the white sage.

"He knew what he was talking about. The plants, I mean." He ran his hand along a blue flowered stalk. "Beautiful."

Laurel glanced down the road.

"What are you thinking?" he said.

"About roadside memorials," she said. "You drive by and it makes you wonder who the person was. Who made the tribute and why?"

"Yes, and who waters and tends them?" he added, wiping sweat from his forehead. "People like us, I guess."

"Yes. Like you and me, Tom." She craned her neck, looked up at the sky. "It'll rain soon."

"You haven't noticed. It's been sprinkling off and on." He held up a hand, caught a few drops in his palm. "See?" He stood and walked to the perimeter where the land they'd cleared met the hillside brush. "Looks good but—"

"Oh, no, Tom." She playfully wagged her finger. "We're done now, finito, basta, no more."

"How about a small cross then? One with Samuel's name, his birthdate and the date he—"

"No. Sam wasn't religious. You know that." She was fussing with her red sweatshirt, rubbing a muddy splotch, making the stain darker and bigger in the process. Without looking up, she asked him about a childhood rhyme. "How does it go, you know, the one about Jack's house with the cat and the rat? It goes on forever. Never ends."

"Uh-huh, and this is your subtle way of telling me we're going beyond what we'd planned. Overkill, right?"

Laurel bent down and picked up the watering can. "Okay...maybe a plaque would work, but that's it." She turned and headed for the truck.

"You're too far out in the road, Laurel. Better be careful."

"There hasn't been a car all afternoon." She kept walking.

"Humor me and get out of the road. You never know when one will zip around the bend up there."

"What did I just say, Tom?" Her voice suddenly cracked, the sound high-pitched, almost primal. "Have you seen a car today? Well, have you?"

"No, you're right," he said, and then set about collecting the gardening tools and the empty pots and carried them back to the truck. When he'd finished, he looked around, saw a red dot walking down the road— Laurel on her way home.

\* \* \*

The office grew dark, and he switched on the desk lamp. Rain drizzled down the window behind him. A knock at the door and he shoved aside the file folders he'd been working on.

Laurel came in holding a plastic sack. "I hate interrupting, Tom, especially when you're grading papers."

"Let's sit and talk since we can't work on our project today." He motioned to the small sofa, and then came over and sat next to her. "What did you bring with you?"

She pulled out a caboose, part of a child's train set. "I thought maybe we could add this to Sam's memorial. Not sure where the rest is." A couple of baseball caps, both frayed at the brim and stained from wear, came out next. "What do you think?" she asked.

"Great idea. Maybe near the plaque."

She looked down at her hand, twisted her wedding ring. "The train, yes. Not so sure about the hats. How would we manage it?"

"We'll attach them to wooden stakes, like we did with the sage."

"Okay," she said, and sat back as if for a long chat. "You looked busy when I came in."

"Do you want to talk about Samuel?"

She picked up one of the baseball caps, ran her fingers around the brim. "Yes," she said. Then, "No."

He laughed. "Okay." He shrugged. "What do you want to tell me?"

"I...I'm sorry about yesterday. Running off, leaving you there. Alone."

"It's all right," he said. "No reason to apologize."

She nodded. "If you say so."

"Would you like to see the plaque?" He went to the desk and opened a drawer.

"Not now, Tom, maybe later." She asked if he'd heard the weather

report.

"It's not supposed to rain as heavily tomorrow. We'll be all right for the afternoon."

"Good. I want to go back as soon as possible," she said, "I want to do it right this time."

"What do you mean, do it right?" he asked.

She sat up straight and took a deep breath as if gathering courage. "I won't lose my temper again. I promise."

"So you want a do-over?" he asked, and the lines around his mouth crinkled.

"Yes."

"Then we'll indeed go tomorrow if the weather's clear."

She said nothing and started searching through the sack by her feet, as if looking for something specific. "But what if it isn't clear tomorrow? I don't want to spend another day indoors. I want to finish our work."

"We will, but we have to wait. Just until—"

"I don't want to wait." Her voice loud now. She shook her head.

He took her hand and held it. "Do your breathing exercises."

"In with the good," she said, taking a long breath, and after she exhaled, "Out with the bad."

"Feel better?"

"Yes, Tom. I do."

He went back to his desk, moved papers around until he found what he wanted. "I have great news. A reporter from *The Adobe* called, asked if he could do a short article on Samuel. Interview us about the memorial. What do you—"

"No." Laurel jumped up from the sofa, knocking over the sack and spilling the contents as she headed for the door. "Absolutely not. Nothing in the papers. No one can know," and then she was gone.

He shrugged and went back to work, sorting through files, but stopped when he heard voices outside his window. He turned. A blurry figure flashed by. Someone called out, "Laurel," and he rushed from his office.

\* \* \*

Laurel wore no raincoat or hat. Her clothes were drenched. She knelt in the mud, tearing at the native plants, pulling them out by their stalks and roots.

"Laurel?" He bent down next to her. "Laurel, look at me!"

"Everything has to die," she said. "Why, goddamn it? Why?" She moved on to the seedlings, ripping, tearing, and chanting softly:

"This is the maiden all forlorn
That milked the cow with the crumpled horn
That tossed the dog that worried the cat
That killed the rat that ate the malt
That lay in the house that Jack built."

She paused, looked up at him. "If only—"

"If only what, Laurel?"

"If only...I don't know. You're supposed to have the answers, aren't you?" She rose slowly, unsteadily, and then collapsed in his arms. "I killed them."

"No," he said. "You didn't. It was an accident. You weren't responsible then and you aren't responsible now." He held her close, tried to comfort her, shield her with nothing but his soggy white coat.

"But they're dead just the same," she said.

"Yes, they're gone. Tom and Samuel."

She looked up at him. Their eyes met. "Do you think any of this was worth it, Doctor?"

\* \* \*

Jack Adamson, MD, PhD had been working steadily on Laurel Dean's progress report since dinner. A quick glance at his calendar indicated he was scheduled for eight patients the following day. *No time tomorrow. Better finish now.* He scanned several pages of notes, including the treatment summary he'd almost completed.

On Laurel's admission to the hospital, he'd made an initial diagnosis of severe melancholia, coupled with guilt and long-term depression—the source being an automobile accident that killed her husband, Tom, and son, Samuel, aged twenty-three. Laurel had been driving.

Dr. Adamson was aware at the outset of the dangers of therapeutic role-play. If he pushed too hard, Laurel might retreat further into a state of despondency. If she identified too closely with him in the role of her husband, this could bring up relationship issues he was unable to resolve. Yet in their early sessions, Laurel had proved resistant, unwilling to connect to her grief in a constructive manner. So he took a chance and was encouraged when, after explaining the therapy and the memorial for Samuel, Laurel had agreed and said, "Sounds like a plan, Tom."

Today, Laurel had made significant progress toward healing. When he'd looked in on her after dinner, she'd appeared to be sleeping peacefully and without additional sedation. He felt she was ready for individual therapy, and perhaps, in time, he would see her occasionally as an outpatient—a new long-term goal.

After signing the report and closing Laurel's file, he took off his glasses and rubbed his eyes. Tomorrow, he would ask the orderlies to remove every trace of the memorial. It was no longer needed. The site wasn't far from the hospital. It was only a few miles down the road.

# K.M. Kavanaugh

K.M. Kavanagh's stories are featured in SinC-CCC anthologies *Gone Coastal, Never Safe* and *Somewhere in Crime* and in magazines. Kavanagh is focusing on a sequel to *Rock of Morro Bay,* the debut novel of her Central Coast mystery series and *Wing It 1,* her episodic fantasy novel. She loves reading mysteries, historical romances, fantasy and sci-fi novels. When time permits, she and her husband take nature walks, visit museums and attend classic car events. Favorite getaway? Cruising Hwy. 1 in their '49 Woodie, on the lookout for deer and zebra herds.

Cathy Oles suggested I write a murder mystery occurring on the Guadalupe Nipomo Dunes. She hooked me with the story of De Milles "lost city" being buried beneath them. In the research stage, I discovered:*The Ten Commandments* premiered in '23; Carter and Carnarvon opened King Tut's tomb in '22; Carnarvon owned Highclere Castle; '23 movie set pieces were unveiled in 2013 at the Dunes Center. All this made the story impossible to resist; I started writing. At some point, my series characters (*Rock of Morro Bay*) took charge and left me in the dune dust. I blame any weird stuff on them.

# Rockin' the Casbah
by
## K.M. Kavanagh

*September 25, 2000*

We spotted the transient digging near a dune through our binoculars. He wore the street uniform of camos and faded military surplus. He reached down, oversized jacket billowing, and pocketed something. His street wariness must've kicked in because he spotted us and rabbited.We gave chase on foot, but before we got there, an old Jeep pulled up and he jumped in. The vehicle peeled out, leaving us behind in a swirling cloud of dust and sand.

I choked out to Harry, "Catch the license plate?"

My best friend coughed and shook his head. I wiped my eyes, cleared my throat and asked, "What the hell did he want *here*?"

"Egyptian treasure, Rock."

"What??"

"De Mille's Lost City. Set pieces, huge sphinxes, maybe Egyptian-style jewelry. Maybe somebody hid something real with all the fake stuff."

I shook my head. Harry loved paranormal, local legends and anything else that had never been proved. I needed solid evidence. "Harry, you're chasing ghosts and rumors again.'

Rumor had it that when Cecil B. De Mille and crew left the Guadalupe Nipomo Dunes after filming the '23 version of *The Ten Commandments*, they didn't take everything. According to locals and film buffs, De Mille ordered the 120' high and 720' wide set to be dismantled and buried. In the late '80's a survey had been done; authorities were convinced that parts of the set were intact, but much had deteriorated. Just like the funding that never brought forth one piece of Hollywood history.

"Lot of shovel work here, it's our duty as guards to look around." I pointed to where we'd seen the transient digging and other holes nearby.

An hour later, we still hadn't found treasure or clues. Big surprise.Then nature took over and kicked the breeze into a shrill wind blast. I whipped aside hair that had been blown into a dark mask impeding my vision. I brushed off sand that had assaulted the rest of me. As we walked the perimeter of our assigned grid, sweat dripped, plastering my shirt against my back. I was as uncomfortable as hell and growled in frustration. Harry smirked.

I shrugged, thinking nobody can measure up to my best friend. Every muscled inch of his 6' 6" frame looked calm, cool and collected, giving him the appearance of half super hero/half Nordic god. Yesterday, one toss of his sun-kissed hair or glance from his steely blue gaze had brought ladies running.We'd featured in one sideshow of Monday's circus; today, the Guadalupe Nipomo dunes seemed deserted by comparison.

Harry cracked a smile and said, "We're still banished from the set, huh?"

"You know *the set* has yet to be built."

Stars, local extras, on-location footage and expert CGI would not help another remake movie succeed. Loved the original *The Ten Commandments* from '23, but nothing compared to De Mille's '56 version.

"Sucks though. One minute you're in contention for a major part, in the next, you're consigned to guard duty."

"I'm a PI, not an actor. I had no intention of taking that part." During investigations, I take on personas. But a few lines in front of a camera, and I'd turned into a gibbering idiot.

"Well, Miss Croft wanted you."

I refused to comment. Maybe Harry would give up.

"Maybe it's those killer violet eyes. Ladies love them," he said.

"You should've seen your face, Rock." Harry wasn't giving up.

There's no denying that I have a temper. Soon after I gave in to the casting director's request to raise my sunglasses, temper took charge.

Harry imitated the guy's nasally voice, "Hey, check this guy out. He's got *Lizzie eyes*."

My buddy liked to tease. He knew about the fanfare connected to possessing Taylor eyes and my opinion of it.The ensuing madness—film personnel taking head and body shots and commentary about my nonexistent acting skills didn't bother me. None of that had started the boil within.Wasn't until the casting director said something *really* personal that I'd had enough. Somehow my fist connected with his nose right before I stalked off.

"Willie Bathgate deserved that punch.Lewd comments about your mother? Unforgivable."

Yes, Mother's a sensitive topic.She's doing poorly at home, and meds to control psychotic episodes added up. But Bathgate had said something else, something I wouldn't dare report to Harry. Instead, I said nothing and concentrated on skirting around what appeared to be an abandoned Plover nest.

"I'm surprised we got a call back," Harry said.

"They're filling guard positions with locals. They don't bring in pros until they start filming stars."

"That's shooting, Rock."

Despite the late autumn heat, I shivered. Shooting made me think of deaths we'd both rather forget. I sincerely hoped Harry's words didn't jinx us.

* * *

No stars had been shot, but someone who worked with them had.We'd shown up early Wednesday for guard duty, hoping to grab breakfast from the canteen. The tent was surprisingly empty, and the line for food almost nonexistent. The pretty young blonde in front of us shoved chips, yogurts and almond bags into a suitcase-sized purse. As she turned, her emerald eyes lit up and she said, "You missed the excitement by about 20 minutes."

"Excitement?" I asked, thinking her low-cut blouse was pretty damn exciting. Harry ogled her until I cleared my throat and snapped my own eyes away from the enticing double-D's.

"Yeah, excitement. You know, screaming, people vomiting, dumb morons scrambling for cover."

"Dumb morons?"

"There's a dead body on the casting couch. No shots were being fired; obviously the bastard had been shot hours before.What a bloody mess." She licked her lips, then continued, "Who would think bullets caused that much damage? Real noisy outside the tent, too—frantic cell phone calls to 9-1-1, rumors pinging around until police cars skidded to a stop, then everybody clammed up."

"Who was killed?"

"Don't know. Gotta jam." Back to us, Blondie stretched up for apples, her jeans exposing a tramp stamp that read, *"Bite me."* She zipped her purse, waggled her fingers and sauntered out.

"Just as it was getting interesting," Harry grumbled. He grabbed tongs and stuck muffins on two plates.

"I know you love petite girls with big assets, but maybe you shouldn't stare."

"Me? Your gaze was glued to those babies."

"I'm a trained P.I., we observe things." I grabbed butter pats and poured steaming Columbian into our mugs.

"Oh, that's rich. What did you observe besides her breast size?"

"A red dot on her left breast; another on her right."

"Tight bra?" he asked.

"Nope, tattoos."

We inhaled muffins and coffee, pocketed fruit, then joined people standing behind crime-scene tape. I scanned the area with binoculars. White tents huddled, a small encampment with a larger tent isolated. Several bullets had pierced white canvas on the tent's side. The back and front flap were tied open to give techies access for CS photos.

With law enforcement officers milling about, we couldn't get closer or eavesdrop. Our binocular-enhanced view, though limited, still allowed us to see detectives study something on a blood-soaked couch. When the photographers finished, the ME moved in. As he adjusted the body, CSI techs rolled in a large privacy screen. Harry and I put binoculars to use and before they blocked it, we caught a clear glimpse of the nude corpse. We grimaced together.

"Someone else didn't like Willie Bathgate," said Harry.

"That casting call is probably long," I answered.

"We'll never know how long —"

"— don't say it!"

"I'm just saying, who would cut off a guy's— "

"Junk! That's what she'll think," a homeless man muttered loudly several yards away. Until we'd swiveled our heads to look, he didn't understand how far his voice had carried. Behind us, the desolate landscape—dunes stretching out as far as the eye could see—served as biblical desert and sound amplificaton. His eyes widened, recognizing us before we recognized him and moved forward. Nowhere to run, but the guy tried.

Took moments to overtake him. When he shrugged out of his filthy jacket, Harry appeared stupefied. Something fell out of the jacket, and the homeless man grabbed for it. I tackled him knee level and down to the sand. I secured the gaunt man, while pocketing a bag of almonds that felt too heavy. As I pulled the guy up, I took shallow breaths. The stench of piss, birdshit and other prurient smells made for a quick delivery to the authorities.

Our friend Lt. Joe Valdez smiled, but Joe's cousin and man-in-charge, Detective Luis Valdez with the SLO Sheriff's Department didn't. The cousins looked almost like twins except for Luis's crooked nose. Luis had wider shoulders, but his trim physique indicated he hit the gym as frequently as Joe.

"That guy stole something from the studio's leased property."

"Thanks for the assist. We'll take it from here," Detective Luis said.

"The guy was digging the dunes. He's up to something," said Harry.

"We see people here and on the beach with metal detectors. They dig up coins and old metal. As long as they avoid the Plovers' nesting season, we don't care. We'll find out why he ran, but he's not connected to the murder."

I handed over the almond bag and said, "Check the guy's nuts."

Detective Luis gave me a cold stare that looked identical to his cousin's whenever Joe shifted into *official* mode at SLO P.D.

I shrugged. "Okay, I get it. No help needed."

"That's right. You might get involved in Joe's investigations, but stay out of mine."

"I always warn him, too, Cuz," said Joe, his moustache stretching with his grin. "That's how it all begins."

Detective Luis Valdez's dark gaze caught mine. "You

both need to give statements."

"Now or later?"

"Tomorrow morning. Joe'll get details tonight unofficially, but I need official. Understand?"

"Yes."

"I heard about Monday's argument with the vic. You've been Joe's friend for forever, but if you did this, he can't save you."

"I wouldn't kill the vic because he was a dick—"

"—and now he doesn't have one," blurted Harry.

Shit. How would we explain knowing *that* detail?

"That's it. You're going in now. Meet me at the station in ten minutes or my men will hunt you down." Detective L.Valdez handed me a card and stomped away.

"Meet you there," I called out after him. I asked Joe, "Drinks and darts afterwards?"

"I'll find a local watering hole. Call when you're done."

"Okay."

Joe leaned in closer with his I'm-serious look. "And Rock?"

"Yes, Joe."

"Play it straight, and you'll be okay. Remember, my cousin's even more official than me."

I gulped. Valdez in official mode bordered scary. I never messed with Joe when he was serious, and I planned to treat Luis the same.

* * *

Plans are overrated. Detective Luis Valdez walked in with attitude that was hard to ignore. I wanted to intro him to my own 'tude, but he's running a murder investigation. Not worth the trouble. I stared at the graffiti-carved table until he forced me to look.

"How'd you know that Mr. Bathgate's genitals had been mutilated?"

"Before the CSI techs rolled out the privacy screen, they took location shots.We watched through binoculars."

"Did you know him before the casting call?"

"No."

"What were you doing there? Aspiring to be an actor?"

"No, security work," I said.

"Why were you reading lines?"

"They commandeered me as a stand-in when a character actor quit. I'm the same size and possess his general looks."

"Why'd he quit?"

"The guy caught Bathgate groping his lady. Threatened to kill Willie."

"Acting pays better than guard duty.Why'd *you* quit?" he asked.

I didn't answer.

"A witness claimed you hit Willie Bathgate because he insulted your eyes."

"Nope. Been dealing with that stuff since grade school."

"Another witness stated you lost it after Bathgate said your Mom slept with Elizabeth Taylor's Dad."

"Heard that before, too. Doesn't bother us. Besides, mother loves Hollywood drama. She's nuts about it."

"Care to explain?" he asked.

*Dammit, he'd zeroed in on what I wanted to avoid.* "Sometimes my mother thinks she's an actress, and the world is her movie set."

"What does that mean?"

"I recently brought Mother home to see if she could handle living there. I never know if I'll be greeted by Doris Day, Katherine Hepburn or Bette Davis to name a few."

Detective Luis' face briefly struggled not to smile.

"And that's a problem?"

"It is when the quack my sister hired says I have to play along."

"So there's tension at home. Is that why you hit Willie?"

"No. When he didn't get a rise with Mom taunts, he tried something else."

"And what would that be?" he asked, leaning closer.

"Told me he'd heard that Harry's boy, Dickens, is a good-looking kid."

"He was going to make Dickens an extra?"

"Yeah."

"What's wrong with that?"

"He whispered that he liked sexually controlling anyone smaller than him –women, boys, girls, really didn't matter."

When Detective Luis flushed, I knew he was angry. "That's why you hit him?"

"No one touches my godson."

The detective nodded before his fist slammed onto the table. He calmed, then looked up. "I hate pedophiles. I would've hit the bastard too, but there's more going on with you."

"What's that?"

"Some people went after Dickens before, and you shot one of them."

"Didn't aim to kill. Want more details? Ask Joe. Anything else?"

"Where were you last night?"

"Harry talked me into going to the unofficial casting party. I needed a break from Mother; he wanted to check out babes. When we saw my ex-girlfriend, Bev, we took off."

"You let an 'ex' chase you away?" he asked.

"Since Bev divorced, she got into Goth. It's weird."

"When did you leave?"

"About ten. From there, we stopped at *Foghorn Blast* in Los Osos. Harry bought me a beer to thank me. When we came outside, we saw somebody had broken into my truck."

"Anything stolen?"

"Nothing worth mentioning."

"What happened next?"

"We headed to my place. Harry woke up Dickens, and they headed across the street."

"You left Dickens with your crazy mother?"

"One, Mother's delusional, but harmless; two, she loves Dickens like a grandson; and three, Mike and Ike were there, too."

"Who's Mike and Ike?"

"His best friends."

"You can go. We'll contact you if anything else comes up."

Maybe I should've told him that Mike and Ike were my semi-psychic, wise-cracking parrots. Maybe I should've told Luis someone had stolen my Dad's gun. And my reluctance to discuss the shooting? Probably wouldn't matter. Still, I needed to share everything with Joe.

\* \* \*

Thwack! "Another bullseye," said Joe, looking as surprised as the bleary-eyed drunks who'd gathered to bet on us.

"Have you been practicing?" asked Harry.

Thwack! "Bullseye again,"I said.

"Okay, you win," said Joe with a sigh. A few losing bettors echoed the sound.

"Pay up."

"Cash or info?" asked J.Valdez as he gathered the darts and people dispersed.

"Info."

"Really? Needing cash is what got us into this," said Harry.

"I'll land a case soon. You'll get a flip or new project. End of discussion," I said.

"I followed up on a great stock tip; paid well. I can spare a little," offered Joe.

"Not necessary. Guard duty brought in some cash."

"Let me know if you want in, Juanita's new client has earned us a nice nest egg."

Joe's wife had diverted her nursing career from hospital to private patients. Paid off for the Valdez family in a big way. Juanita's shrewd, but I wouldn't risk savings on speculation. "I'll let you know. Now no more stalling."

Joe smiled sheepishly. "This stays between us. Six shots through the side of the tent. Possibly, a revolver, but we're waiting on ballistics. Three bullets hit Willie Bathgate. Coroner's report will tell us which killed him."

"Six shots through the side of a tent? Why not a couple from inside to make sure he went down?" I asked.

"Maybe someone just wanted to scare him," said Joe.

"What about his missing genitals?" I asked.

"That went beyond scare tactics."

"What do you mean?"

"The ME believes Willie was still alive, judging by all the blood pooled around him."

"Somebody shy with a gun, but skilled and comfortable with a knife? A gun's remote; a knife's personal. I'd bet on two people," I said.

"Yes, but the blade work wasn't skilled. There were hesitation marks."

"That or he was squirming. What guy wouldn't be?" asked Harry.

"Possibly both hesitation and squirming. We'll know more if they find his parts." The three of us grimaced. Harry looked a little green.

"Rock, why'd you pick info? Curiosity?" Joe turned with Harry and waited.

"I miss looking through your cold files, Joe."

"I miss it, too. You helped jumpstart a few cases and close a couple. Made us look good."

"Joe, while Luis interrogated me, I had a thought. I didn't mention it."

Joe set down his beer and took a calming breath. "What?"

"I think Bathgate was trying to shut down the set early. At the party, Harry heard some things."

Joe sipped his beer and waited.

"Bathgate tore up a costume, claiming it was shit. He verbally abused two actresses he'd had running lines during tryouts," said Harry.

"Okay, so he's one of *those* directors. Doesn't explain why he'd stop the casting call."

"Just a gut feeling," I explained.

"I never argue with your intuition."

"I appreciate that."

"What else didn't you mention to Luis?"

Joe's own intuition had kicked in. He removed the darts from the dart board. So far, Joe was keeping control of his blood pressure.

"I didn't go into details about Mike and Ike."

"That's good."

"The shooting came up. I told him to talk with you."

"Luis is thorough. He'll peruse the files and question you later if he needs something."

"One last thing, someone broke into my truck Tuesday night."

Joe's face flushed. "Did you call it in?"

"I'm reporting it to you."

"Dammit, Rock. You better hope this doesn't come back to bite you or me."

"I'll take responsibility, not you," I said.

"Damn straight." Three darts flew in rapid succession. Thwack! Thwack! Thwack!

Joe was right. All three shots were straight; one bullseye.

\* \* \*

When I woke, I ran, stretched and showered. On the way to the kitchen, I glimpsed at the living room and did a double-take. Mother had caught the Egyptian revival spurred on by Hollyweird's visit to Nipomo. How late had Mother stayed up? She'd hung sheers, stacked pillows around the room and covered the wing chair with a gold tablecloth, bric-a-brac and tassels—her version of a Pharoah's throne. Which movie? The *King and I*  or *The Ten Commandments*? Thankfully, imitating Yul Brynner was easy. Would Mother be Anna? Neferiti? Salome? Possibly the actresses who portrayed those roles, Deborah Kerr, Anne Baxter or Yvonne Di Carlo? I made a mental note to check out movie facts for both films.

I made the rounds quickly, peeking into the master bedroom, then crept from the back porch to the kitchen. Mother, Mike and Ike were asleep; I'd deal with them later. Yesterday's newspaper lay open on the table. Black lines encircled articles about the casting call murder. Had Mother connected to something current? Odd, usually she takes on personas from a past movie memory. As I chewed on a toaster waffle between sips of coffee, I read about Monday's extras call for locals, Tuesday's casting party, Bathgate's murder and sidebars about the '23 and '56 movie productions. There was a lot of speculation about digging up De Mille's lost city.

After a few phone calls, I was almost ready. I put out birdseed for Mike and Ike and left Mother cereal. I turned turkey leftovers into three sandwiches; one went into the fridge and two I bagged for myself. Mother eats without assistance, but preparing food needs supervision. Open flames? Risky. I childproofed the stove before opening the door to leave.something must've alerted the boys. As I left, Mike or Ike shrieked a new movie misquote.

"Bury yourself in the ground, and eons later even you'd be worth something, D.J!"

"BRAWWK!"

I kept going, but couldn't help smiling. Obviously Dickens and pals had watched *Raiders of the Lost Ark*. Now I was sure Harry's son also fed my boys movie misquotes.

\* \* \*

When I called the studio folks earlier, they'd welcomed additional security. Some tents were off limits until the police removed the crime scene tape, but the studio would move forward with the extras call.We walked past a crowd gathered by the front gate. Harry and I clocked in, then shuffled past the gate toward the parking lot. New protestors had joined the crowd and held signs. Variations on the same subject: *dig up the lost city*. A contingent of homeless looked on while eating apples and bags of almonds, one resembled the guy we'd collared yesterday.

We headed out in Big Silver, my 4 x 4 Silverado truck. We moved past dry landscape and rolling dunes. Seemed nothing had changed much, until we reached the outskirts. We spotted a Jeep idling near where we'd seen the homeless man digging. It took off. Big Silver ate up the distance, but the other vehicle had a good lead.

"Binoculars, Harry!"

"K-kangaroo, A-Arthur, T-Timothy, H-Henry;2, 2."

"I'll pull over; you use your cell phone."

"Why pull over? I'll call; you hunt," said Harry.

"Got a hunch brewing. When we stop, call in the license to Joe."

I pulled over, but stopped Harry from making his call. A gut feeling had hit me full force. Why were the digging spots calling to me? "Grab my camera from the boot? I need to think…"

Harry fetched the camera. I zoomed in on the digs not far from us. I pictured the homeless man, the Jeep and guessed they'd been digging fairly close together, but not quite the same spot. I knew something was off, but what?

"Call Joe and give him the license. Then give me the phone."

"I thought you didn't need a cell phone—"

"—not now, Harry, I'm onto something."

"Gotcha." After Harry talked to Joe, he handed me the phone.

"Hey, Joe. Did Detective Luis talk to the homeless guy yet?"

"George Herbert was a waste of time. Crazy, you know? Wouldn't talk unless Luis called him by his street name, 'Magpie'."

"What else did Magpie say?"

"Magpie kept muttering about junk jewelry, a gold-marbled cat and something should be left buried. He's still in jail because they found pot on him. Must take other drugs, Rock. His mind is messed up."

"Can't search his home for more drugs because Magpie doesn't have one."

"Right."

*Homeless, Magpie…Oh.* The light went on. "Gotta run, Joe. This is intuition talking. Tell Luis to stall or lose Herbert's paperwork. Do not release him."

"Wait! You're onto something; aren't you?"

"Yeah, I'll call if it's helpful, Lt." I handed the phone back to Harry.

"I saw that look. You've figured out something."

"Not sure what yet. Harry, know what Magpies do with shiny objects?"

"No, Dickens is the birdwatcher now."

"Dickens told me about birds' unique habits. Magpies hide shiny objects."

"I'm confused."

"Harry, pretend you're homeless. No home to stash stuff; shelters are temporary.You either carry it or find a hidey hole."

"Hole?" he asked his grin widening.

"Something bothered me about the digging. While talking to Joe, it hit me. Magpie wasn't digging, he was *burying* something."

"Too bad we don't have shovels."

"Thought we could dig after shift, so I stashed them in the truck. Here's the key to the shell. I'll take pictures."

I photographed wherever dirt had been disturbed. So many holes, it looked like a colony of beserk gophers.What difference would two more holes make? I took Magpie's area and Harry worked almost where Jeep guy had, digging deep until his shovel hit with a loud clinking sound. He eased off and slowly unearthed a garbage bag containing vintage preserve jars. Inside of these, we found plain clay beads, smaller blue beads and what appeared to be golden metal chunks and guaze-wrapped figurines. We filled the rest of a half-filled jar with loose clay beads. I pocketed two for later examination. Harry explored further, but found nothing more. We dug my area together and soon heard a clunk.We gently excavated and looked down into the hole.

Harry's face turned green. Hairs stood up along my spine. We touched nothing, just stared at the hole's contents in shock. First item? Not surprising. Another preserve jar filled with more clay beads. With the camera, I zoomed in on the lid where a bird and other symbols were carved. I hesitated a moment, thinking my next zoom-in might hasten my desire to upchuck breakfast.Then reality hit, this was my only chance to see the goods close-up. I took a deep breath and continued my perusal. The first large jar contained a gun; the second, a Bubbie's pickle jar, contained pickle juice and what might be Bathgate's genitals.

The pickle jar creeped out Harry, but I was worried about the gun. We called Lt. Joe and Detective Luis; Joe arrived first. He looked into the hole and then at me. "I knew this would come back to bite you."

We both knew the ballistics test would prove it was Dad's gun. I ran my fingers through my hair and didn't say anything.

"Lucky for you, I filed a theft report after we spoke. But, Rock, why would someone steal your gun to commit a crime?"

"I wish I knew."

"What I say next is off record; agreed?"

I nodded.

"I'm helping the sheriffs department, so don't repeat this to anyone.After you talk to Luis, leave. We both know this could get ugly for you."

Not surprising news. As soon as I'd seen the gun, I'd known. Joe's a SLOPD detective and just confirmed it. Means, opportunity and motive. I was three for three.

\* \* \*

A uniform that arrived with Detective Luis took our statements, while he listened. He threw out a few questions, probably a preliminary to an intense grilling later.

"Why didn't you contact us before digging?"

"Wasn't a sure thing, just a hunch."

"You're good at that; right?"

I shrugged my shoulders, then said, "You said people

dig around here without hassle. Think of me as just another lucky prospector."

A twitch started along Joe's jawline; his cousin's eyes narrowed. "I'm betting that'll change soon."

"How's that?"

"Luck is a fickle lady." Luis slashed his hand through the air in a dismissal wave. Harry and I took off in Big Silver without looking back.

"That was your Dad's gun; wasn't it?" asked Harry.

"Afraid so."

"How the hell did Magpie get it?"

"Don't know, but before the ballistics report gets back, I need to know everything about Magpie. Where he went to school, his family tree, does he have any priors? You know the drill. Maybe Joe will help, too."

"There's no way Luis'll let you question Magpie."

"Okay, so maybe I'll get access to the interview tape and file folder."

Harry grinned and gave me the Magnum-eyebrow wiggle. "Unofficially, of course."

Though Harry never spoke of his government work, I'd heard he had connections that P.I.'s like me only dreamed about. Sometimes, I took what he offered. For Joe's sake, I drew the line. "You know the rules."

"Unless it's a life-and-death situation, nothing illegal," he said.

"Especially no break-ins at the Sheriffs Department."

"Gee, Rock, you're no fun."

"Fun is overrated when you're facing jail."

"Don't worry. Something will shake loose and we'll figure it out." We jumped into Big Silver and headed home.

\* \* \*

"Hi, Uncle Rock." Dickens smiled up at me as I tousled

his dark curls. *Two gifts in one.* Smiles were a recent addition to the break-throughs made at his grief and trauma counseling. And speech? I'd never known how joyful hearing a child's voice could be especially when we thought we'd lost that sound forever.

"Hi, Dickens." I smiled, we high-fived, then I walked past the couch to give father and son privacy.

"Hi, Dad. Tough day?" Harry's face smoothed out. Even after a year plus, he still had moments of panic. Afraid his son had disappeared a second time. Wondering later, if his boy would ever talk again after being locked inside his grandfather's car at a murder scene.

Harry hugged his boy, then they high-fived. "Son, we're a tough family. Together we can handle it; right?"

"You bet, Dad. We're superheroes tough."

I decided then that other than guard work; I had to keep Harry out of this.

Harry looked at me and said, "Don't even think about cutting me loose."

"Harry—"

"You need all the help you can get. We started together; we finish together."

"Uncle Rock?"

"Dickens?" I couldn't help smiling as he petted my parrots' heads. The boys made a sound somewhat like a cat purring; parrotspeak for they loved attention.

"Can you bring Mike and Ike over? You work on your computer and Dad can work on ours. Maybe you'll find clues."

"What about Mother?"

"Yul Brynner movies on the TCM channel tonight."

Mother loved Yul Brynner movies; dynamite wouldn't move her from the TV. "That okay with you, Harry?" I asked.

"Good plan."

I didn't know how much time it would take before Luis closed in on me. Any action sounded good. I threw together a quick dinner of Hamburger Helper and salad, then we left Mother to watch her movies. As we walked over, I calculated how long it might take the ballistics report to get back to Detective Luis. Labs are swamped with work and that was in my favor. But how far would Joe's loyalty to our friendship extend? Luis was his cousin; blood ties are stronger than friendship. I decided to cross that bridge when we reached it.

Once we'd arrived at Harry's mobile home, one similar to what Mother and I shared, we went to work. I settled the parrots next to Dickens on the couch. "What do you want me to do?" he asked.

"You pick a movie to watch with the boys and keep them quiet. Harry, dig up any facts about the aftermath of De Mille's movie. Exactly what they did with the set, costumes and jewelry, who attended the movie parties and events, anything newsworthy around that time period. I'll check out George Herbert."

A couple hours later, Harry and I compared notes. "Set dismantled and buried, costumes and jewelry packed and sent back to Hollywood. Before they took apart the set, they had a huge Hollywood-style party among the sphinxes. Guess who was on the guest list."

"You tell me."

"Howard Carter."

Harry had ways of tapping into info that I didn't. He'd struck gold with this one.

I raised an eyebrow.

"Yes. *The* archealogist, Howard Carter."

"Timeline's right. *The Ten Commandments* came out in '23. Howard Carter, with the financial assistance of Lord Carnarvon, discovered King Tutenkamen's tomb in 1922. Carter was quite the celebrity after that," I said.

"What about Lord Carnarvon?"

"He died months later after a mosquito bite became infected. Many claimed he was cursed because he'd stolen from Tut's tomb."

"Stealing?" he asked.

"Oh, yeah. Back then, excavators had a finders/keepers attitude toward discoveries. Not everything was catalogued, and those items left with the archeologists. This practice wasn't considered wrong except by museum officials of the host country. In fact, Lord Carnarvon funded many excursions by selling antiquities to rich tourists wanting to add to private collections."

Harry's eyes narrowed. "How do you know all this?"

"I looked up 'George Herbert.' In addition to public intoxication by our current George, Howard Carter partnered with George Herbert aka Lord Carnarvon #5 and owner of Highclere Castle."

Harry grinned. I said, "Print out stuff on Carter and Carnarvon, while I focus on Egyptian jewelry."

"Egyptian jewelry? Like in the pharoah's scene? Or are we talking even older?"

"Don't be ridiculous. How could something from Tut's time end up in the Nipomo Dunes? Makes no sense. I'm thinking jewelry used in the De Milles''23 movie. Remember the clay beads? I think they painted them whatever colors worked for the costume. Not a Tut find, but Hollywood memorabilia sells for pretty big bucks."

"Now that makes sense."

\* \* \*

After tossing down a couple beers and forwarding theories that bordered on crazy, we called it a night. He tucked in his boy; I took my "boys" home. I bribed them with birdseed and cuddles, and they went into the large cage without fuss. Mike said, "Don't bite the hand that feeds you."

"Has mother lost her marbles?" squawked Ike.

I shut the door to the enclosed back porch and hoped not. Still, she must've been the one to mutter that phrase since it wasn't a movie misquote. Putting off the inevitable, I went looking for Mother in the kitchen. Clean and everything in place except a bowl with popcorn seeds. I checked the microwave for scorch marks, and finding none, moved into the living room. The movie set remained intact. Mother had fallen asleep on the "throne."remote in hand and silver head leaned forward. She wore an old necklace with Egyptian influence over nightgown and robe. If that was the extent of her costume, that was okay with me.

She stirred a little when I took the remote and said, "Yul?"

"Not tonight, Mother."

I switched off an old Bob Hope movie. Mother didn't stir again except to shuffle off to bed with my help. I was relieved she was herself and not an onscreen persona. I rehooked up my computer in the office and headed to bed.

Trouble plagued my sleep with a neverending dream that spiraled out from one event to another. Featured players: De Mille '23's movie premiere attendees-Goth women wearing long gowns with Egyptian-influenced jewelry; Howard Carter writing diary entries from the stone perch called "Castle Carter"; Lord Carnarvon directing movers with a long succession of wooden crates entering a side entrance of Highclere castle. A worker dropped one smaller crate and beads burst through from the broken side. Lord Carnarvon cursed the man; Howard Carter reappeared to jot down notes.

I don't believe dreams are a doorway to answers. Nocturnal escapes take whatever's been thrown into the mind sieve during daytime, add tension, worries, grind together into a stew of confusion. Instead of pondering about the dream's meaning, I shook it off and tied up a loose end instead. Joe answered immediately.

"Hey, Rock, I was going to call. The license plate is registered to Katherine *Herbert*. And guess what?"

"You tell me."

"It's good news/bad news."

"The good?"

"A patron at *Foghorn Blast* witnessed two thiefs breaking into your truck."

"Good.What's the bad?"

"The guy was drunk or crazy. Claimed he'd seen ghosts. No bodies, just angry white faces. One topped with flaming red hair. Sorry, Rock."

Me, too, and *deja vu*. Not wanting to raise Joe's blood pressure, I thanked him and hung up. Brewskies aside, the witness had seen real people. Probably at a distance through the side-door window, bodies hidden by the truck. The flaming red hair fit. The white spooky faces? My ex-girlfriend Bev and friend in goth. The *deja vu* moment courtesy of Bev's ex-husband. He'd once broken into my truck and stolen Dad's gun; I'd broken his nose. I wouldn't do that to Bev, but I would force her to answer questions.

The Cambrian grapevine has a long reach, so I called someone who'd worked with Bev at *Linns Fruit Bin*. She told me about Bev's current workplace. I called *Foghorn Blast* and caught a back-office guy offguard. "Found glasses in your parking lot Tuesday night. Saw them on a red-haired waitress earlier that evening."

"Donate them to our lost-and-found."

"What if I give them to you to pass on? She might be appreciative."

"Appeciative? Wouldn't go near that bitch if you paid me. Give them to her yourself. She's working tonight."

"Thanks."

"And pal? We have bouncers, so no funny business."
He hung up.

\* \* \*

Despite the friendly atmosphere of sawdust-covered floors, wine barrel tables covered with appetizers, filled beer mugs and wine glasses keeping patrons happy, Bev looked pissed. When interrogating someone unofficially, be direct. If he/she is hostile, go with offense. "The police have a witness who saw you two break into my truck. I want Dad's gun back, Bev."

"I don't have it; Kat does."

Bev must be emotional to cave so early. "Get it back; I won't press charges."

I watched Bev squirm, knowing what I'd ask was impossible.

"They're into something I refused to do. If I give you Kat and her boyfriend, Devon, would that help?"

"I want Dad's gun, too."

"Maybe they know where her stupid uncle hid it, but I don't."

Whoa. In that moment, many pieces came together. I checked my hunch.

"Magpie seems good at protecting things, but I think Kat's headed for jail."

Bev looked frightened. I said, "We weren't always enemies; we used to talk. You changed when Svensen came along."

"You didn't change enough," she said.

I shrugged. "Hey, my offer stands for the next hour."

Bev took a dinner break and spent a few minutes filling in details about how she met the couple at a Goth bar. Initially, they all hit it off, got close, but they turned strange. I stopped her there. "Strange? Goth is pretty strange."

"No, that's fantasy. Kat and Devon like danger. Real stuff; you know?" She sniffed and wiped her eyes on a cocktail napkin.

"What kind of danger?" I asked.

"Anything involving pain and fear. I can't talk; they'll hurt me."

I raised my eyebrow, but Bev shook her head. "Promise you'll turn them in, and I'll give you their Saturday night hangout."

Since today was Friday, it worked. I nodded. As she leaned forward to write on her order pad, I couldn't help checking her out. She winked and said through a weak smile, "Wait until you see hers. Tit-tats, unforgettable."

"Breast tattoos?"

"Yeah, connect dots together with her tramp stamp, and you'll understand, Rock. Bring back-up, she's a bloodsucking bitch!"

"Thanks for the warning, Bev."

\* \* \*

Listening to Bev's warning, I called Joe and Harry. Joe called Luis. After much back-and-forth arguing, Detective Luis set up an observation interview with Magpie for tomorrow. Highly unorthodox, but Luis had been getting nowhere. Saturday afternoon ,we reread the research Harry and I'd gathered, then strategized. Luis and Harry sat behind the mirror, and Joe and I carried waters into an interrogation room with earth tones and outdated furniture.

Magpie smelled better without his nasty jacket. His lined, sunburned face looked calm and resigned to fate. Joe introduced us. Magpie smiled, reached for the water and said, "Good. That other suit pissed me off."

Joe confirmed Magpie was George Herbert, then asked standard questions similar to what Luis asked, but varied for comparison. Magpie seemed antsy. "Asked and answered; try something new." George chugged down water. Joe gave me the go-ahead look and opened his notebook.

"Okay if I call you, Magpie?"

He smiled, "I prefer it."

"Magpie, I'm an interview observer. We're two guys talking, and I'm nosy. But you're not obligated to answer my questions; okay?"

"Alright."

"Found your stuff in the dunes. How'd it get there?"

"Hid everything from my niece."

"Why?"

"Doesn't belong to her. Everything's stolen!" He'd worked up to a rant, then calmed himself.

"Can you tell me when things were buried?"

"Yes."

"Go ahead."

"Don't want to rat her out, but the weirdness is getting dangerous. For everyone, you know?"

"What if I ask yes-and-no questions and you nod or shake your head?"

He nodded.

"Your niece is Katherine Herbert?" Nod.

"You call her Kat?" Nod.

"Kat took the gun?" Nod.

"Kat used the gun?" Shrug.

"Kat likes knives?" Shrug.

"You stole all the stuff in the jars?" Negative shake.

"Someone else did and you hid it?" Nod.

Something niggled in my brain from an earlier phone conservation. "Now we need explanations. I didn't see a gold-marbled cat among the items in the jars. Is it covered in guaze?"

Magpie laughed. "Must've been high. Thought I'd said

cold-as-marble Kat."

"Your niece?" Nod.

"So when did she steal the loot-filled preserve jars?"

"We're not graverobbers. My *grandfather* stole it long ago…" His eyes took on a far away look, then suddenly focused. "After he died from the curse, grandmother wanted to stop the deaths. Told Carter to take it all. Guess they missed something."

"Did you find the stash?"

"Kat found it. Tucked away in an old attic trunk."

"Why wasn't the loot found earlier?"

"Ever see pictures of Highclere Castle?"

"Nope."

"Lot of nooks and crannies for hiding things there."

"What's in the jars?"

"Most are artifacts that should've remained with Tut. I stole from Kat to give it all back. Mrs. Carter sold things to a NYmuseum, maybe they'd send theirs and our loot to Egypt. Belongs with Tut, so he can rest easy."

"Tell me about the reglued almond bag."

"Fooled Kat. Started sending things back secretly."

"What's in there?"

"Everyone will know soon."

"What about the pickle jar and the gun in the other jar?"

"Devon brought them over Tuesday night and said to hide 'em. He'd tried to get Kat's knife, but she wouldn't give it up. Even with those brown streaks. Guess it's like my lucky jacket."

"How's that?"

"Can't clean it or you'll wash off the luck."

After much wheedling, I convinced Magpie to give Luis an official recorded interview. After they finished, the three of us would hunt with Harry.

\* \* \*

The rural SLO-based club, *Dreaded Undead,* wasn't what I'd expected. No Halloweenish decorations except the females who'd chosen to wear trailing silk peignoirs, white face makeup with red dots and trails on their necks. Except for a few zombies and vampires, men wore the dark suits similar to our undercover attire. The upscale hangout sported clean lines, thick glass bars outlined in neon blue lighting and elongated metal pub tables and chairs. Many goblets served "dripping blood." Dancers gyrated to the beat of very loud techno music that bled my ears. A very realistic Dracula bared his fangs as we walked past his music booth on the way to the dungeon.

Luis' and Joe's badges got us into the exclusive "cellars." Alighting from the long stairway, we were surrounded by moaning, screams and wicked laughter. We stalked silently through foggy corridors past dark, velvet-draped alcoves and glass-bricked Sado-masochistic rooms. Our ghostly guide faded away when we reached the large room on the end. Chain-wrapped chairs and a couch filled the interior and an empty viewing chair sat behind a curtain of whips. A table of delicate cutting tools was attended by a long-legged vixen encased in black leather with long strips torn out. She must've bound her breasts together because the red dot tattoos pushed close, forming a forever love bite. She grinned and pointed toward her muscled partner clad in only a leather loin cloth.

I recognized her victim as the actor who'd quit the casting call. Devon bled from slight cuts on his arms and his back bore whipping welts. Momentarily distracted by his giddy smile and ugly wounds, my three colleagues didn't see Kat reach for something in her thigh-long boot. I leaped forward, pinned her arm and removed a stiletto. She fought muscles that outmatched hers, and I didn't give into her pleading to "finish him." One-punch Harry knocked out Devon who'd struggled to rescue Kat; Joe and Luis had both suspects cuffed and read in under two minutes.

\* \* \*

Their first "thrill-kill" hadn't gone smoothly, but it took days for Devon and Kat to finally crack. The threat of DNA evidence, Magpie's confession and Bev's sworn statement finally sealed the deal.

After talking with Joe, I finished watching a Rockford rerun with Mother and the boys. Ike cackled, "Has Mother lost her marbles?"

Mother grasped her necklace, looking stunned. I probably looked more stunned. It felt as if my third eye had opened and direct sunlight seared an idea into my brain. I excused myself and scrambled for the Nipomo dunes souvenirs that I'd casually tossed into an envelope on my desk. Though needing to verify my hunch, instinct told me I was right when I examined our find. I called local authorities and a NY museum's antiquities department. The latter sounded excited; the former pretended they weren't contemplating headaches. Other Nipomo officials and the Dunes Center exhibitors would be ecstatic. Tourist dollars would be assured for years.

I called Harry, but his machine answered. As I joined the gang in the den, Mike called out, "Has Mother lost her marbles?"

Mother grasped her necklace, then calmed as she realized it was intact. "Mother didn't lose any marbles; she helped find them!" I said.

Mother smiled. "Thank you, *Rock*." I hugged and held her, silently celebrating her moment of clarity. I thought about how precious mother/son relationships were and how they'd connected from present to centuries long gone. The phone rang. I kissed her on the forehead, then answered.

"You rang?"

"Guess what, Harry?" I blew Mother a kiss, then went into my office.

"What?"

"I owe you an apology."

"Oh?" I heard clothes rustle as he sat up.

"We found ancient Egyptian treasure in the dunes."

"We're rich!! We struck gold, Rock.—"

'—Harry, stop! We're not talking gold here."

"Are you kidding? Ancient Egypt used gold on everything, including Tut's death mask."

"Funny you should mention him." I pulled the envelope from the desk drawer.

"If we're talking Tut, we're talking gold. His tomb was filled with that and precious artifacts."

"What's more precious than gold to a nine-year-old boy?" I asked, rolling the artifacts in my palm.

"You tell me."

"A gift from a surrogate mother that would be treasured forever."

"What gift?"

"Marbles."

"Have you lost yours?"

"Nope. The clay beads had no holes. I believe they're Tut's marbles."

"Good. Now old Tut can rest easy."

Harry couldn't see me roll my eyes, but somehow, sensed it. We still debated the tomb curse on the way over to meet the Valdez cousins. Joe and Luis bought the first couple rounds at *Foghorn Blast* ; we paid for the next ones. As we laughed and drank in celebration of a case closed, I thought about young Tut. How long before all the Boy King's toys had been returned, and he could truly R.I.P.?

# Susan Tuttle

This piece was written in one of my classes when we did what I call a "free write." We take a slip of paper from my infamous "peppermint box" and what is printed on it becomes the opening line or phrase of the piece. We then have 5, 10 or 15 minutes to simply write whatever comes into our heads. Some amazing stuff arises when we set aside our conscious minds and let our subconscious take over. "My father was away, like he always was..." is the slip I drew. Set timer, and write!

# The Writer
## by
### Susan Tuttle

My father was away, like he always was the fourth weekend of every month. He said it was for work, but I knew he had a girlfriend. She lived about fifty miles south of us and he did meet her through one of his work trips, so I guess works had something to do with it. But his fourth weekends were all about her, not earning money.

I don't know why he kept Brenda (I'd snooped in his briefcase and found her name when I was twelve) a secret. Mom had died eight years before, when Joey was three. At seven I took over most of the household duties. From my way of thinking, it would have been nice to relegate myself back to chores and childhood. A step-mother would have allowed that. But Dad must have thought we'd disapprove of him moving on, so he kept the girlfriend a secret.

I was seventeen the night Dad left yet again to meet Brenda. Joey was spending the night at a friend's house, so I had the place to myself. I have to admit it was fun for a while. No baby brother to fight with or have to feed. No sharing the TV. No policing bedtime. I felt grown up for the very first time, instead of a child playing at adulthood.

I sat out on the front porch after dinner, rocking in the glider as I wrote the next chapter in my book. I want to be a published author and I read once that to be a writer you have to write, so that's what I did. I wrote.

This was the fifth book in my ongoing series titled, *Oh, Antony!,* and I think each one was better than the one before, if I do say so myself. I had come to the part where Amber and Antony were finally alone together and something interesting could actually happen in that deserted farmhouse where they'd holed up from the Mexican banditos who were chasing them, and where they had only a bag of taco chips and salsa to eat and an old cast-iron tub to sleep in—together —when footsteps interrupted my train of thought.

I looked up and my heart stood still. He walked up the front porch steps with a measured beat, one slow step at a time. He had dark stormy eyes and high cheekbones with dimpled cheeks and a square jaw. He was lean and mean and power rolled off him in waves. His black hair tumbled to his shoulders in curls any woman in her right mind would kill for—or maybe kiss for. He wore a black t-shirt that had seen better days and jeans so tight they had to be painted on.

"H-hello?" I managed to warble.

"I've been waiting for you," he crooned, his voice pure silk.

"You have?" My heart lurched. This wasn't happening, couldn't be happening. "Who are you?"

"You know who I am." He sat beside me on the glider and captured my hand.

"Antony?" I whispered.

He kissed me, took possession of my lips, my heart, my soul, just as he had Amber's and so many other paper women before her. Before me. He tasted exactly the way I'd written him. When I opened my eyes and looked into his, I knew I was lost.

Danger made him irresistible; after all, I'd written him to fit my every mood, my every desire. When he rose, my hand still in his, I wondered where we would go. How many places we would rob. How many people we would flee from before my life ended.

Who knew being a writer could be so wonderful? And so dangerous?

# Barbara M. Hodges

Barbara M. Hodges is the author or co-author of ten works of fiction. *The Blue Flame, The Emerald Dagger* and *The Silver Angel*, are the first three young adult books in her Daradawn fantasy series. *Ice* and *One Last Sin* are crime fiction, co-written with Randolph Tower. Barbara and Maggie Pucillo are the authors of *A Spiral of Echoes*, a paranormal romance that takes place in Baja, Mexico. Along with Darrell Bain, Barbara wrote *Shadow Worlds*, a science fiction thriller. She also has a book of shorter fiction out, *Aftermath*, and a epic fantasy, *Return of the Ancients*. In fall of 2015, Barbara and Cathleen Thompson released a children's picture book, titled, *A Forever Home for Gracie Lou*. All of Barbara's books are in print and e-formats, and A Spiral of Echoes, Ice, and *One Last Sin* are available as audio books.

Barbara lives on the central coast of California, and shares her life with her husband Jeff and two basset hounds, Hamlet and Heidi. When she isn't writing, she enjoys designing and making jewelry and watching NASCAR races.

About the story: "Twenty-one Days" introduces you to Sherice Soloman. Sherice is one of the main characters in *Ice*. When Randolph Tower, who is in my local writer's group, and I decided to write a book together, I knew exactly what I wanted to write. A story about a female serial killer. I'd been bouncing it around in my head for quite some time. Getting to know Sherice fascinated me. She is very complex. I hope you enjoy meeting her also.

# Twenty-One Days and Counting
by
Barbara M. Hodges

Why don't they have a support group for serial killers? I mean druggies have one, abusers of alcohol have AA, but we don't. There are hotlines for a soul who feels suicidal; someone to talk you out of killing yourself, but no one to talk you out of killing someone else. No sponsors for us to call.

Imagine what a meeting of serial killers would be like —more men than women, of course.

I walk up to the microphone and say, "Hi, I'm Sherice Solomon. I haven't killed someone in twenty days."

They all politely reply, "Hello, Sherice."

With a smile I shake my head and turn onto the road that winds through the county park. I see a parking lot, stop and climb from my car. Down a slight slope there is a bench beneath an ancient oak. I walk to the bench and settle myself.

A man walks toward me, a tri-colored basset hound at his side. The man is tall, thin, and as he walks closer and I see his chiseled features, truly a hunk, not at all my type. He smiles, then as the hound bristles and growls, he frowns, glances at me again as he moves by.

"Thank you," I call to his back.

He turns, a perplexed look on his face, then with a shrug he and the basset hound break into a run.

The sun filters through the oak tree and warms my head. I lift my face to its brightness as a slight breeze lifts my hair. A gorgeous day for a stroll through the park, and that's all it will be I assure myself, a calm, uneventful walk.

I pull out my cell phone and look at the date again. May third. Yes, twenty days since my last kill. A new record. This time I can do it. I will kick the habit. Get the monkey off my back. I'm not hearing Arahni's voice much anymore, only when I get too close to the chest where the ornate blade lies. A shafra it is called.

I've given up killing because I like it here on the Central Coast. The weather is beautiful, the people friendly. I don't want to move on.

I gaze across the baseball diamond.

They haven't found my last kill yet. I wonder why. He isn't in a grave. I left him in high grass among eucalyptus trees on the mesa.

I sigh.

I shouldn't have killed him, but he put me in such a predicament.

Could it have been different?

I think back.

The night is mild. It has been a bad day, Arahni nagging, the Hunger building inside of me. I feel the need of a solitary walk among the eucalyptus trees.

I park my car alongside the road.

Exit.

Begin my stroll.

Feel the start of peace.

Yes, I can do this. Tomorrow will be better.

Then he comes.

He slows his car beside me and rolls down the window. "Are you lost?"

I continue to walk, ignore him.

"I'm William."

I stop. Look at him. His face is flushed. His gaze sweeps over me and he licks his lips.

"Go away, William," I say.

His answer is to slam the car's door into me.

Then William is behind me. He pulls my body back against his, holds a knife to my throat.

"Don't scream and you'll live." He motions with his head toward a darker area between the trees. "Go there."

I do not scream, but inside me the Hunger does, as Arahni purrs inside my head. Damn, not even ten days this time.

I do as he commands and in the darkness he cannot see me smile.

I feel his heart pound against my back. His arousal presses against my backside. In the darkness of the glade, I bend my knees, twist, sweep his feet from beneath him.

William goes down hard. The knife flies from his hand. I pivot, dash to the blade and scoop it up. The Hunger screams to be fed. Before William can comprehend, I slice the knife across his throat, jump back as blood spurts. There is no finesse. It is all so crude. Not my style at all.

The Hunger is appeased, but I have to start my count all over.

The memory drifts away. Today the time stretches ahead of me. I sigh and reach to pick up a brown pine cone. What can I do to fill this day? At these moments I long for someone to share it all with. Maybe I will go to confession. I am not Catholic, but it seems it would be fun to say, "Forgive me father, for I have sinned. It's been twenty days since I last killed someone."

"Excuse me. Excuse me."

The breathless words come from behind me. I turn. A woman hurries toward me. She looks to be in her late forties, short and chunky, with a flushed face.

In my head I feel Arahni stir.

The woman stops beside me. "Please, could you walk with me?"

"What?"

"There's a guy over there." She motions with her hand. "He's been following me since I passed the dog area."

I look in the direction she points. A man stands there. He glances our way, then turns and goes into the bathroom. A rapist? I glance around. We are alone. I hate men who prey on women. The shafra is in my car. I refuse to dwell on why I have brought the blade with me. The Hunger wakes at my thoughts.

"Has he said anything to you?" I ask.

"He asked me what time it was."

"I have my cell phone. We could call the police."

The woman looks uneasy. "What if I'm wrong? I'd feel so stupid."

"Better stupid then dead," I say.

"No. If you'd just walk with me for a little while. It'd be safer for you too." She glances again toward the bathrooms. "I'm Bethany. I haven't seen you in the park before."

"Sherice," I reply. "It's my first time here. I live in Cambria. Was out for a drive and stopped to stretch my legs."

"Cambria is pretty. Although for a true beach feel I love Cayucos." A look of alarm crosses her face. "There he is. He's coming toward us."

I watch the man near.

He stops beside us. "Ladies, it'll be dark soon. You should head home."

"Excuse me?" I say.

"The park closes at dusk."

"Are you the park host?" Bethany asks.

"No. I'm Detective Wes Smith. I live close by."

"Is there something we should fear, Detective?" I ask.

Before he can respond his phone rings. He walks a few steps away from us before he answers, "Detective Smith."

"I'm right around the corner from there." I hear him say and then. "I'll call Darcie."

He ends his call and punches in another number.

I eavesdrop unashamedly.

"Darcie, it's Wes. They've got a body on the mesa. I'm heading there now." He pockets his phone.

"Is everything okay, Detective?" Bethany says.

He looks at us, then frowns. "You ladies should go home."

Bethany raises a hand to her lips. "Did you say they'd found a dead body?"

It seems I wasn't the only one eavesdropping.

The detective's frown deepens. "Go home, ladies."

"Of course, Detective," I say.

We both watch him hurry away.

I touch Bethany's arm. "I'll walk you to your car."

She shakes her head. "I jogged over."

I smile. "They why don't you let me drive you home?"

"Would you? That would be great. I don't feel safe knowing someone got killed so close by."

"I know what you mean." I point to the parking lot. "My car's over there."

"Thanks so much, Sherice. My husband's out of town. Why don't you come in and have a glass of wine with me?"

"I'd love to."

As we turn toward my car, the alarm on my cell phone goes off.

"What's that for?" Bethany says.

"I made it through another day. I'm trying to break a bad habit."

She nods. "I so get it. I quit smoking two weeks ago."

At my car, I unlock it, and open the door wide. As Bethany climbs inside, I look into the darkening sky. Should I do this? You don't usually put a bottle of Scotch before a weak alcoholic. My gaze shifts to my tote bag where the blade waits. Oh, what the hell. I love a challenge.

Twenty-one days and counting.

# AUTHOR SHOWCASE

As all authors, we love to hear from our readers. Here's how to contact the writers in this volume, and how to find their other works.

1. Diane Boyles: website: dianebroyles.com

2. Ruth Cowne: Email, abuela10@att.net

3. Paul Alan Fahey: Website: http://pualalanfahey.com; email: paulfa1189@gmail.com; Goodreads blog: www.goodreads.com/author/show/6452410.Paul_Alan_Fahey/blog

4. Judythe Guarnera: Contact Judy through email: j.guarnera@sbcglobal.net, or Facebook: JudytheGuarnera

5. Victoria Heckman: Visit her website: www.victoriahekman.com; find her on Facebook, Twitter and Instagram

6. Barbara M. Hodges: Website: http://barbaramhodges.com; Facebook, barbara.m.hodges; Twitter, BarbaraHodges

7. K. M. Kavanaugh:

8. Sue McGinty: Website: www.suemcginty.com; Facebook, sue.mcginty.author

9. Cora Ramos: Website: www.coraramos.com; Blog: coraramos-cora.blogspot.com; Facebook: CoraJRamos.Author.

10. Candace Sargent: Email: cvedrin@gmail.com

11. Susan Tuttle: Website/blog: www.SusanTuttleWrites.com; Facebook: susanwriter; Twitter: @STuttleWriter; LinkedIn; Goodreads.

www.ingramcontent.com/pod-product-compliance
Lightning Source LLC
Chambersburg PA
CBHW072134170626
46813CB00004BA/1566